DEAD ON
YOUR FEET

Also by Grant Michaels:

A Body to Dye For
Love You to Death

Grant Michaels

DEAD ON
YOUR FEET

St. Martin's Press
New York

Design by Junie Lee

Library of Congress Cataloging-in-Publication Data

Michaels, Grant.
    Dead on your feet / Grant Michaels.
       p.   cm.
    ISBN 0-312-09781-6
    1. Ballet companies—Massachusetts—Boston—Fiction.
2. Beauty operators—Massachusetts—Boston—Fiction.
3. Gay men—Massachusetts—Boston—Fiction. 4. Boston
(Mass.)—Fiction. I. Title.
PS3563.I3317D4 1993
813'.54—dc20   93-8979
                                                             CIP

First Edition: September 1993

10 9 8 7 6 5 4 3 2 1

In memory of Tatjana and Andre,
with gratitude and respect and love.

Thanks to the patience and
generosity of my friends.

CONTENTS

1

Shall We Dance?

I think my lover is killing me.

I don't mean literally, with a knife or a gun or poison. It's a more refined yet relentless termination of my life the way it was before I knew him. Not that there was so much to kill. My existence was mostly work and home, work and home, the dull routine broken by an occasional quiet evening with a few close friends, or the rare night of reckless frolic with a noisy gang of heavy drinkers. But at the heart of it, despite the patient love of my friends, despite the extreme social nature of my work as a hairstylist, despite the enduring love of my family and the vague love of my pet, I was lonely for another kind of love. Physical passion had been dormant so long my nether regions were feeling wizen. Then along came Rafik—that's his name, rhymes with technique—who quickly relieved the anguish of physical loneliness. The cure, however, was not without complication.

It was late March, a rare blue-sky morning to mark the first day of spring. An all-night rain had scrubbed the air and left it sweet. Boston weather had passed that critical point when we natives can safely put away our scarves, gloves, and mukluks, put all of it back into storage until next winter, which on the first day of spring in New England is honestly only six short months away. I was on my way to work, to

Snips Salon, on the posh lower end of Newbury Street just around the corner from the Public Garden and the Ritz-Carlton Hotel. I was early and I knew I had no customers booked that morning, so I decided to pay a surprise visit to Rafik where he works, at the studios of the Boston City Ballet, deep in the South End.

Rafik had been a dancer in Montreal until he injured his hip in a nasty fall during rehearsal five years ago. I hadn't met him yet, but sometimes I wish I had so that I could have nursed him back to health. He was in his late twenties, just entering the mature phase of his performing career, the best years. But his destiny had abruptly changed course in that moment when an old moving van had back-fired wildly outside the studio, and Rafik had lost his precious concentration during his third revolution in midair, and gravity had taken over. He landed badly from the complex aerial tour, crashed directly onto the pelvic crest of his right hip, and cracked it clear through to the ball-and-socket joint. The injury no longer affects his everyday life. But for a performer of classical dance, where at any moment the body's equilibrium might be directed by only three or four muscle fibers, that kind of injury was the death knell. So to remain with his art, Rafik turned to choreography and teaching. Outwardly he seemed satisfied with the decision, yet I sense that some part of his psyche was scarred and desensitized, some aspect of his emotional growth arrested when his life on stage was interrupted in its progress to artistic fruition. Perhaps that's one reason he moved to Boston—to give his life a fresh start in a new place. His arrival here certainly changed mine.

So there I was, ruminating about love and art and destiny, neglecting the womby scent of moist soil and the green sprouting things along the sidewalk, blind to tree limbs gauzy with pale buds, unfazed by all the optimistic signs of springtime that pervaded my stroll, as though I could not believe that winter was finally over—that's when I found myself at the entrance to the studios of the Boston City Ballet. Parked outside the main doorway was Rafik's motorcycle, which I have nicknamed Big Red. The name comes partly from the color of the paint, and partly from those indelible memories of Rafik's courtship, when he'd appear unannounced, dressed in "high leather" and balancing the big red machine between his densely muscled thighs.

At his request I rarely visit Rafik at the ballet studios. He seems intent to keep his personal life, including me, separate from the ballet company. That early spring day though, I was waxing romantic, more so than usual, and I wanted to see him. Maybe the arrival of warm weather had got my vital juices moving again after a winter's siege. But I knew one thing: A whiff of my man would jazz me up that morning.

I pushed my body against one of the massive glass doors and entered the building. The entire structure had been renovated recently inside and out, forged into an exemplar of late-twentieth-century architectural safety. Every aspect of the new design had been color-coordinated, thematically unified, and accessorized. I was certain that someone had used a computer to obtain such flawless and consistent results. It was a long way from the ballet studios of yesteryear, where numerous flights of creaky wooden stairs usually led to a musty old hall. A sense of history prevailed in those places, a lingering of old and sacred ritual. I wondered how the modernized surroundings of the Boston City Ballet affected the artists who worked there. Were their temperaments yanked out from the past, aborted from the long tradition that had conceived their art, and then flung down into the computer-assisted environment of today?

Inside the austere lobby was another world, one unaffected by changes of season. Here were only open space and mundane bodies, lacking all sentiment but in pursuit of absolute beauty, catalyzed by music and refracted into grace and movement—kind of like a fabulous color and cut by me. The receptionist recognized me as Rafik's friend and told me that company class, which is the ballet class reserved for the performing members of a ballet company, was just about ready to break before "center."

I trotted up the broad stairway to Studio A, also dubbed the Grand Studio, where company class was always held. Even before I got to the landing, I could hear through the studio's open door the sound of a concert grand piano, slightly out of tune but swelling and receding with musical phrases of oceanic dimension. Above that turbulent drama I heard the strident voice of an old woman.

"Straaaaaaaaaytch!"

From that bestial wail I knew that Rafik was not teaching company class today. I looked in through the open door. The stratospheric ceiling suggested a cathedral, or else an airplane hangar. From windows cut into the roof high overhead, broad ribbons of yellow sunlight cut diagonally into the huge space and illuminated some of the dancers, as spotlights would on a stage. The scent of clean sweat mingled with the pungency of crushed rosin on the raw wood floor. It had been one of the Boston City Ballet's most controversial extravagances to install hardwood flooring in the renovated Grand Studio rather than opt for the cheaper but more modern vinyl covering widely used in most other studios and on stages. Rafik had once remarked that dancing on unfinished wood was the best. The aroma and the texture of the long slats of pale wood over the expanse of floor did seem to maintain a link with the past. Perhaps history was still alive here after all, both in the flooring and in the movements being made upon it.

There were about forty-five dancers in the studio, two-thirds ballerinas and one-third ballerinos. Their attire ranged from classic— black tights and white T's for the men, pink tights and black leotards for the women—to postmodern—shimmering unisex bodysuits of iridescent colors found nowhere in nature, not even in tropical forests. Some of the dancers donned baggy cotton sweats strategically torn to expose the critical knee and hip joints, and a few more, the more brazenly exhibitionist, sported flimsy shorts of skin-tight jersey and even skimpier tops, all sweat-soaked and showing the muscular workings of shoulder, back, chest, buttock, and thigh. All was inspired by a sophisticated pretense of modesty that created more eroticism that actual nakedness would have.

Madame Ekaterina Rubinskaya, the aged ballet mistress of the Boston City Ballet, was conducting class, or more correctly directing the show, since the combined forces of music, color, and space made everything inside the ballet studio larger than life, like a Cinema-Scope, Technicolor, and SurroundSound spectacular. I had met Madame once before, back when Rafik first started working for the company, but I had never seen the old woman in action. Now she was supervising a complex set of stretches at the barre, the last exercise for the dancers before the center.

Madame Rubinskaya, or Rubi, as Rafik secretly called her, carried a switch of flexible springy willow as she strutted like a field marshal among the dancers, ready to deliver a light swat to an unstretched knee or a raised shoulder, or to any of a few hundred other ill-placed joints and muscles. Her clever eyes caught every movement in that cavernous studio. Even the pianist watched her warily, as though she might deliver a smart slap to his knuckles at a wrong note or a missed beat. Madame noticed me too, the instant I arrived at the open doorway. She walked toward me as she screamed blood curdling orders to the dancers.

"Up! Is all up! Hold back strong! Eeeeeeeeeee, poooosh!"

So this was art.

She stopped at the open door and faced me directly. She was surprisingly short so close up, and I felt myself drawn downward to her, almost against my will. Her entire torso—bust, waist, and hips— was homogenized into a single, shapeless unit, but one that looked firm and strong despite its age. Her face was a prehistoric terrain heavily coated with foundation makeup, a vain attempt to camouflage the ravages of time. But with no other makeup, her features receded into the mask that was her face. Only her eyes remained wide and alert. Our heads were suddenly close, and I could smell the soft wool of her wine-colored cardigan. She whispered like a conspirator, but I heard her clearly in spite of a rush of notes from the piano at that moment.

"You come for Rafik?" Her heavy accent sounded like a bad parody of a Russian spy.

I blushed and found myself speechless, a rare event for me. I glanced nervously at the slender willow shaft that quivered in her hand, ready to strike. I straightened up to military attention and forced a polite smile.

"Yes, for Rafik."

She responded with a sly grin and murmured, "Then I will not kill him today." She turned abruptly on her heels and screeched, "Eyegaaaaaaain!" causing the piano music to surge with renewed passion. Madame strutted back onto the studio floor, and I felt a strange relief, as though I'd survived a surprise attack. How did the dancers endure this kind of treatment every day? If Madame Rubinskaya's tactics were any indication, the abuse went far beyond muscle and bone. Perhaps a dancer's training required the unconditional surrender of the personality as well?

With the threat of Madame's switch gone, I focused back on the activity in the studio. I scanned the bodies and saw Rafik stretching carefully at one of the portable barres in the center of the floor. Like a Persian prince or an Egyptian Fayumic portrait, Rafik has fine dark features whose chiseled familiarity is one of my life's pleasures. But I noticed some unfamiliar lines on his face too. Experience and disillusion were already marking Rafik's countenance. But his body remains supple. Like a cat he is long-legged and equally clever with all four limbs. Sometimes during sex I can't tell if it's a hand or a foot or a knee or an elbow that he's plying on me. And his male organ is like a fifth limb, one fluent in a unique kinesthetic vernacular. He can even make it dance—but then, he is a choreographer.

To reduce the strain on his injured hip Rafik was working his leg on the portable barre's lower level. He slid the raised leg along the barre and stretched his thighs open to the limit of his split. He claims that it had once been perfectly open—an easy one hundred eighty degrees—but now it stops short of one hundred twenty. Perfect split or not, Rafik still possesses the lithe, sculpted muscles of a performing dancer. Besides, in the everyday world what practical use is a perfect split?

From far across the floor Rafik caught my admiring gaze and replied with a wink. All was well between us. My crotch stirred too, the proof that I was still infatuated. Since hooking up with Rafik I was generally in a semi-turgid state. In fact, to help check my newfound spunk I'd even developed a new mantra—"Quell the swell. Quell the swell"—but it rarely worked. Before my shameless arousal became noticeable to anyone in the studio that morning, I aimed my attention away from Rafik.

Working opposite the barre from him and facing him was a young male dancer. I immediately noticed the similarity of his body to mine, though his was devoid of any fat. Still, I could see by his frame and flesh that he shared my tendency to retain weight. Someday, when he stopped dancing, he too would be plagued with those same twelve or so pounds that refuse to leave my hips. Right now though, his haunches looked fine—full and round and tight. His legs could have belonged to my twin, if he existed. Relative to his trunk they were extra long, and plump with muscle, especially the calves. And like me, he had small feet that were broad as a brick and had an aggressively high instep. There was however a major difference between me and my dancing doppelgänger. His entire musculature was obviously rock hard, while mine is just pleasantly firm. With a little longing I wondered if that young dancer represented my own body if I had ever pushed it to the ultimate conditioning that ballet produces. But a sudden bark from Madame Rubinskaya snapped me out of my reverie the instant the music stopped.

"Take away barre!" she commanded.

Perhaps a finely tuned body wasn't worth the sacrifices required to attain and maintain it.

Long before I'd met Rafik I'd learned from other dancer friends that all ballet classes comprise two distinct parts: barre and center. The barre, pronounced the same as the place where you can get a drink, is the first part of class, when the dancers perform their movements next to a stout wooden railing called a barre. The barres are usually attached permanently along the studio walls, but they can be portable and freestanding on the studio floor as well. The barre exercises warm up the dancers' muscles and develop their strength. The center, or *centre*, if you want to be absolutely French about it, takes place on the studio floor proper. The center resembles actual dancing, when the dancers travel across the floor and through space, and they must rely on their own stability and strength. This is where the jumps and the turns happen too, along with the thrills and spills of classical dance.

Rafik and the young dancer were about to move their portable barre off the floor, but another dancer, a lissome blond ballerina, was still executing her personal version of the stretches. While the class disbanded for a short break, with most of the dancers pouring out the doorway and roughly pushing me aside with a kind of mob momentum, that singular ballerina blithely continued her graceful movements, bending backward like a contortionist to touch the back of her knee with a softly held wrist. Rafik and the young male dancer watched her intently. Then their eyes met and ... Did Rafik just wink at him? Couldn't be. It was my insecurity at work again, misconstruing a wink and weakening my belief that I could be loved by someone like Rafik. His wink was more likely a wince of pain from the recent stretches. But then the young man made a remark, and Rafik responded with a generous smile and a comment that caused both the young man and the blond ballerina to giggle. The ballerina pulled herself upright from her bent back position and retorted sharply, which caused both Rafik and the young man to laugh out loud. And throughout this brief vignette, to my shame, I found myself feeling alienated and jealous of their easy, playful camaraderie.

Madame Rubinskaya, still holding the willow switch in one hand, stopped beside me upon leaving the studio. She looked down at my feet, then directed her gaze back into my eyes with a cold stare.

"Is rubber?" she said accusingly.

"Excuse me?" I replied.

"Your shoe is rubber?"

"Ah . . . yes," I said with another forced smile. I inverted one foot to show her the spongy white sole of my sneakers. She approved with a sharp nod.

"Then you can go in studio."

Her permission granted, she moved brusquely on. My eyes followed her down the bright wide hallway. She paused and turned back toward me in half-profile. She tucked the willow switch under one arm, then fetched a package of cigarettes from a pocket of her cardigan. She lit up and inhaled deeply while she put the pack away. Then she exhaled a voluminous cloud of smoke. I watched her grasp the cigarette between her thumb and index finger and pull it smartly from her lips, as though portraying a tough from the old movies. (I'd once seen John Garfield hold a fag just like that, with his palm curled protectively over the glowing tip.) Madame retrieved the switch from under her arm, then resumed her deliberate pace toward a closed door a short distance away, arrived there, opened it, and vanished within. A blue-white cloud of smoke was all that remained in her wake.

Meanwhile numerous dancers had settled themselves on the carpeted floor of the lobby. Some of them lay belly-down and stretched into wide open splits, some of them lay belly-up with legs propped up against a wall, and most of them, as though imitating Madame's example, had lit up and were smoking freely. Here were specimens of the most extraordinary physical development engaging in—if you could believe the surgeon general—one of civilization's most hazardous pleasures. Even I had tried many times to smoke as part of my image as a hairstylist, but had failed. I could never achieve that cool, elegant poise that comes from truly enjoying a cigarette. I generally coughed and gagged, and I always got teary, like an oversensitive wimp.

Just as I was heading inside the Grand Studio, Rafik emerged with the young male dancer alongside him. They both wore big happy smiles on their faces. However, when Rafik saw me his easy smile changed to a look of surprise, and not one of pure pleasure. The young dancer who'd come out with him eyed me cautiously, then

moved away from Rafik and settled down on the carpet to stretch
some more. Rafik approached me.

"You are not at work?" he said with his French accent.

"The day is so beautiful I thought of you."

Rafik smiled cynically. "You are *romantique.*"

"So are you," I said, hoping for a hug or a touch.

He shook his head. *"Non.* I feel now—how you say?—*pragmatique."*

"Maybe you're working too hard again."

He shrugged. "Work. Life. Is all the same."

Right then and there, at that horrible lapse of understanding, I
wanted to hold Rafik close to me and make him tell me that it
mattered to him that I loved him, that I wanted to be with him
forever, that I wanted to save him from the pit of pragmatism that he
was plummeting ever deeper into. But he spoke first and stole the
moment from me.

"We must change our plans tonight."

I sighed heavily, a sigh of exasperation. Rafik had already post-
poned twice an "anniversary" celebration we had planned to mark
our first year together. Tonight was to be the third try, and I was
beginning to sense that he didn't share my enthusiasm about our
togetherness.

He went on. "I have important meeting with Max Harkey. He is
director—"

"I know who he is."

My gruffness surprised him. It did me too, but I had to resist his
charms. Otherwise I'd passively accept yet another cancelled date
with him. Rafik continued quietly.

"It is dinner," he said, then added, "You are invited."

"Oh," I said with chagrin.

"It is business. Maybe you have no interest." (Rafik pronounced
the word "mebby.") "The new conductor for this season has arrived.
We will talk about the music for the spring program."

"Well, I don't mind, as long as I'm with you."

"There will be much ballet talk. You will be bored."

I had to concede a point there. For a nondancer, there's almost
nothing duller than being around dancers talking about dance.
They'll blab endlessly about muscles and ligaments and body place-

ment, like an open forum in anatomy. At least when hairdressers socialize, they exchange juicy gossip, all sex and money.

"Rafik, I'll even listen to dance talk if it means we don't have to cancel our anniversary again."

"You think I do not have grief from that? I want to celebrate, Stani, but I must do my work."

He had cleverly used the nickname bestowed by my Czech grand-mother. Rafik always said it correctly too, accenting the second syllable: "Stuh-*nee*." Only three people ever called me by that name, and they all seemed to do it when they wanted to gain a point during an argument.

"Rafik, would you rather I didn't come?"

It was Rafik's turn for a heavy sigh now, but his was a sigh of deference. "Max Harkey has asked for you. We are dining at eight o'clock at his home. He expects us at seven-thirty."

"Where do you want to meet?"

"Chez Harkey."

"Why don't we go together?"

Rafik set his mouth tensely and replied through his tightened lips, "I will depart from the studio."

"Then I'll meet you here."

"You should go there yourself," he said firmly.

I wondered why he was being so difficult. Was it so much to expect that my lover might want me along on a social event, even if it was affiliated with the ballet company? I mean, were we a couple or not? I pulled out the small pad I always carry with me and asked Rafik for the address, then wrote it down. Just as I finished, Madame Rubin-skaya arrived in the lobby where we were standing outside the studio. She was about to resume class.

She said to Rafik, "You will do adagio?"

Rafik replied no.

"Is most important part," she said, and glanced at me as though I would keep him from class.

"I know, Madame," Rafik said. "But I must prepare for rehearsal."

Madame Rubinskaya seemed to accept this reason. "And I must prepare your dancers," she said, then Madame re-entered the Grand Studio. Immediately followed a flurry of cigarettes being extin-guished in the lobby. Then all the sprawled-out, split-open, curled-up or twisted dancers' bodies were on their feet and then back in the studio at attention. During the break Madame Rubinskaya had exchanged her whiplike switch for a sturdy walking stick of ebony topped with a silver finial. She used the stick to support herself in the center of the floor while she set the first combination of steps, the Grand Adagio.

Standing next to me outside the studio, Rafik watched her intently as she filled thirty-two counts of powerful music with space-filling poses and unexpected turns of body, eternal balances, and sweeping circles of the upper body and arms. In spite of her ancient body, Madame had captivated Rafik's attention. He was lost in her movements the way I wanted him to be lost in my presence. When Madame had marked all the steps and poses, the large class split into groups and performed the difficult adagio.

Rafik said, "I must go. I have rehearsal."

"Can I watch?"

He became almost violently defensive. *"Non!* I have told you already. Not this piece."

Rafik was keeping his most recent work a complete secret from me. Since its conception many months ago he had discussed neither title nor subject nor music with me. I was to experience this choreographic event along with the rest of the viewing public on opening night, in a few weeks. Until then I was to wait patiently and loyally, to tolerate Rafik's moods and his despair, and to love him unconditionally through it all because he was a great artist who had to do this great thing. Well, I'm just an ordinary mortal. I want a flesh-and-blood man as my lover, not a creative demon.

Rafik continued, "Today I am working with Toni."

"Tony?"

"The conductor, from Italia."

Tony? Could it be true? Could my old flame Tony, the former church organist and choir director, now an internationally acclaimed opera conductor—could he be in Boston to conduct for the ballet? Then why hadn't he called me? And why did Rafik's eyes twinkle at the mention of his name?

"I know him," I said.

"Is not him," replied Rafik. "Is *she,*" he said emphatically and with correct grammar, even if he had chosen the wrong gender. Then he pointed behind me. I turned and looked in the direction he indicated, expecting to see a sexy man, which my Tony certainly was. But instead I saw a radiant and voluptuous redheaded woman approaching us. She sure wasn't a ballerina, not with that frame and that bosom and those hips, and certainly not with that walk. Everything—hair, head, shoulders, hips, thighs—all of it was moving in fluid figure eights. No ballerina ever reveled in her own flesh that way. A ballerina's body was an instrument of artistic expression, while this woman's was obviously used to pleasure—big pleasure and lots of it.

My suspicions that Rafik was hanging out with my former fantasy man were unfounded, and I felt stupid to have doubted him. Rafik introduced us. Her name was Toni di Natale. Then he explained to her—a bit glibly, I thought—that I was a "friend" and I was just about to leave. Here's your hat, what's your hurry?

Toni di Natale extended her big hand toward me. "How do you do?" she said with a husky voice that bore no trace of accent.

"Hi," I said taking her hand, which matched mine in size and strength. "I don't hear the sunny Mediterranean in your speech."

She smiled broadly and replied with her dry contralto, "I was born in New York, but I spend most of my time abroad. If anything," she said, and then changed her vocal inflection as she continued, "I occasionally lapse into high Brit." Then she laughed heartily and shook her head and shimmied her shoulders and tossed her mane of lustrous red hair, all with exaggerated playfulness.

I replied, "My friend Nicole does that too—the Brit bit."

Rafik interrupted us and said to her, "Shall we go to work?"

"Sure," replied Toni, but her hips did most of the talking with the monosyllabic answer. Then she asked me, "Are you coming along too?"

Rafik intercepted her question before I could answer myself. "No," he said sharply.

All at once I understood how a woman might feel if her husband ever related to another man in a vaguely sexual way, and then proceeded to exclude her from their company. Rafik and I were lovers, yet this woman was attempting to arouse Rafik's interest, and was very possibly succeeding. And now *he* was trying to keep *me* out of it. Already the two of them treated each other with a familiarity that I had assumed was mine alone with Rafik. For the briefest moment I wondered if Rafik might be bisexual. After all, Ramon, the shampoo boy at Snips, claimed to be bisexual, and he was from Paris, which is where Rafik was born and lived before going to Montreal. Maybe bisexuality ran higher among Francophones?

The awkward moment that followed Rafik's blunt "no" was broken by the voice of Madame Rubinskaya braying from within the Grand Studio. "Straytch, straytch, straaaaytch! Stay! Finish!"

The music stopped and there was silence.

Toni di Natale remarked offhandedly, "She's a living relic."

To my surprise, Rafik glowered at her. "Her family was favored by the czar," he said in staunch defense of the old woman.

Toni replied firmly, "The czar is gone. The arts world needs people like you now."

Flirtation disguised as fact and flattery.

A tense frown creased Rafik's brow. Perhaps her adulation bothered him? Or did he sense my uneasiness that they might have already done the horizontal tango?

"Nice to meet you," Toni said to me. Then she hooked her arm into Rafik's and turned to lead him away. He looked almost helpless in her power, and no part of Rafik is ever helpless.

"See you both at dinner tonight," I blurted.

Toni di Natale turned back toward me with a big swirl, using Rafik's body as her pivot point. "Are you going too?" she said. "How nice!" But her enthusiasm, like everything else about her so far, was veneer.

Rafik told her to go and wait in his small office, just down the hall, where he'd meet her in a few minutes. "Don't keep me waiting too long," she said. "I still have jet lag." She laughed noisily, and Rafik nodded back with a big grin, one that I recognized from when he first seduced me.

Toni di Natale continued on toward Rafik's office, leaving us alone outside the Grand Studio. Rafik waited until the music for the adagio started again, then he said to me, "I see what you are thinking."

"What am I thinking?"

"You think of sex."

"That's right. Especially sex with me, and how long it's been since that happened. I wouldn't mind a little more interest from you. We are still lovers, aren't we?"

Rafik stared directly into my eyes.

"You hurt me with these words," he said.

"I miss you when you are so involved in your work."

"It will pass."

"But I want you now."

"Tonight, Stani. I promise. After dinner at Max Harkey's."

Again the nickname. I never liked the idea of making an appointment or a promise to have sex with someone I love. But I was lonely for Rafik, and he seemed to be spilling his affection everywhere but on the home front.

"You still want to meet chez Harkey?" I asked.

"Yes."

Why was he insisting on separate arrivals? So we wouldn't be perceived as a couple? Or was it just another odd way of punishing me for not living with him?

"I'll see you later then," I said coolly.

Then, as if to belie all our misunderstood words, we suddenly embraced there in the hallway, holding each other close and hard. I listened to his breath, felt his lips graze the side of my neck, absorbed his moisture, took in his scent. Rafik's skin exudes miraculous scents—the lively citrus of bergamot, the cool green of clover, the pungent bite of nutmeg, the sweetness of vanilla—an olfactory smorgasbord that challenges me to keep my lips and tongue and teeth to myself when I'm near him. Holding Rafik for those few seconds outside the Grand Studio of the Boston City Ballet made everything in the world fine again. Never mind the axiom that says electrical vigor between two bodies must diminish with time; if Rafik was giving me a manicure, I'd probably climax three times.

"You'd better go change," I whispered. "I don't want you catching cold in these sweaty duds."

I left the studios and headed back across town to Snips. I was mildly disgusted by all the jealous turmoil I'd just put us through. I knew it was all irrational. If Rafik wanted to play around with anyone—the male dancers, or the females, or even Toni di Natale, for that matter—he'd have plenty of time to do it at the studios. So his suggestion that we arrive separately at Max Harkey's place must have been a matter of convenience and nothing more. I'd do better to focus my obsessions on the nature of Rafik's secret choreography—the new work he refused to share with me—than to fret about his love.

2

My Little Corner of the World

Snips Salon has thrived on Newbury Street since the day Nicole Albright opened its doors. From the very beginning Nikki never let on to the clientele that she owned the place. Instead she has always portrayed the resident manicurist, which somehow gets her customers to talk more openly with her. I don't quite understand why the ploy works, but it does.

Last winter Nikki officially promoted me to salon manager. It's mostly a paper title, since I've always helped manage the shop. But these days she wants even less to do with running the business, so she's passed the major part of management on to me. The change is good for me since I earn more money and spend less time on the shop floor. When I do work out front, I see only the customers I want—no more anonymous walk-ins unless I find them irresistible.

That morning, after my visit to the ballet studios, I breezed into the shop around eleven o'clock. My nostrils flared at the familiar sharp tingle as I inhaled the vapors of the myriad and sometimes noxious chemicals used to beautify our clients. I often wonder if the thousands of beauty salons around the world might be in Olympic competition with the heavier industries like petroleum or nuclear energy in terms of creating ecological disharmony. True, the newer beauty products are more considerate of Mother Nature, but many of them still reek of destruction. Perhaps the only saving grace is that stylists and

estheticians exercise their environmental wantonness in the name of
beauty, unlike the energy cartels. I mean, when was the last time you
filled the tank and felt sexy? When were you last enraptured by a
flawless meltdown?

I saw Nicole manicuring a client. She looked up for a moment and
scanned me quickly with her bright blue eyes, peering over the top
of her half-frame magnifying glasses like an ever-alert feline. She
smiled softly and nodded to me, missing not one surgical swipe of her
cuticle trimmers. Nicole's usual boisterous mood was somewhat subdued these days, ever since her young lover Chaz had gone off to
Hollywood to make millions practicing entertainment law. I thought
his departure a blessing, since I saw only his ego-ridden and obnoxious side. I never trusted him either, probably because he was young
enough to be Nicole's son. She's on that side of fifty and Chaz wasn't
yet thirty, which put him just younger than me. Besides, he was
good-looking and well-built and cocksure of himself. But then, good-
looking, well-built men usually are cocksure of themselves, probably
because they so rarely experience the rejection that we pedestrian
types do. But Chaz had been good for Nicole's libido, even if his
sexual tenure did cause a rift between us. Fortunately, Rafik had
come along and had partly filled the emotional gap I felt during
Nicole's affair with Chaz. But once her lawyer-lover departed, Nikki
became the one who incurred a void in her life, and our feisty big
sis–little brother relationship had easily resumed.

On the way to my office at the back of the shop I passed by Nicole's
manicure table, where she keeps a tumbler full of emery boards at
hand. They always remind me of the afternoon Rafik used one so
inventively on my tender body parts.

"Sorry I'm late, doll," I said cheerfully.

"Tied to the bedposts again?" she replied, keeping her cool gaze on
the gnarly ancient hand that writhed in her grasp.

"I went to the ballet studios," I said.

Nicole didn't respond, but her elderly client looked up and spoke
to me in a voice overcome with tremolo.

"Are you a dancer?"

I recognized her as one of our generic dowager clients who kept
a suite at the Ritz-Carlton. This one's hair had recently been modernized from silver-blue to silver-blond. The new color job was probably
the work of Ramon, the once-upon-a-time shampoo boy who had

stepped up to part-time stylist after I accepted the mantle of salon manager. As for the old woman's question, I wondered if she was legally blind, since anyone with sight and half a brain would know that I do not have a dancer's silhouette. I'm tall enough with a leggy five-foot-ten-inch frame, but I carry several extra kilos around my middle that would drive a dancer to liposuction if not to suicide. Fortunately Rafik doesn't care about the fat-to-muscle ratio around my midriff. Perhaps he even gets a perverse thrill from it, since vanity still forbids such a mortal flaw on his body. Or maybe it's simply the Jack Sprat syndrome, where opposites attract: He is dark and sinewy and hairy, while I am pink and porpoise-sleek.

"No, ma'am," I said to Nicole's elderly client. "I'm not a dancer. But my husband is."

She gasped slightly, as though the idea of two men together had never occurred to her, not even here in Snips, one of the gay strongholds in Beantown, Massachusetts. She may have been sporting the *moderne* Brahmin look, but her thinking was as calcified as ever.

Nicole said, "The office awaits you, Stanley."

Even my salon name, Vannos, had vanished like an old actor's mask when I assumed the position as salon manager. Thus dismissed, I headed toward the little chamber in the back of the shop, formerly one of the storage rooms, which Nicole had converted to an office where I could tend my managerial duties. On the way I saw Ramon, who was happily chatting up one of his new customers. He gave me a big smile as I passed by. Ramon had become a lot friendlier since he started doing his own creative work, and especially since he began receiving his tips directly from his own customers instead of from the other stylists. But despite the new improved Ramon, my client list remained sacrosanct, as did any customer who explicitly requested me. Ramon would have to cultivate his own following, just as we all did in the beginning.

I entered the office and surveyed my domain. The tiny cubicle is equipped with all the essentials: a luxurious mauve leather chair, a European coffeemaker, a small refrigerator, a multiline telephone, and the usual desk and computer. The other accessories include a sisal floor mat and a darling but useless little side chair of anodized pink steel tubing with seat and back surfaces of narrow satin ribbon, all multicolored and interwoven. Everything combines synergistically to create a look of relaxed urbanity, distinctly cozy and gay.

Among the debris on my desktop is the usual gallery of framed photos that grace any good executive's office: a color snapshot of my mom lounging with a frosty cocktail during a summer barbecue at the New Jersey homestead, while my father is in the background, enveloped in clouds of smoke wafting from the meat-laden grille; a sepia-toned studio portrait of my sister and her husband and their two princess daughters, all of them reeking of the complacent bourgeois life they desperately seek and seem to have attained; and finally a photo-collage of my Burmese cat, Sugar Baby, in various endearing poses throughout her idyllic life with me. Rafik's likeness is not on the desk among the other family portraits, but instead holds a place of honor all its own. On the back of my office door I've mounted a life-sized poster created from a photo of him, a full-body shot taken during his glorious dancing days. When the dramas and intrigues of salon life become too distracting—usually on a daily basis—I cloister myself in this private sanctuary and let the icon transfix me.

My dominion surveyed, I launched into my morning ritual: Fill the coffeemaker with bottled spring water; scoop in excessive amounts of freshly ground, custom-blended coffee; set out one of the homemade pastries my mother sends every week; start up the computer; sort and open the mail; and that's about as far as I got for the next ten minutes. I just couldn't settle down. I opened the window that overlooks the back alley and also keeps me connected to the weather, which in Boston can be a full-time preoccupation. I thought some fresh air might help me get down to business, but the cool breeze carried the scent of young green growth from outside, which only distracted me further from the dull paperwork awaiting me. I filled my mug with coffee and then took a big forkful of poppy-seed strudel. The buttery pastry and the sticky black seeds tasted extra good that morning.

I closed my office door and gazed at the poster of Rafik that hung there. He was standing beside a barre, one elbow placed on it and the other on his hip. The classic dance attire—white T-shirt, black tights, white socks, and white kidskin ballet slippers—belied his suggestive stance. His weight was on one leg; the other was slightly bent to give a rakish tilt to his hips. His head was cocked to one side, and he grinned directly into the camera lens. The look was an open invitation to pleasure. My heart pumped a little faster. I wondered, Was it true? Were Rafik and I really together? Had we actually met and connected? Of all the available men in Boston, why had Rafik chosen me? He is complex, almost Byzantine, where I am simple and direct. His paradoxical self contains youthful spontaneity, guru like wisdom and acceptance, compulsive creativity, martial destructiveness, lustful joie de vivre, and even despair. He is demon and angel, teacher and student, lover and enemy, child and father. I sometimes worry that an ordinary person like me might obstruct the potential of someone like him. But he claims that I provide a lightness and a humor that refresh him and revitalize him. So why do I feel that gnawing inside me? Perhaps the equations that finally explain us are simple: Rafik is gorgeous and I worship him; he expends creative energy and I replenish it; he lives in the tradition of grand opera while I run a sudsy sitcom parody of it.

Nicole opened the door and broke my daydream.

"Wake up, darling." Nikki often entered my sanctum without knocking—a forgivable intrusion since she owns the place. On her five-foot-four-inch physical self she wore a classy skirt-and-blouse ensemble. The long-sleeved silk blouse had been screened with big blocks of dense color—blue, red, and yellow—all outlined in black, like a Mondrian painting. The fitted skirt of charcoal gray worsted had a curiously slimming effect around her hips. Alas, "svelte" had left Nicole years ago, after she stopped modeling on the Paris runways and began eating and drinking whatever she wanted. These days, her idea of exercise and dietary control is to walk a few blocks to the health-food store and buy a package of rice crackers. She might nibble at one or two, but the rest becomes bird food while she telephones for Italian take-out. Fortunately, her metabolism keeps her just this side of plump.

"I wasn't napping," I said. "I was ruminating."

"You do too much of that," she said. I offered her some of my strudel. She shook her head no. "You know I've cut out sweets this month, but that coffee smells heavenly."

"That's as close as either of us will get there," I said as I filled a mug with the steamy beverage and poured a dollop of heavy cream into it, just the way she likes it.

"Thank you, darling," she said and took the mug, then tried to settle herself in the little side chair. She scowled and winced for a few seconds, squirming and fussing with her hips, trying to get comfortable in the tiny seat of slippery satin ribbons.

"Just set your butt down and leave it there, doll."

"It's a horrid little chair," she said. "I'm going to replace it."

"But it's the *objet piquant* of the room."

"And you can't sit in it."

If Nicole really hated the chair, she never would have bought it. I think what she wanted that morning was the comfy leather that was cushioning my fanny at the moment. Fat chance.

She sipped her coffee then asked me, "Is everything all right with Rafik?"

"Sure," I said happily. "Why?"

"You went to see him at the studio this morning."

"The beautiful weather inspired me to seek my beloved."

"So you weren't together last night?"

"Everything is fine, doll."

We sat quietly for a few moments, sipping the rich coffee and breathing in the moist lively air that wafted in through the open window. A little bird in one of the bushes outside fluttered nervously among the branches and cheeped noisily. The very peacefulness seemed to unnerve me.

"Okay, doll. You guessed right. Rafik and I are on another bumpy patch."

"Jealousy again?"

I nodded. "I feel so juvenile I'm ashamed."

"What brought it on this time?"

"The same old thing. He's in one of his creative periods, which means we're not having sex. And when that happens my old insecurities come home to roost and I think he's having sex with every young thing at the studio, and then I realize that my whole concept of love and partnership is based on sex, and then I hate myself."

Nicole shook her head and clucked her tongue quietly.

"Stanley, why don't you just move in together? What are you waiting for?"

"Our domestic temperaments are too different. He has that old-world attitude about marriage. He expects the homey comfort and security of a wife to keep things smooth. And I know I'm not exactly a model of virility, but I'm certainly not a homemaker for somebody else."

"There must be some middle ground."

"We try to spend three or four nights a week together, but he still argues how impractical it is to keep separate apartments. I figure the separateness is precisely what keeps us together."

"How's that?"

"I don't want to know everything that goes on backstage in his life."

"Are you afraid of intimacy?"

"Cut the psychobabble, doll. I just wouldn't want to stumble home early some afternoon and find him, well, with a guest."

"Darling, you're sounding Victorian. What difference would it make as long as he's being safe and discreet about it? Rafik adores you and he wouldn't do a thing to hurt you. I think you expect too much from people."

"That's a platitude, Nikki. Besides, rationalizing about love is like wearing sensible shoes. It fills a need, but it completely discounts the emotions. None of it matters anyway, since I can't be or think anything other than what I am."

"What you are is fatalistic and lazy. We all have control over our lives."

"Doll, no one creates his or her own reality, unless you're refering to things like hair color, or hemline, or heel height. But when it comes down to the nitty-gritty stuff, about how we feel and act and respond with each other, I don't think any of us has much control over any of it. It's all genetically determined, sperm meets egg, the luck of the draw, including the ability to overlook or endure sexual infidelity from a spouse."

"Stanley, please—"

"It's true, Nikki. My rational side knows that promiscuity, even by my lover, doesn't really matter in the grand chaos of things. But my romantic side cares only about love and all other things irrational. So, I'm a mess, and it's all controlled by my DNA, not by any learned response. No matter what I might want to do or try to do about it, my life is rooted in Slavic melancholy, and I'll probably never be truly happy or content as long as I'm alive."

"Rubbish!" replied Nicole. "You have too much idle time, and you're whining."

"Maybe I need a corpse to distract me."

Nicole's long-lashed eyelids opened wide at my flippant remark. "I should think you'd had enough of that," she said. Then she pushed her coffee mug toward me. "Do something useful and pour some cognac in this."

"So early in the day?"

"I don't have a customer until one."

"You never used to drink like this, not until Chaz left town. I hope you're not resorting to booze to compensate for lost love."

"Since when do you lecture me about that?"

"You never let me get away with self-pity."

"Darling, before you met Rafik, I tolerated your long-suffering dreariness without judgment. Is it so much to ask for a little compassion now?"

She was right. Before my current soap-opera life of doubt, I lived a soap-opera life of frustration. And Nicole had watched every tedious episode, plus the reruns.

"Touché, doll," I said, and I fetched the bottle of fine champagne cognac from a locked overhead cupboard. I poured a few glug-glugs of the amber-colored elixir into her coffee. If her one o'clock customer even vaguely alluded to the scent of cognac, Nikki would probably offer her a shot as well.

The phone on my desk beeped. It was the receptionist announcing a walk-in request for Vannos.

"Vannos doesn't work here anymore," I said.

"He's a referral," replied the receptionist.

Whoever it was, I'd have to give him a look at least. The best way to keep a client list exclusive is to take new customers only on referral. I left Nicole in the office and went out to the shop floor. Awaiting me at the reception desk was a tall, virile man in his late forties with a headful of thick pepper-and-salt hair and a matching mustache. He appeared to be what in gay parlance is called a butch-daddy type. He wore standard-issue denims, but they were immaculate and pressed with creases sharp enough to inflict fatal wounds if he walked too fast in them. The shiny black calfskin boots and the massive sterling silver belt buckle meant that this contrived casual look had cost him well over a thousand dollars.

I introduced myself.

He replied, "You come highly recommended." His voice came out oddly light and breathy for such a tall man with such well-cultivated shoulders.

"What can I do for you?" I asked.

He moved closer to me. "I'd like to try blond," he said with a quiet giggle. "Donaldson says you're a wonder with color."

I didn't answer for a moment. Donaldson—not Don, not Donny, not even Donald, but Donaldson—was a longtime client of mine whose life as a bottle blond had gone through the entire spectrum of light, lighter, and lightest. Donaldson was also an extremely femme decorator whose fluttery mannerisms would fatigue a desperate mayfly in heat. I stood back and took a cold hard look at the handsome man standing before me. I was partial to his phenotype, that generic, square-framed, masculine quality that some lucky men get from the genes they're dealt. Then I imagined him a blond. But even with my expert eye, I couldn't see it. To make this man a blond might suit some other facet of his personality, but it would also ruin the present picture of him, the one I happened to like.

"I'm sorry," I said. "I can't do it."

"What do you mean?" he demanded. "Donaldson said you could do anything."

"Technically speaking, I can, but I think your hair is fine the way it is."

"Gray like this?" he said. His voice was becoming strident. "It makes me look too old."

"I wouldn't touch the color. It's perfect."

The man seemed unconvinced. "I can pay," he ventured.

"I'm sure you can, but I won't color your hair. I'd be glad to style it—"

"No," he interrupted. "I want to be blond. Is there anyone else who can do it?"

I paused, wondering how to change his mind, then realized it was hopeless. "I'll get Ramon," I said glumly.

An hour and a half later the man was a blond. Ramon had shaved his mustache too, so his horsey upper lip was now exposed, which gave his face a long, sagging, almost sad quality. I may be in the business of beauty and artifice, but I never interfere with nature because of someone's silly urge to look young.

The day went on. I finished my office work and saw a few customers too. But by the time Nicole and I closed up the place, I had become restive again, probably in anticipation of the evening ahead. Somewhat uneasy, I headed home to begin the Grand Preparation.

Home is a spacious one-bedroom apartment on Marlborough

Street. I'm on the top floor, which is a mixed blessing. On the good side, it's quiet, bright, and airy. On the bad, there's no elevator in the building. Since I've got good legs the four flights of stairs don't usually bother me, but sometimes I wonder about getting another place. Then I consider what I'd lose if I moved out: The rent is strictly controlled and there's great solidarity among the tenants. So chances are I'll live there forever. Besides, I'm high above most of the street noise, and I even have a river view. You have to look out the bathroom window, but it's there.

I opened the door and was greeted by Sugar Baby, whose short taupe fur is the same color as the candy. I picked her up and cooed to her while I checked my telephone messages, of which there were none that night. Then I carried her purring body to the kitchen, which is where most of my domestic life seems to transpire when I'm home alone. I'll eat there, talk on the telephone there, watch television there, even read there. It's probably a family holdover from growing up in working-class New Jersey, where everything happened in the kitchen. Back then the living room was reserved for guests and special occasions. The same is still true for me.

Two big decisions faced me after I'd opened my mail and had mixed myself a frosty martini, my preferred libation once the snow has gone. The first question was which food to serve Sugar Baby. I decided to leave the decision up to her by parading the five cans in front of her and making suitable enticing sounds for each one. I'm sure the gin was enhancing that little vignette. By far the most enthusiastic response, gauged by Sugar Baby's guttural vocalizing, was elicited by a kidney-and-bacon combination, so that's what my favorite girl got for dinner that night. I hoped that the menu at Max Harkey's place would be chosen with more discernment.

The second and more critical decision facing me was what to wear. How should I present myself to a crowd of dancers and related groupies, the most body-conscious of the evolved primates? Should I try to blend in with a slim look, which meant wearing all black, just the way most of them would? But that might appear too contrived. Besides, with my full, healthy figure, attempting the slim look was mostly a vain pursuit. Perhaps I should portray an admiring outsider, which is what I really was anyway. That choice would allow me to wear anything in my closet that still fit. I decided to meditate on it during my shower.

After a thorough scrubbing under a fine, steamy spray with French-milled soap scented with wild fern, my body was rosy and refreshed. I poured myself another cocktail to enjoy while I dried off. At one point I caught a glimpse of myself in the dressing mirror. My body is decent enough, though certainly not the stuff of which porn stars and fashion models are made. So what part of it appealed to Rafik? Maybe he liked my square, manly jaw or the full lips adorned with a droopy red mustache that matches my coppery hair. Or was it the green eyes? The big dopey grin? My guess is that it's probably my naturally good legs and feet that gain the approval of his dancer's eyes. And my robust backside. And perhaps my *équipage* too, which ranks high in profile and proportion and friendliness, if not gross dimension. Then again, maybe what Rafik cherishes most of all is my beautiful soul.

I shrugged at another unanswered mystery of love, then went to assemble my outfit. I chose a cotton shirt with broad stripes of turquoise, purple, and gold—all complementary to my short red hair. For slacks I took the pleated and cuffed charcoal-gray twills. Soft black suede slip-ons cushioned my feet. Thanks in part to my long Slavic limbs and the two martinis, the whole package of Stan Kraychik looked pretty good in my dressing mirror. For fragrance I chose an Italian cologne whose piny balsam scent reminded me of a cop I once knew—very straight of very straight. A spritz of that stuff on my neck was as close as I'd ever get to him.

So, fastidiously douched and dressed, I set out by foot on the evening of that fine spring day, once again heading toward the South End, this time to Max Harkey's place, where I would rejoin my beloved Rafik and his unbridled animal magnetism.

3

Dinner at Eight

Max Harkey lived atop a four-story brownstone called the Appleton. The building had been gutted and lavishly refitted during the golden days of the Boston Housing Authority, when slum property was proclaimed historic landmark willy-nilly, then mindlessly purged of its history to be rezoned, rebuilt, and reassessed. This one time historic treasure now boasted an architectural disfigurement—a glass-walled penthouse erected upon the original roof. That anachronistic superstructure was Max Harkey's place, which seemed an appropriate home for the controversial director of the Boston City Ballet. Lesser mortals occupied the original four levels of the building, though my interior-designer friends claim that every flat in the Appleton is a decorator's dream. The building lies within two convenient blocks of the Boston Center for the Arts on a narrow cul-de-sac dubbed Appleton Mews, a reference to the numerous converted carriage houses that line the street. The location also puts it within a few blocks of Station D, headquarters of the Boston Police Department.

It was almost eight o'clock when I arrived there, fashionably on time. I noticed Big Red parked on the sidewalk outside the building and felt a tingle around my left nipple. Strange what a symbol of love can do.

I entered the foyer and pressed the button for number five. Within seconds a voice with a slight and pleasant accent came over the intercom.

"Who is there, please?"

"Stan Kraychik."

There was a long pause before he asked, "Your name again, please?"

"Stan Kraychik. I'm with Rafik Panossian."

After another pause the buzzer sounded and I went in. I hoped I wouldn't need a passport and visa to get into the penthouse. I found the lobby elevator, which was a small cubicle paneled in bird's-eye maple. Once inside I pressed the button marked "PH," which obviously stood for penthouse. Yet the label didn't seem right for a fifth-floor apartment that had been stuck onto the roof of an old brownstone. Forty-fifth floor, maybe. But I live on a fifth floor, and I sure don't consider my place a penthouse.

The elevator door closed with a fluid whoosh, and the tiny chamber slid upward noiselessly, without any mechanical sound or vibration. The manufacturer's name engraved on a brass plate above the panel of buttons explained the odd lack of noise. The elevator had been built by HydraLift Ltd of Liverpool, England. It must have worked by hydraulics instead of motors and pulleys and cables. The elevator came to a smooth stop and bobbed for just a second until the pressurized fluid stopped moving, kind of like a waterbed. The door slid open onto a vestibule from which wafted the scents of dried spice and wool carpeting. Atop a black-lacquered console sat a large vase of winter cherry and three long branches of eucalyptus. Also on the console was a copper-and-glass art deco lamp that gave a soft pinkish glow to the small area. I saw my reflection in a large mirror framed in verdigris-finished wood, and I felt rich.

The door to Max Harkey's apartment swung open and discharged all the noises and jabber of a party in progress. A small, sturdy-framed young man with tawny skin and bold blue-green eyes stood in the open doorway and greeted me.

"You are Stan?" he said.

I nodded. I could tell he'd paid a lot to have his blond hair waved and colored, and the look suited him.

He said, "I am Rico." His accent was gossamer and appealing. "Please come in?" he said like a question.

"Where are you from?" I asked.

"Brazil."

I entered Max Harkey's apartment and was engulfed by a world of visual art. Covering most of the wall facing me in the large foyer was a panel by David Hockney, one of the famous swimming-pools. Rico beckoned me toward the drawing room, where the other guests were gathered. On the way I passed a small alcove that showcased two pieces—a pair of Roman warriors cast in bronze, each figure about two feet high. The men were poised for battle, with their plumed helmets and unsheathed weapons, but they could have been ready for sex too, with their strongly arched backs and their muscular buttocks tense and exposed.

I continued into the drawing room. Despite the people talking and drinking and chatting energetically in there, my attention was taken by a gigantic Bösendorfer piano, shiny black and as long as a mobile home. It sat regally surrounded by freestanding sculpture, the most notable of which was a large piece in rosewood—a stylized danseur, noble and aloof, perhaps inspired by Max Harkey in his youth. A vague memory from a college art course brought the name Ivan Meštrović to mind, perhaps because the sculptor was a fellow Slav. Then my eyes wandered to the huge Morris Louis canvas that occupied the far wall. Max Harkey's place was a goddamn museum and the guests didn't even seem to notice.

A striking man in his early fifties with a square-angled face and a leonine mane of silver hair approached me. The cleft in his chin looked so matinee-idol that I wondered if it was natural. The skin around his jaw and throat was still taut against the muscles and bones beneath. His pale blue eyes stared into mine with a cold, almost threatening gaze.

"You must be Stan," he said and extended his hand. "I am Max Harkey."

I shook his hand and replied, "Thank you for inviting me."

"And high time," he said. "I know Rafik so well, I should meet his other half."

He portrayed the gracious host perfectly, complete with appliquéd sincerity.

He led me to the wet bar, where Rico had already resumed mixing drinks. That young thing certainly moved fast. I ordered a martini and while Rico set it up, one of the other guests came over. Max Harkey introduced him as Marshall Zander, a longtime friend and the major benefactor of the Boston City Ballet. Marshall Zander looked about the same age as Max Harkey, but with thinning brown hair that would be mostly gone before it ever became a distinguished gray. His body seemed lumbering and awkward, unused to any kind of movement. Clearly he had never danced. Though his clothes were obviously expensive, they were dowdy and fit him badly. He was like a big, sloppy dog—one that had a fancy pedigree but lacked any grace.

"What brings you here?" he asked, which seemed an odd question to ask a guest. Perhaps he didn't know that I was coupled with Rafik, or perhaps he didn't care, or perhaps it was just his clumsy attempt at friendliness.

"I'm with Rafik," I replied.

"Oh," he said without interest and then turned his attention to Rico, who at that moment was placing my martini in front of me. He gestured for me to take the drink, which I did. Then I sipped. It was perfect—super dry and with a twist.

Max Harkey then took me to meet Madame Rubinskaya, whom I'd already seen that morning at the ballet studios. Madame was ensconced in a capacious easy chair upholstered in velvety azure mohair. She'd positioned her legs to show off the calves and ankles and feet, which were exquisite despite her age. She alternated between smoking a long cigarette in an ivory holder and sipping what looked like sweet vermouth poured over ice. When Max Harkey introduced me, the old woman forced a smile.

"Of course," she said, pronouncing her "r" in two syllables. She offered me her hand while she fixed her eyes somewhere beyond my face. "We have met before."

I took her hand, not sure whether I should kiss it, shake it, or simply hold it. It was strangely firm and beautiful, strong too, without the slightest bump of arthritis. Her nails had been meticulously enameled with a muted red polish, and the pale crescent moons peeked out near the cuticles. Her face, however, was another matter. Madame had applied a chaotic array of makeup for the occasion, presumably her evening look, one intended to impart a sense of Continental glamour, but which instead made her look like a porcelain doll that had survived a blitzkrieg. It was hardly an improvement on the stark mask she had worn earlier that day, and in a weak moment of esthetic compassion, I almost offered her a free makeup session at Snips. But I quickly realized my folly and said nothing. I gave her hand a friendly squeeze and released it finally. She placed it back on the arm of the chair, and I caught her ever so slightly wiping her palm against the soft, nappy fabric. Perhaps it was a nervous reflex. Or perhaps she felt contaminated.

Just then I felt a familiar warm arm snake itself around my waist and I knew that Rafik was near me. I turned and looked directly into his handsome face. What luck to love him!

"Hi," I said.

"Finally you have come," he said. "I was worried."

So he did think about me!

"Choosing my outfit took longer than I thought," I said. I glanced quickly around the room and noted that all the guests except Marshall Zander and myself were wearing black. Sure, there were startling jags of color among the accessories, but the basic color scheme tonight was as I had predicted—black on black.

Hanging onto Rafik's other arm was Toni di Natale, the conductor whom I had also met at the ballet studios earlier that day. Even Toni's color choice proved that she belonged properly to this group. She wore a long-sleeved gray silk blouse and a formal evening skirt of black wool crepe. Her concession to color was the silk scarf of variegated bright blues and purples that she'd knotted loosely around the collar of her blouse.

"Good to see you again," she said with practiced geniality. It was obvious that she was using her high Brit that night. Toni di Natale gave a theatrical toss to her headful of lush red hair. The gesture was already too familiar to me, like an irritating tic. She probably did it a lot when conducting from the podium . . . or the headboard. I wondered if her friendliness with me was just a ploy to improve her chances with Rafik. It wouldn't be the first time one spouse had been charmed to clear a pathway to the other.

"Nice scarf," I retorted with the same mock familiarity, though the scarf was truly gorgeous.

She smiled broadly at me then pulled Rafik away with her toward the wall of glass windows that lined one side of the room. Rafik winked back at me. "See you later," he said as Toni led him away.

Left in their wake, I answered softly, "I'm counting on it." I recalled his promise to spend the night in celebration of our anniversary already passed. It wasn't looking hopeful.

Max Harkey reappeared and murmured to me, "Fine young man."
"I know," I said. I wondered if Toni di Natale's flirtation with my
lover was bothering me because she represented the kind of woman
I might have been had I been a woman. One's own obnoxious flaws
seen in others can often provoke irrational dislike for them.

Among the remaining guests were two dancers from the ballet class
I'd watched that morning, the two who'd stood at the same barre with
Rafik—one the young man whose body resembled the most ideal
incarnation of mine, and the other the blond ballerina who had
continued her stretches while the other dancers left the studio. Tonight they stood together, apparently inseparable. They were drinking what looked like plain mineral water. I asked Max Harkey about
them.

"The boy is Scott Molloy," he said, "and the girl Alissa Kortland."

I knew the terms "boy" and "girl" were often used throughout the
dance world without disparagement, but coming from Max Harkey
they still sounded pejorative. "I've seen them both on stage," I said,
"but I didn't even recognize them."

"Performance often brings out aspects of the personality not evi-
dent in ballet class or ordinary society," replied Max Harkey. "By the
end of the evening you may know more about them than you care to."
He made a small laugh. "I've seated you between them at dinner."
Then he added, almost to himself, "Interesting how much Scott
Molloy resembles you in basic body type."

I thought, Except for my love handles, you mean. Sometimes I
wonder if I should just lose the weight—*actualize* myself, as it were—
and open a Twelve Step weight-loss clinic.

Suddenly we all heard the rich sonorities of the grand piano filling
the large reception room. The one remaining guest I hadn't formally
met had seated himself at the massive Bösendorfer and had launched
into a dazzling piece of music that energized the air like a musical
aperitif.

"Jason Sears," whispered Max Harkey. "Brilliant talent. Recently
arrived from London with Maestra di Natale. He hopes to gain entrée
to Boston's concert scene."

The pianist was a surprise to me. When I'd first seen him among
the other guests I assumed he was a model who'd been invited as a
kind of decoration, so super-groomed were his looks and demeanor.
That Jason Sears was also a virtuoso seemed redundant. His fingers

flew over the keyboard, nearly igniting it with a tour de force that urged climax upon musical climax. The piece was so unabashedly romantic that I found myself almost lightheaded from its sentimentality. Yet there was something about the shameless passion of the music that connected to me deeply, something I wanted to believe in and yield to, but was too embarrassed to admit. I watched Rafik and saw that he too was enthralled with the music, responding physically to every sound. Next to him Toni di Natale listened with the analytical detachment of a judge at a piano competition. Meanwhile Marshall Zander leaned against the wet bar smoking a cigarette and gulping his liquor. His vacuous face seemed impervious to the wild rush of notes, and my first impression of him changed. I saw that he resembled an evolved primate more than a canine. He might even be related to those big brutes, the Kong family.

Elsewhere Scott Molloy and Alissa Kortland stood side by side, still drinking mineral water and whispering to each other, unaffected by Jason Sears's fiery performance. Then I noticed that Madame Rubinskaya had vanished from the room, as had Rico the houseboy. That young man sure moved fast. Then again, so had the old woman.

Five minutes and several thousand notes later, Jason Sears finished the piece with a grand flourish of crashing chords. He let the final sounds ring through the air for several long seconds before damping the strings into silence. It took most of us a few moments to recover from it all. Then we burst into applause that lasted almost as long as the brief piece itself had. When all the enthusiasm and the congratulatory comments had subsided, Rico the houseboy reappeared and announced that dinner was served.

Jason Sears approached Max Harkey and excused himself from dinner because he had an early flight the next morning.

"Besides," he said, "I have horrible jet lag."

Max Harkey replied, "It certainly didn't show in your playing."

"That's just good technique," said the pianist. He bade good-bye to the group of us, and then made a personal farewell to Toni di Natale, who was still hanging onto Rafik's arm. "I'll see you at the hotel later," he said to her while eyeing Rafik dubiously.

I wondered, what else did this dashing young lion excel at? I half expected to hear about his prowess at differential equations. There seemed only one more superlative left to this paragon, and I couldn't keep my eyes from wandering to that region of his anatomy where lurked the most superficial measure of a man. But the drape of his pleated trousers concealed all.

Toni di Natale said to him, "Get some rest, Jason." Then she added, as if to counteract her obvious coolness, "The Liszt went well tonight."

"Thanks," he said, but his smirk showed more irritation than gratitude. Then he departed quickly.

The rest of us filed into the dining room. The table was a monolith of oiled mahogany that rested on six massive square legs. Tens of flames from two elaborate candelabras washed the room in warm light and caused the place settings of porcelain, silver, and crystal to glitter softly and give a welcome feeling to the room. Someone had raided the vault at Tiffany & Company.

We took our seats according to the place markers—hand-lettered cards edged with a Florentine stripe of marbled green and gold leaf. Max Harkey sat at one end and Madame Rubinskaya at the other. Along one side, starting at Max Harkey's end, was Marshall Zander, then Toni di Natale, and then Rafik, at Madame's end. On the other side were Alissa Kortland, then me, and finally Scott Molloy, also near Madame Rubinskaya.

Scott Molloy quietly asked me to change places with him so that he and Alissa Kortland could sit together. But I was certain that Max Harkey had choreographed his table seating with the same care he used when positioning his dancers on stage. So I replied to Scott Molloy, "I'm fine, thank you."

Max Harkey overheard the surreptitious exchange and asked, "Is there a problem?"

For an awkward moment neither Scott Molloy nor I could answer. Then I said, "Not at all," and I took my seat. Scott Molloy sat down too, but he turned his body slightly away from me, so that he angled more toward Madame Rubinskaya. Max Harkey made a small frown at the slight disturbance, but said nothing more about it. The meal began at last.

Rico served us, and his talent at vanishing and reappearing by magic was tested to its limit with eight guests. The first course was a cold soup, creamy pink and sweet and sour all at once. I commented on it, partly to ease my social discomfort, partly to compliment Max Harkey's cuisine.

"It's delicious," I said.

"Is only borscht," said Madame Rubinskaya with a small shrug, as if to emphasize the inanity of my remark.

"Mousseline de borscht," corrected Max Harkey with a quick wink to Madame.

"Mousseline," repeated Madame with the tiniest smile and nod back to Max Harkey.

"It's her own recipe," said Max Harkey, addressing everyone. "Top secret, too."

Suddenly everyone else at the table was making suitable complimentary sounds about Madame's excellent soup. I watched Rafik and Toni di Natale put down their spoons and applaud Madame and smile openly at each other. Their movements harmonized with the same natural ease that happens between siblings or lovers. On either side of me Scott Molloy and Alissa Kortland imitated their actions precisely and joined in the applause. Meanwhile, Madame Rubinskaya accepted everyone's praise with austere cordiality. My original and sincere if simple comment had been blown out of proportion, and I felt like a bumpkin.

Once we all resumed our discreet sippings and scoopings of the cool pink concoction, Marshall Zander said suddenly, "So what do you do, Stan?" His words came out a bit too loud and with an obvious effort to keep them from slurring from all the liquor he'd had, but he did succeed in turning everyone's attention back toward me. I waited until every spoon was still with suspense before delivering my answer.

"I burn hair."

"You what?" said Marshall Zander.

"I'm a hairstylist," I answered. "On Newbury Street."

Rafik interjected, "He is very good."

Toni di Natale gave Rafik a playful nudge with her shoulder. "I'm sure he is," she said. Then she asked me with her broad, fake British accent, "Mine is the devil to get right. Would you do it some time?" Once again she gave her wavy red tresses that well-practiced shake. I was already tired of Toni di Natale.

"And would you do mine too?" added Alissa Kortland, blatantly mimicking Toni di Natale's accent du jour.

"And mine?" added Marshall Zander with a glazed, mooning stare.

"And leave mine alone," said Scott Molloy with a scowl.

"I'd be glad to do you all," I said. Some of them tittered politely at the double entendre, but the topic of my career was summarily dropped, as was any further inclusion of me in the conversation. The talk switched quickly to the gossip of the dance world, about which I knew little and for which I cared even less. The only other person who didn't join in the conversation was Marshall Zander, who was gaping at me from across the table, and who was now quenching his thirst with Max Harkey's fine wine. I certainly didn't want to encourage him with friendly chatter, so I sat quietly and listened and observed everybody else.

The talk focused on dance activity in New York, of which Boston was apparently a mere province. It was all about dancers and recent performances, who was doing what with whom both onstage and off, who was really good, and who was a fake. But despite the clever remarks, the words generally rang empty, as though the guests were all playing prerecorded tapes for each other, showing off their verbal pirouettes. Throughout the sophisticated banter I watched their faces, which seemed to tell more than their words. Toni di Natale was obviously smitten with Rafik, who was in the thick of the dance talk. I saw her being entranced by Rafik's mouth and the shapes it made when he spoke. I knew exactly what she was thinking too—how those lips might taste and feel, and the things they might do. I found myself gazing at my lover's mouth and then at Toni di Natale's infatuation with it. When I finally looked elsewhere around the table, I caught Max Harkey and Alissa Kortland exchanging unlikely glances that betrayed desire and submission on both their parts. Then to my horror I caught Marshall Zander studying me with the same intent. Our eyes met and locked for a moment and I thought, No!

Just then Rico entered the dining room carrying a Venetian glass charger in his strong young arms. Upon the large platter sat an edible dome of molded filets of meat, oven-crusted and succulent. It was surrounded by spearettes of asparagus, caramelized onions, and braised endive. All was arranged on a bed of broad flat noodles. A narrow wedge of the meaty dome had been cut away and laid flat to show the stuffing of pâté and pistachio nuts.

Max Harkey said, "We must thank Madame for sharing another treasure with us—*Escalopes de Veau* Rubinski."

Madame Rubinskaya replied, "The czar's cook make this for my grandmother. She was the czar's favorite ballerina."

"Brava! Brava!" said Marshall Zander, and he applauded loudly.

Everyone at the table joined him. Then Marshall stood up, still applauding, and gestured for the rest of us to do the same. But we kept our places, wanting simply to eat and not to continue with the theatrical event that dinner had become.

When the applause stopped, Madame Rubinskaya added wryly, "You should instead give ovation to Rico. He goes all morning to find veal. Then he does everything exactly how I say. No question. I think maybe he will make good dancer too." She laughed lightly at her own joke. Rico smiled in gratitude from the console where he was slicing the veal and filling our plates.

The meal proceeded in a grand manner, with the additional courses including a buttery *gratin* of sliced artichokes and *duxelles*, a sorbet, and a salad. The wines were French and Californian. All were of excellent vintages, and all played a major role in the culinary event far beyond that of a simple beverage, or so we were told.

But despite the refined airs, and the extraordinary food and wine, and the fabulous surroundings, I really wasn't enjoying myself, especially since I had to watch Toni di Natale and Rafik sitting together across from me. Their whispered exchanges seemed rude enough, but the real test came in trying to ignore Toni's sex-laden smirk when she passed Rafik the boat of creamy dill dressing, all milky white and viscous and suggestive.

Rico the houseboy offered me the only moment of comic relief by flirting in a direct and playful way that reminded me of a brief romance I'd had with a young Balinese. It had been a simpler kind of love than the one I now shared with Rafik—who at one point noticed Rico lingering over my shoulder long after a plate had been set properly in front of me.

Rafik said, "I think Rico likes Stan."

To his simple taunt I replied too quickly and too loudly, before my higher self could edit and censor my words.

"What do you care?" I said.

Everyone was instantly silent, eager to witness a private quarrel in public.

"Excuse me?" Rafik asked, as though he had misunderstood me.

"You and Toni have been flirting all night."

At that instant Toni di Natale removed her hand from where it had been resting affectionately atop Rafik's forearm.

"Don't be a child, Stani," he said, then with obvious defiance placed Toni di Natale's hand back onto his forearm and patted it there securely. But that didn't bother me half as much as hearing him use my nickname so callously in front of the others. He knew it would provoke me. For some reason Rafik was purposely trying to hurt me. Nicole had been wrong about that. But it was neither the time nor the place to press him for his reasons, so I let it go for the moment. I did ask Rico for more wine though, and I made a point of grasping his arm and holding it tenderly when I made the request, and then again when he refilled my glass. Two could play at Rafik's game.

The brief and tension-ridden exchange between us had caused various reactions around the table. Marshall Zander seemed inordinately pleased by it, as though a minor squabble increased my availability to him. Max Harkey seemed bored by it, as though homosexual misunderstandings were a tedious if necessary part of the dance world. Scott Molloy was intrigued by our male-to-male tiff in a vicarious sort of way, while Alissa Kortland studied Scott Molloy's interest with a keen, judgmental eye. Toni di Natale seemed amused by the whole episode, and Madame Rubinskaya remained above it all, impervious, unnoticing, as though an awkward moment like ours never really occurred in polite society.

Dinner continued in an atmosphere of congeniality, however forced or mistrustful. When at last we'd finished and were sitting nearly comatose around the big table, Rico once again appeared at the perfect moment and cleared the plates noiselessly.

Max Harkey said, "Before we take dessert in the salon, I have some announcements about the spring program." His voice assumed a pontifical tone as he continued. "As you all know, or at least most of you do"—here he eyed me politely—"I have just returned from London and I am delighted to bring good news."

The relief in the air was palpable, as though some imminent disaster had been averted and everyone could once again breathe normally. Just then Rico entered the room. His face, usually playful and animated, now showed concern. He leaned toward Max Harkey and whispered into his ear. The result was that Max Harkey then excused himself to accept a telephone call in another part of the penthouse. With him gone, a strange constricting pressure also left the room.

"Sheesh!" said Scott Molloy. "When he mentioned the spring program I thought sure the ax was going to fall."

"What do you mean?" asked Alissa Kortland.

"I heard he wants to cancel our new piece with Rafik."

Alissa Kortland began, "Not *Uomo gio—*"

"Please!" interrupted Rafik. "Do not talk about my work here." He shot a quick irritated glance at me. Then he asked Scott Molloy, "Did Mr. Harkey say something I do not know?"

Scott said, "I've seen his reaction during our rehearsals. I don't think he approves of your theme." At this remark Marshall Zander tried unsuccessfully to stifle a laugh. Scott Molloy scowled back at him and continued, "I think Mr. Harkey might be conservative about those things."

Marshall Zander then burst into laughter that continued until he lost his breath and began to cough. Then he lapsed into a series of gurgling and wheezing and gulping noises. When he finally recovered himself, he took a big drink of the fine red wine and said to Scott Molloy, "You're too much, kid. Too much." Then he shook his head in disbelief at the young dancer's last remarks.

Rafik continued the original conversation as though it hadn't been interrupted by a near medical emergency. "I think Mr. Harkey would tell me if he changed his mind."

"Don't be so sure," replied Alissa Kortland. "He's been known to change a program on opening night. Anything is possible with him and his moods." As if to prove her remark, she pouted like a child who'd been denied an ice cream.

Madame Rubinskaya spoke sharply. "Is enough now, all of you! If you cannot say to his face, don't say at all."

Marshall Zander retorted with a wine-swollen tongue. "The Geshtapo has shpoken."

Madame Rubinskaya glared angrily back at him. I thought Marshall Zander might stick out his tongue at the old woman, but he didn't.

Toni di Natale said, "I think it's peculiar, the way you all treat him like a daddy." Her high-Brit was really flying now. "Then as soon as he's gone, you all go at him like a roomful of naughty children."

Except for me, I thought dizzily. I asked Rico for just one more glass of wine. Rafik gave me a tiny shake of his head, a discreet warning for me to stop drinking. I raised my empty glass toward him as though making a toast, a toast to our mutual defiance.

Toni di Natale continued, "From my experience with him, Max is perfectly approachable. All our interactions have been honest, straightforward, and adult."

"Well, then," said Alissa Kortland, still imitating Toni di Natale's affected speech, "you've obviously gone beyond the daddy stage with him."

"What?" said a startled Toni.

Alissa replied, "I see the way he looks at you, and you at him."

"My dear, our relationship is strictly professional."

"Then it's just a question of who's paying, isn't it?" said Alissa.

Toni di Natale replied airily, "Why, Alissa, I believe you're jealous."

"Should I be?"

Toni di Natale giggled. "You silly girl! There's not a thing between Max and me."

Madame Rubinskaya said, "Stop! Is shame to talk like this!"

"Shame on the bloody lot of you," I said and guzzled my drink.

Rafik said, "No more for you."

I blew him a kiss.

Toni di Natale said, "Just for your information, Alissa, I'm engaged to Jason Sears."

"Then why are you flirting with my lover?" I demanded.

Toni di Natale tossed her red hair and replied blithely, "Because Rafik is so adorable and because it's fun. No harm, Stani."

I replied flatly, "My name is Stan."

Madame Rubinskaya shook her head in disdain.

When Max Harkey returned to the table, his face was ashen. He sat down and stared into space for a few worried minutes before speaking. The telephone call had obviously disturbed him, and everyone at the table attended him as they would the Delphic oracle.

"As I was saying before that unfortunate interruption, I had some good news to relate to you all. While I was in London I managed to engage the *assoluta* of choice for our spring program." Max Harkey looked directly at Madame Rubinskaya at the other end of the long table. He went on, "Mireille Rubinskaya, Madame's own grand-niece, was to join us in the title role for our revival of *The Phoenix.*"

Madame Rubinskaya's warm smile lapsed quickly into a confused frown. "What you mean 'was to,' Maxi?"

Max Harkey replied, "I'm afraid that's the bad news. That telephone call was long distance from London. Our dear Mireille was injured during rehearsal this afternoon."

"*Bozhe!*" said Madame. "How this happen?"

Max Harkey shook his head with profound regret. "Her partner . . ." he began, then had to compose himself before continuing. "It seems she made a bad preparation for a lift and, well, he just couldn't get her up. She landed directly on her knee."

I saw Rafik shiver in empathetic pain for the dancer and her injury.

Madame Rubinskaya said, "I will call her now."

"You can't," said Max Harkey. "It's too late."

"Too late?" she said with increasing alarm.

"I mean the time," he replied.

"Why?" she countered. "They call you."

"It's five hours later in London. Mireille is resting quietly now. They waited until after the surgery to call so they'd have a full report. You can call Mireille tomorrow."

"How it can happen?" said Madame Rubinskaya.

Max Harkey answered sadly, "It just happens, you know that."

Madame replied, "New ballet is not good. Too fast."

Rafik asked Mary Harkey, "Will she dance again?"

He answered solemnly. "It doesn't look good. She's probably got to stop for four months at least. One thing is hopeful, though. The ligaments are all intact." Then he added as if talking to himself, "Thank God she didn't hurt—" Then he checked himself, "—anything else."

"So much for the revival of *The Phoenix,*" said Marshall Zander.

Toni di Natale added, "I suppose it saves me rehearsing a new score. Maybe I can have some fun instead."

"Callous bitch!" said Alissa Kortland.

"Come off it, Alissa," said Toni di Natale. "You don't even know the girl."

"It's still bad luck when another dancer is injured, no matter who it is," said Alissa.

"I'm glad to see your concern, Alissa," said Max Harkey. "Because I intend to go on with the performance exactly as planned. Except that you will dance the lead."

"What!" said Alissa Kortland in astonishment.

Max Harkey stared directly across the long table at Madame

Rubinskaya. Then, keeping his eyes on the old woman, he nodded and said, "Yes, Alissa, you will dance *The Phoenix.*"

Madame Rubinskaya uttered a horrified, "No! It cannot be."

Everyone at the table turned toward her.

"But it can," said Max Harkey.

"You know, Maxi. You know very well. That role is for Mireille alone. It cannot be for other ballerina. You know the contract. It says for Mireille alone. And you promise."

"I regret this news of her injury more than any of you can imagine. It is a personal blow to me."

"Oh, Max," said Marshall Zander. "It's *her* damn knee, not yours."

Max Harkey replied, "I'm afraid there is much more to this matter than Mireille's knee. Nonetheless, the program will proceed as scheduled. *The Phoenix* will go on."

"You cannot do that, Maxi," said Madame Rubinskaya gravely.

"But I can," he replied.

"You know. You promise!" she said.

"I know that the promise was not unconditional. The circumstances have changed, so the original agreement no longer holds."

"How? How!" The old woman was almost screeching.

Max Harkey spoke to her with the calm surety of a son who has control of his mother. "Please, Ekaterina, not here."

Madame Rubinskaya and Max Harkey fixed their gaze on each other. They said nothing. The showdown lasted twenty excruciating seconds. Then Madame pushed herself away from the table and stood up.

"You please will excuse me," she said quietly. "All of you. I am very tired now." She walked away from the table and left the apartment directly, not even getting her coat.

With superb diplomacy, as though Madame Rubinskaya had left to use the lavatory, Max Harkey said to the remaining guests, "Shall we retire to the salon for dessert?"

As we got up from our seats and headed for the salon where this travesty of etiquette was apparently to continue, I leaned toward Alissa Kortland and muttered, "It's just like *The Red Shoes*. A ballerina goes down but the show goes on."

"You're horrible," she said, and walked away arm-in-arm with Scott Molloy.

The numerous martinis and glasses of wine I'd been imbibing all night had finally taken their toll on my social graces and on my kidneys as well. So before going to the salon with the rest of the guests, I wandered through Max Harkey's expansive apartment looking for a bathroom. I found one midway down a long hallway, quite far from the rest of the guests. Just as I was about to relieve myself I heard two people arguing loudly. It was Max Harkey and Marshall Zander. Their voices were coming from the open window of a nearby room that faced the same airshaft as the lavatory. With utter concentration I retightened my sphincter to avert the noisy splash. Tipsy as I was, I wanted to eavesdrop on the two men, and I nipped the gush of my water just in time.

Marshall Zander was threatening to withdraw his support from the ballet company if Max decided to cancel Rafik's new work, a piece called *Uomo giocoso*. (So that was its name!) Max was arguing that he was in charge of the art, and Marshall the money, and that Marshall should mind his own business. Marshall demanded to know what Max had against Rafik.

Max answered, "When he yields to me unconditionally, Rafik can have whatever he wants."

"You love him, then," said Marshall Zander with a pathetic whine.

"Don't be absurd, Marshall. Rafik needs to be humbled."

I wondered for a horrified moment if that was true. Was I supposed to be dominating Rafik?

"So you've appointed yourself the task," said Marshall Zander. "You are certainly the best at putting people down."

"Will you ever recover from my rejection of you, Marshall? That I consciously chose, in spite of your splendid sexual passivity and your ever-engorged trust fund, the youth and beauty of my girls over the intelligence and dedication you offered me? You more than anyone should know that my sexual preference is normal. It must infuriate you to see Rafik like that, with his blood at a constant simmer, just how you like them, and then find him involved with a hairdresser, no less. Hah!"

Then I heard a sudden loud crash—something large being thrown against a wall and shattering. The noise startled me and caused me to relax just the tiniest erg, just enough to let go of that little muscle that was holding back the white-water rapids. And then out it all came at once, cascading noisily into the hopper. When I finished, the two men were silent. Were they waiting for me to flush? Was one of them injured? Unconscious? Dead? I remained motionless for another moment. Finally Max Harkey spoke.

"That vase was worth a month's salary, Marshall."

"Then put it on your expense account, Max, along with your whores and the wardrobes you supply them."

"That's enough. You're boring me."

"We'll see how bored you are at the next trustees' meeting."

"Don't threaten me, Marshall. The company is endowed now, thanks to you. You shouldn't have done such a good job."

"We'll discuss this later, Max."

"As you wish. Our guests are waiting."

I saw the light in their room go out, so I flushed the toilet, then rinsed my hands and returned to the so-called party.

When I got back to the main salon everyone was already seated within the rough semicircle described by the expensive furniture. On the long sofa sat Marshall Zander, alone. Flanking the sofa were two overstuffed easy chairs, one occupied by Max Harkey and the other by Rafik, with Toni di Natale settled cozily on the matching ottoman next to his legs. Opposite that arrangement Scott Molloy and Alissa Kortland occupied a loveseat together. The only seats available were various odd side chairs, none of which looked too comfy, and I was feeling like I needed a lot of comfort at that moment. But short of asking Toni di Natale to move and let me sit by my lover, or else sharing the sofa with Marshall Zander, I had no choice but to take one of those hard, straight-backed side chairs.

Rico had wheeled in a small serving cart laden with assorted desserts: a silver bowl full of chocolate mousse; an open-faced apple tart with warm caramel sauce; fresh apricots, grapes, pears, and kiwis; and finally, two cheeses. The cart also carried hot beverages and after-dinner liqueurs. If the Boston City Ballet ever had to close its doors, it was clear that Max Harkey—or rather his houseboy Rico—could easily manage a fine restaurant.

Rafik was talking to Max Harkey.

"Is it possible Madame will stop *The Phoenix* on this program?"

"She'll come 'round to my way of thinking," replied Max Harkey. "Don't worry about that."

"I don't," said Rafik. "I worry about my own work on the program."

Max Harkey raised an eyebrow. "We'll see," he said.

Rafik continued, "I need Alissa in my piece, and it is too much for her to do both roles in the same program."

Max Harkey set his jaw firmly. "I said we'll see."

Marshall Zander said, "It seems to be a simple choice of reviving something old or showing something new. And you know where my allegiance lies, Max."

"Yes, I do," replied the other man.

Marshall Zander continued, "Showcasing new work is the main reason I continue to support the company."

"That's enough, Marshall."

"You shut the old woman up, Max, and now you're shutting me up. Who's next? The board of directors?"

"Perhaps you should go home, Marshall. You seem tired."

"But I haven't had my dessert yet, Max. You're not going to withhold your fine hospitality, are you? Not after all I've done for you and the company?"

"Is this bickering necessary?" asked Toni di Natale. "Can't we discuss the program without personal conflict?"

Scott Molloy said, "But it *is* all personal, so how can you avoid it?"

Alissa Kortland added, as though the intervening remarks had never been made, "I think I could do both roles on the same program. It would be no different from doing Odette and Odile."

Rafik answered quickly, "No. They are too strenuous. One role will suffer because of the other."

Max Harkey added, "Besides, my dear Alissa, you are not nearly ready to perform the two swans."

"And I'll never get there if you keep limiting me."

"Alissa, I told you, you will be performing *The Phoenix*, and the limitation there is certainly not in the role."

Alissa Kortland reddened and said nothing more.

Meanwhile I was wondering what had happened to propriety. First the artistic director and the chief benefactor of the ballet company were arguing publicly about some very private matters. And their candor was contagious, so now the dancers were chiming in with candid if feckless opinions. I figured, Why not add my own noise to the fracas?

"Which piece will attract a bigger audience?" I blurted.

All faces turned to me in astonishment.

Marshall Zander said, "Now there's a consideration! The audience."

I turned to Rafik. "Not that your work isn't excellent, love. But if you can have only one of these ballets on the program, shouldn't you consider audience appeal?"

Toni di Natale shifted slightly away from Rafik, as though sensing his growing anger.

Rafik glowered at me. "My work is not practical or political. It is personal. If you knew about my work, you would not say these things."

"But I don't know about it, do I? And whose fault is that? You've kept it all a big secret from me so far. So what am I supposed to think?"

"You should keep quiet when you don't know," said Rafik.

Scott Molloy added, "Rafik is right. You don't know what you're talking about."

"Well, why is it such a secret from me?"

Rafik answered. "Sometimes a work of art must grow in a private place, away from the eyes of others."

"So now I'm just 'others'?" I said. "You make it sound so damn mystical, Rafik, when it's probably nothing more than self-glory. Highbrow art is usually just vanity anyway." God, what was I saying? I knew how hard Rafik worked on his choreography. I only wanted to tell him that I loved him, but instead I was making harsh and critical remarks about his art, perhaps about his life.

Rafik replied, "Vanity is what you do in a beauty salon!"

"At least I focus my creative energy on another person, not on myself."

"And why?" asked Rafik. "Why? For a bigger tip. That is vanity!"

God, I was drunk. How could I be so drunk and be thinking and behaving so abominably, yet still have the capacity to realize that I was drunk? I bit my lip, fighting back tears of frustration. Here I was among intelligent, creative people, and with my lover, and I was being a boor. I was utterly unable to assume the mask appropriate. There was only one thing to do to escape from this self-imposed misery: have another drink. I got up from the disciplinarian chair and asked Rico to pour me a double shot of the strongest liqueur.

I toasted the group at large. "Here's to art and to tips!"

I gulped the syrupy liqueur all at once. Then I excused myself and left the party. Rafik did nothing. He didn't say anything, he didn't get up, he didn't try to stop me. It was Toni di Natale, of all people, who helped me out.

"Let me call you a cab," she said.

"Better to walk when I'm like this," I mumbled back. "Burn some of it off. Just get me out of here."

On the way out I once again noticed the gigantic shape of Max Harkey's grand piano, now quite blurry. A musical score almost the size of a newspaper folio and with a colorful cover was lying flat on the music stand.

"Whazzat?" I asked her.

"The score to *The Phoenix*," she said, then added somberly, "It's the music that started the whole argument."

Then to my surprise, she hugged me. I figured it was a holdover from her Italian upbringing. She murmured into my inebriated ear, "You are lucky to have Rafik." Her words and her warm breath caused my ear to burn. "He is a very sexy man."

I felt a tingling around my nipples, that sure sign of strong emotion. "Everyone else seems to think so too," I said.

Rico arrived with my coat. He gave me a big friendly smile, but I was too drunk and too self-absorbed to appreciate it.

Outside on the street the sight of Big Red almost caused me to burst into tears. But I bit the inside of my lip and pinched the bridge of my nose to keep the tears at bay. I wasn't about to be seen stumbling home with hot tears streaming down my cheeks, looking like any other jilted queen. When I got home, I found myself bewildered by what had just happened. I had somehow killed my dream of love. How had it happened? What demons lurked within me to accomplish such a thing? I stumbled into bed, and then, remembering that this was to be my anniversary night with my lover, I finally broke down and sobbed and wailed into my pillow. Even Sugar Baby did not join me that night.

4

Singing in the Rain

Next morning the telephone blasted me out of a fitful sleep, like a panic alert for a nuclear attack. Its tormented electronic bleating launched a dull unfocused pressure at the back of my skull. With a queasy stomach, all I could recall was the vast quantity and variety of alcohol and food that I had consumed just a few hours earlier. Groggily I hoped the phone call would be Rafik, eager to apologize for his role in the horrible misunderstanding we'd had last night. At numerous points during the night I'd awaken startled and anxious and tense. I'd get as far as punching his number, but then logic would take over and I'd hang up before the call went through. After all, what if he wasn't home? That would be even worse than the torture of regret. So throughout the long, lonely night I tried to assure myself that we'd soon be frantically apologizing and forgiving each other. And everything would be back to normal.

The phone was still ringing. I grabbed clumsily and dropped it, accidentally bumping Sugar Baby, who at some point during the night had deigned to settle on the empty pillow next to mine, Rafik's place. From her cat sleep she sprang from the pillow, leaped over my head, landed on the Turkish carpet that covers my bedroom floor, and scampered away. I put the phone to my ear, but before I'd even said hello, I heard Rafik speaking excitedly with his heavy French accent.

"Stani," he said, "there is great trouble. Max Harkey is dead!"

My first reaction was that Rafik was playing a prank to distract me and win back my affection. If so, it was one unworthy of his fertile imagination. Then again, perhaps it was that cultural difference between us that made his joke sound flat to me, some Francophone subtlety I still couldn't appreciate. But I wondered—and Max Harkey be damned—What about *us?* Aren't you sorry about last night? Have you forgotten how you hurt me?

"Stani?" he said uncertainly, as though the phone might be out of order and the connection never properly made.

"I'm here," I replied coolly, thinking to myself, And so far you haven't said the words I want to hear.

"Stani, I find him like this. Is horrible!"

"Where are you?"

"At his apartment."

I set my blurry vision toward the alarm clock. There seemed to be only one hand, pointing downward. It was 6:30.

"What are you doing there at this hour?"

The line was quiet. After a few seconds of waiting for his answer, I felt the throbbing at the back of my head move forward to my temple. Then an unexpected wave of nausea washed over me, and I felt a cold sweat break out on my forehead. I envisioned every goddam glass of alcohol I'd had last night. They all swirled in a vortex in my mind's eye, from the first martinis at my apartment, to the additional cocktails at Max Harkey's, to the numerous glasses of wine with dinner, to the tumbler of liqueur afterwards. It all came back with nauseating clarity. Oh, to be unconscious! All I wanted was to put the phone down and go back to sleep. Maybe then all of last night's mistakes—especially my boozy belligerence—would fade away back into a dream. Then I could wake up again later to a bright new world where everything was blue skies and songbirds. The idea was so appealing that I almost nodded off.

"Stani?" said Rafik.

I returned to the present, to the unpleasantness of why Rafik was at Max Harkey's place at six-thirty in the morning. Somewhere I recalled Max Harkey saying that Rafik needed to be humbled. Had the challenge been met last night, only to culminate in the man's death? I confronted Rafik directly.

"Did you spend the night with him?" I said.

"How you can ask such a thing?" he yelled. A tremor of pain rammed itself through my swollen brain. "Stani, his blood is everyplace."

The new tension in Rafik's voice told me that perhaps he wasn't kidding. I sat up in the bed. Sugar Baby must have sensed my alarm, because she jumped back up onto the bed and nestled against my thigh. I rested my forehead against my free hand.

"Tell me what happened, Rafik."

"I tell you, he is dead."

If he was telling the truth, there was only one thing to do. I'd been in those exact circumstances myself, facing a corpse. Back then I thought I'd done the right thing by being responsible and calling the police, but then I always learn the hard way.

"Rafik, if Max Harkey is really dead—"

"He is, Stani. Believe me."

"Then you must do exactly what I say."

"But Stani—"

"No buts, Rafik. Just listen and do. First, you wipe your fingerprints off everything you've touched in that place. *Everything.* Understand? And then you get out of there. Now! I'll be waiting for you here."

"I cannot do that, Stani."

"Why not?"

"The police are here," said the master of selective omission. "They do not know I am calling you. They ask me many questions. Will you come? Please?"

I paused, not quite sure what to do or say. My arrival at Max Harkey's place might only complicate things, especially with the police there. The line was quiet while I deliberated. When Rafik spoke again, I heard a new timbre in his voice, wily modulation, cryptic but musical, a kind of aural snare distilled from a legacy of Middle Eastern genes and the myriad ruses employed by clever harem boys to spare themselves painful punishment or even castration.

"Stani," he said, "I am sorry for last night. I did not mean those things." His words flowed like dark notes from a wood flute, and their exotic coloration left me defenseless. "I love you. I will stop my work. I will leave the ballet."

After our falling-out I'd hoped for a more dramatic reconciliation, a physical event where Rafik would arrive at my threshold repentant and contrite. Even at three o'clock in the morning he would beg forgiveness and let me show him just how much and how willingly I could forgive. But instead, Rafik was now inducing me to rescue him from a bad situation with the police, at the home of the very man with whom he might have had the ultimate confrontation, and who was now dead.

"Okay, Rafik. Don't quit your job yet. I'm on my way."

I hung up the phone and got out of bed. I turned on the shower, then decided that this situation precluded my usual morning ablutions. Instead I rinsed my face with cold water, put on some clean clothes, and was ready to leave within minutes. As I opened the door I noticed Sugar Baby's wide bewildered eyes following me. "Yes, doll," I said to her. "I am going without feeding you."

From my apartment to Max Harkey's penthouse is a brisk fifteen- to twenty-minute walk. Finding a cab to take me there was going to take just as long, so I opted for Slavic locomotion. The sun hadn't come up yet, and the air outside was misty and gray. The pavement felt damp and cold through the leather soles of my old loafers. The last dregs of last night's excess still coursed through my veins, altering my perceptions and my steady stride. I urged my legs to move faster, figuring the exercise might burn off the alcoholic poison and the gnawing doubt in my blood.

Despite my muddled thinking though, two facts were clear enough: Rafik needed me, and I wanted to help him. But this latest complication in the melodrama, *Life with Rafik,* was jangling my psyche. Before meeting him I had narrowly connected sex with love. Coupling was almost a spiritual act for me, a shared experience of two souls, elevated and sacred. But Rafik brought expanded dimension to the notion of elevated. His sturdy rig and his four smooth-moving limbs sang with the same true and natural ease as a born musician uses perfect pitch, except that Rafik's kind of body-song relates more to the hunt than to poetry. When he slides his supple self through space, he stalks everything in his path, and when he connects with his prey, it's pure fulguration, like a magnesium ribbon that flares white-hot.

Even after a year with Rafik the sex is so satisfying and surprising that I can't imagine doing it with anyone else. But I still insist on being safe. It annoys Rafik, who trusts our blood tests and who vows he is and always will be sexual only with me. But just as the idea of monogamy is no proof of love, neither is unsafe sex. The condoms are a disputed point between us.

The glamour and desirability of Max Harkey's address, so glitteringly evident last night, were now obscured by numerous police cruisers and a medical-rescue van that had completely blocked the narrow pavement and sidewalk for the entire length of Appleton Mews. Flashers whirled and noisy engines idled, as if in readiness for imminent departure. Since Appleton Mews was a dead-end street, traffic wasn't a concern, and at that early hour cars were even more unlikely. Still, a few police officers stood around ready to redirect anyone attempting to drive down the quiet street. At the far end of the Mews was the Appleton itself, usually refined and stately, now cordoned off by police markers. The gaudy neon ropes made the building look somewhat like a grande dame in disgrace.

Parked in front of the Appleton was a car that I recognized immediately, an old Alfa Romeo coupé with the designation "Giulia Sprint Veloce." I knew the classic sports car belonged to Detective Lieutenant Vito Branco of the Boston Police Department. Branco must have got a recent raise, because the Alfa's dark green paint had been expertly reconditioned.

Also parked out front was Big Red, in exactly the same place it had been last night. Had Rafik spent the night? The motorcycle caused neither tingles nor tears at that moment. I approached the Appleton's main entrance, where three more police officers were guarding the doorway under the great marble arch. I explained to them that I had a friend in the building and that I wanted permission to enter. I didn't exactly grovel, but past experience has taught me that politeness doesn't hurt when courting the police. One cop checked my identification and agreed to escort me up to Max Harkey's apartment. We went inside and entered the small wood-paneled elevator. As we ascended, the cop and I remained awkwardly silent, but we studied each other furtively. He looked like a walking display for all the accoutrements of authority: gun and holster, blackjack, handcuffs, squawk box, lug-soled boots, wide leather belt with heavy chrome buckle. Though he held his face in a tense scowl, his eyes kept shifting toward me, then darting quickly away, as if he was studying the panel of oiled maple in front of him. But I knew he was sizing me up, and for all my reasonable masculinity, I might as well have been hauling a sandwich board that read "GAY MAN INSIDE." That's probably what was unnerving the poor guy. But then, my sexuality seems to unhinge only the most fervently macho men.

The elevator door slid open onto the small vestibule that connected directly to Max Harkey's apartment. A funereal gray light caused me to look up, and I saw that the ceiling was skylit, which I hadn't noticed last night. The security door to the main foyer of the penthouse was wide open, and the cop led me in. In this very place last night had transpired a social gathering the rules of which I hadn't quite grasped, but nonetheless had managed to violate. This morning the cops were using their own set of peculiar rules, the ones that create pandemonium of any situation.

When I entered the sprawling penthouse, the first thing I saw was Max Harkey slumped at his big grand piano. He appeared almost to be playing the instrument, expressing himself in a deep and moving passage, his head lowered to the keys as if to coax the instrument's very soul to speak. Except that Max Harkey was dead. The Persian carpet at his feet was saturated with a huge dark stain, which I knew was blood.

Then appeared the brawny form of Detective Lieutenant Vito Branco. He didn't notice me as he approached Max Harkey's body and crouched down to examine it closely. His back was to me and he blocked my view of the dead man, but I caught a microsecond glimpse of a huge glistening wound, still red and alive, around Max Harkey's groin. From where I stood, it looked as though he had been castrated. I had to turn my head away and bite my lip hard, then take some deep breaths to quell the nausea. It wouldn't do to vomit here, in front of the cops. In a few moments the cold sweat subsided and I could turn my attention back to the body. Lieutenant Branco was still intent on the corpse, with what appeared to be more than a clinical interest. Was he as disturbed by the wounds as I was? Though Branco was younger than Max Harkey, perhaps he recognized the similarities between them. The victim was a man about the same build as Branco, six feet plus, with the same broad shoulders and sturdy loins. He even had the same strong jaw and cheekbones, same sculpted nostrils and lips. From my meeting last night, I hadn't guessed that Max Harkey still possessed such a muscular body. Branco was now gazing at the victim's legs, blood-drenched and fully exposed by the gaping silk bathrobe that lay open below his waist.

The limbs were obviously strong, yet elegant, almost regal. Oddly, I was saddened by the bloodiness. I wondered about Branco's powerful legs, how much bulkier his muscles probably were, and how his skin was most likely tough and hairy, not smooth like Max Harkey's. When the lieutenant changed position, I got a good look at Max Harkey's body. With great relief I saw that everything in his crotch was still intact. So what had held Branco's attention? Had he been compelled by machismo to make a comparison? Was there cause for envy? The lieutenant quickly moved his gaze away from the lifeless organs, and I wondered if I'd imagined the entire vignette, especially since sex is always on my mind, stimulating—electrocuting—my cerebral cortex to invent perversions where none exist.

I moved closer to the piano. Except for all the blood, Max Harkey's legs could have been sculpted from pale gray-blue marble. Then I saw the wounds close up—one clean deep puncture on the inner face of each thigh, directly into the femoral arteries. Max Harkey had been bled to death.

Branco rose quickly and steadied himself on the nearby piano. He closed his eyes as if to recover from his examination. Was it just the sudden rise to his feet? Or did Branco have a weakness? Did certain kinds of killings bother him more than others? Had anyone but me noticed his lingering interest over the dead man's legs? It wouldn't do to seem so interested in the exposed nakedness of an attractive male body, no matter how dead it was. With a scowl Branco forced his eyes open, and still he didn't see me. But I was getting reacquainted with all the dark masculine features that this cop shared with my lover, and then the million subtleties that distinguish the two handsome men. Branco's face twisted into a frown, and he stifled a belch. He seemed to be having a rough morning.

Branco spoke sharply to his sergeant. "Get him in a bag."

The sergeant replied, "Med-ex hasn't made his report yet, sir."

Branco snapped, "Then just get the damn bag ready!"

The sergeant wilted slightly at Branco's order, then he said, pointing to me, "What about him, Lieutenant?"

Branco turned toward me and stared for a long disbelieving moment before he said, "What are you doing here?"

"My friend called me."

"You tangled up in this?"

"No, but—"

Branco barked another question to his sergeant. "Where are the witnesses?"

Witnesses? Who else was present? And where was Rafik?

The sergeant answered Branco by jerking his head sharply toward the kitchen. Branco turned away from me and with a heavy tread went toward the swinging door that led to the penthouse kitchen. He paused at the swinging door and turned back to us. He pointed to me and said to his sergeant, "Hold him downstairs." Then he pushed the door open. A blaze of morning sun should have burst from the kitchen, but instead the drab monochrome of a drizzly March morning seeped out.

In spite of Branco's order to eject me from the premises, I asked the sergeant if I could see Rafik. The sergeant looked through me and said, "You heard the man." There was no sense in resisting the inevitable, so I let myself be led out from Max Harkey's apartment and back downstairs to be held outside at Branco's leisure. On my way out the front door I noticed that the latch had been jimmied. The officers out there eyed me with suspicion, hoping perhaps that I might do something that would galvanize them to action, to behave like cops. I went and stood near Big Red, as if the motorcycle and I might comfort each other while waiting for Branco. Fine droplets had condensed from the misty air onto the bike's lacquered metal parts and heavy chrome fittings. In the dim morning light Big Red emitted a kind of sanctified glow that enveloped me with its protective aura. How many times had I held onto Rafik's body while riding behind him on that motorcycle, on those fantastic and romantic trips to nowhere? Big Red was like family.

Suddenly the cops' radios squawked loudly, and jolted the three of them to alertness. The faggot and the motorcycle were small potatoes now that they'd got a call from the boss upstairs. A few minutes later two officers came out from the building, and along with them came a big surprise: Between them they were holding Toni di Natale, who was handcuffed. Lieutenant Branco followed behind. Toni di Natale looked confused and disheveled, as though she had been taken unawares. I noticed that she was wearing the same outfit she'd worn last night. She glanced toward me. Our eyes met, then she lowered her head guiltily. I wondered why. Had she killed Max Harkey? Had she had sex with Rafik? Perhaps both? But that vision of her—the confident woman now vulnerable and submissive to the brute force of two big men—well, it struck a chord in me, and I found myself feeling sorry for her.

The cops jammed the young woman into the back seat of a cruiser and drove off. Branco approached me where I was standing near Big Red.

"This your bike?" he said with an approving look.

"My lover's."

Grunt, went the cop.

I said, "I'd like to know how he is."

Branco replied, "You want to tell me what you're doing here?"

"Rafik called me."

Branco clenched his jaw muscles and compressed his lips, obliterating their sensuous fullness. His brow wrinkled. "So you're an accessory?"

"I *create* beauty, Lieutenant. I am not an accessory."

Branco pulled the corners of his mouth back into the hint of a smile, though his eyes maintained their steely blue-gray hardness. "Still the smart-ass, eh, Kraychik?"

"Whenever provoked, Lieutenant."

Then a strange thing happened. The lieutenant's face softened somewhat, and he looked directly into my eyes, as though for a moment he wanted to portray a person and not a cop. "How are you and your friend getting along?" he said.

I stalled. What did Branco care about my personal life? He was a straight cop and I was a gay hairdresser. What did it matter in his realm of the Moral Majority how I was muddling through my life? Or was he just looking for evidence?

"Could be better," I said. But I immediately regretted my candid reply. "How's *your* love life?" I asked, trying to make buddy banter.

Branco didn't reply, but instead jerked his head up and pushed his jaw forward. "I'll find you later," he said. Then he got into the Alfa coupé and drove off.

Shortly after that exchange came yet another surprise. Out the front door of the Appleton, completely unescorted, strolled Marshall Zander.

"I thought I saw you upstairs," he said. "What brings you here?"

"I could ask the same of you," I answered.

He smiled comfortably. "You could," he said. "The difference is that I'll tell you. Max called me this morning. Apparently someone had broken in and attacked him. He sounded pretty bad, so I called the police and came straight over myself."

"Didn't he call the police himself?"

"I don't know," said Marshall Zander. "Max needed help and he needed it fast. I didn't ask questions. I took action."

"Did Max tell you who attacked him?"

"He was already . . . gone . . . when I got here."

"I mean when he phoned you. Did he give you any clue who had done it?"

"No," he said. "I told you, he sounded awful. Scared. I didn't think to ask him anything, only to get here as fast as I could. Now I wish I had. We'd probably have his killer now."

I noticed then that Marshall Zander's brown eyes were filling with tears. His composure was dissolving fast. I'd seen it happen before, the way some people can maintain a façade of strength in the face of horror and even for a long while afterward, and then lose it all at once as soon as their audience has departed, which in this case was the police. His chin quivered while he spoke.

"You know who else was up there?"

I shook my head no.

"Of course you do," he said. "And I want to know what they were doing. Don't *you* wonder what your lover and that woman were doing up there? They were already there when the police arrived, you know."

"That doesn't mean anything," I said coolly, but his words had set my imagination running wild with doubt.

"Who did this to him?" demanded Marshall Zander. "Max, Max!" he wailed and then broke down into grotesque, gasping sobs.

Once again I saw why I had failed as a therapist. I couldn't tolerate the agony and the ugliness of anyone else's pain, real or imagined. I'd wanted to fix everything immediately, at any cost, even if it meant taking the pain onto myself. And that attitude and behavior will destroy the helper fast. A good therapist needs a detached, clinical kind of compassion, but I was cursed with the tendency to sacrifice myself for others. The only way for me to survive was to quit the field altogether, to leave the analyst's couch to the experts and work my miracle cures at the styling chair.

I stood there unmoved by Marshall Zander's breakdown, wishing

with all my cold heart that he would stop his crying and go away. I
didn't want to be involved with him or with Max Harkey's death. I
didn't even want to be there. I only wanted to know that Rafik was
all right, and so far I hadn't found that out. Where was he?

After a few more minutes of histrionic wailing, Marshall Zander
quieted down. He panted in shallow quick breaths like a blundering
slow-witted animal that has miraculously escaped its pursuer. But
once he regained his composure, his eyes became dark and mean, and
the next words he spoke were full of venom.

"If your lover had anything to do with this, so help me, I'll see him
pay for it."

But his threat rang hollow, as though he'd learned his emotions
from a correspondence course in acting. There was nothing in him to
fear, only to pity. He turned and walked away down Appleton Mews.
From behind I watched his body in motion, his sloppy gait a random
series of asynchronous lurches and lunges, the neurokinetic signals
firing without order from his brain and giving no clear shape to his
stride. Perhaps Marshall Zander's generosity to the ballet was his way
of compensating for the physical beauty and coordination he lacked.
He stopped at a new German convertible and got inside. The sleek,
low-slung, two-seater was completely incongruous with the man who
owned it. It too must have been a kind of compensation for what he
lacked in physical attributes. I was ready to bet that he'd had a
horrible childhood, with his peers picking on him mercilessly, and I
wondered with some pity about the person who lived inside that
vague, gelatinous body.

Finally, as if to dispel all the unpleasantness that had transpired so
far that morning, Rafik appeared under the arched entranceway to
the Appleton. The misty air seemed to clear around him, but I'm sure
I was imagining that. If anything, the air should have become murkier
upon his arrival, since my doubts were waxing ever stronger about
why he was there in the first place. I managed a worried little smile
and a wave, and he returned the gestures with a wan look as he
descended the steps and came to where I was standing with Big Red.
Then I opened my arms to him and he threw himself into them. We
stood in the rainy air like that for some time, embracing and rocking
each other's bodies, as though we were the star-crossed lovers in a
British film from the 1940s.

"It was horrible," he said, tickling my chilly ear with his warm lips as he spoke.

I replied, "What were you doing up there?"

"Max called me for help."

"When?"

"I do not know what time. He was so weak I almost did not recognize him."

"Rafik, did he say who attacked him?"

"No. He said that he was hurt, and he has called the police, and please for me to come right now."

For a wounded man, Max Harkey had certainly made a lot of phone calls.

"Why did he call you, Rafik?"

He pulled away from me. His eyes were fiery now. "What are you thinking?" he asked. I felt my face get hot and I had to look away from his gaze. He shook me gently. "Stani, tell me what you are thinking."

I kept my eyes lowered and said, "What was Toni di Natale doing here?" The meekness in my voice was disgusting. Rafik didn't reply, so I looked into his eyes for an answer. I had a right to know, didn't I? "Was she here already?" I said. "Or did she come with you?" I was trying to be direct and strong, yet I felt like a timid fawn in retreat— all because of the bewildering power of Rafik's warm body next to mine.

Still he remained silent.

"It looks suspect," I said.

"You are suspecting everything I do."

"No . . ." I said, but his words had an unhappy truth in them.

Rafik turned and started walking away from me.

"Aren't you going to take the bike?" I asked.

"It does not start," he said, and kept on walking.

That explained why Big Red had spent the night on the sidewalk in front of Max Harkey's apartment building. I caught up to Rafik and walked alongside him in silence. The cold wet air seemed to enhance the discord I had once again set off between us. At the head of Appleton Mews he turned in the direction of his apartment.

"Can you make me a cup of coffee?" I asked.

He looked at me, his whole face sad and angry at the same time, and his forehead appeared almost swollen, as though it could not contain the conflicting secrets that raged within.

"Yes," he said with a defeated sigh and a small shrug.

We walked the wet sidewalks to his place without another word. Rafik kept a one-room apartment a few blocks from the ballet company. The old brick building sat in squalor, and Rafik's personal domain within its walls resembled the lair of a untamed animal. It was overrun with the intriguing detritus of a bachelor artist, and was permeated with his wild exotic scents. The place was so small that the bathroom required a flawless Dior turn before you could close the door behind you. He kept it all clean enough, but it was hopelessly cluttered, and I sometimes wondered if Rafik wanted to live with me simply because I was the better housekeeper, which wasn't saying much.

Once inside, we shucked our jackets and I sat on his bed. He began the ritual of preparing Turkish coffee in the minuscule galley kitchen, measuring first the cold water and then the powdery coffee into a long-handled brass pot called an *ibrik*. I knew that J. S. Bach had written a "Coffee Cantata," but how could any music compare to Rafik's guileless improvisations at the stove? I was entranced by his natural grace, the supple moves of his arm and shoulder as he shifted the pot on and off the flame, the tilt of his head as he watched the brown elixir foam up and then subside from the rim of the pot, and the sway of his hips and body as he transferred his weight from one leg to the other. While Rafik transformed a household chore into a religious experience, I felt there was only one way to show him that I really cared for him and wanted him more than ever. I got up from my chair and went to where he stood at the tiny stove, his attention glued to the small pot. From behind I wrapped my arms around his slender waist and nestled myself against his strong back and his extra-firm butt. His clean masculine scent made me tremble slightly with pleasure and desire and with some uncertainty too.

"What . . . ?" he said while he continued with the coffee.

"Maybe we don't need that now."

Through the starchy cotton of his shirt I located his nipples and pulled gently at them. Usually that's a clear signal to him about what I want. But Rafik proceeded with the coffee preparation as though he was alone and content in his little room. My furtive hands wandered lower down his taut belly and sneaked in through the small openings between the shirt buttons along the front placket. I popped two of them open and plunged my hands into the curly hair on his chest. I grabbed little bunches and yanked gently, then a little harder, then took handfuls of his furry flesh and massaged it in small circular movements.

Yet Rafik was intent on the art of Turkish coffee.

My left hand wandered down below his belt to the front of his slacks, where I discovered that a favorite part of him had already become stronger and was pressing insistently against the fabric. Mine was hard and moist too, but then it usually is when I am touching Rafik.

"I love you," I murmured into his ear.

"And I love you," he said. "So I will make coffee."

"Let's lie down."

"We must talk."

Huh? Hadn't I already said everything that was important?

"Rafik, just turn the coffee off."

"No. You sit. I will bring coffee."

"I don't want coffee now."

He smiled slightly with that knowing smile that meant he was in control for the moment. He said, "But I do."

That did it. My own love barometer deflated at once, and I went and sat down as he instructed me. I had an uncomfortable feeling that his refusal to have sex wasn't due to the usual choreographic exhaustion that had been plaguing him recently. Rafik's sturdy member never lied. He obviously liked the attention I was giving him. No, his reason for not wanting to have sex with me that morning was just plain and simple rejection.

In the next moment, unguarded, perhaps desperate, hoping to allay my worst fears, I asked, "Are you involved with Toni di Natale?"

He turned around from the stove and made a small exasperated chuckle. "You are very silly man," he said.

"Then are you involved with what happened?"

Suddenly he banged the *ibrik* sharply against the stovetop, spilling some of the coffee and making the gas flame sputter and flare under the small pot.

"How can you think like that?" he yelled. "The police are treating me with more respect than my lover does."

"I'm sorry, Rafik."

"No, you are not. You think only of yourself. You come here and then you want sex. You do not try to comfort me. You do not see what trouble I have."

"But I do, I do."

"All you do is accuse me."

"Only because I don't know the facts. You keep things from me, and so I think you're hiding stuff."

"I tell you all that is important for you."

"But I want to know everything."

"You ask for too much."

"Rafik, what are you hiding?"

He turned away from me and leaned against the stove. He stood like that, motionless, until I realized that he was crying silently. I went to him again, held him close from behind, rocked him.

"I'm sorry," I said, and kissed the back of his neck. "I'm a selfish ass."

He mumbled his reply. "I think you should go now."

"Are you putting me out?"

He turned to face me and nodded sadly. "Please go."

"No coffee?"

He shook his head. "I want to be alone."

Great work, Stanley. Your lover has just been through homicidal horrors, and instead of comforting him, you put him through another interrogation based on your pathetic notions of fidelity and unrequited love. Maybe I really didn't deserve a lover, if that was the best I could do in a crisis. Back when I was alone, I was a model of stability and understanding. Now, in love, I was fretful and weak and dependent on the unconditional approval of my partner, no matter the circumstances. And worse, I imagined that anything he kept from me—a story, a phrase, a syllable—would later materialize as yet another reason for his leaving me. The intense attraction that initially bound us was unraveling, and no matter what I did to mend it, it only got worse.

I offered to make him dinner that night, figuring we could face this unpleasantness more objectively after we'd both cooled down. He agreed. Then I left him with his Turkish coffee while I walked back to my apartment under an opaque gray sky. At some point in my gloomy stroll homeward I felt an obscure and unexpected sense of hope, as though after tonight's cozy dinner—I'd be sure to make all his favorite food—everything would turn out all right again. I would express my love for Rafik in a culinary way that would solve all the problems caused by misunderstanding and murder, just the way the sun always managed to burn through the darkest, most impenetrable clouds.

And today I would win the lottery too.

5

Whose Lover Is He?

When I got back home it was almost nine-thirty, which gave me just enough time to feed Sugar Baby, turn a quick triple S (that's shit, shower, and shave), then head off to Snips. My official hours at the salon are ten to six, but I don't think I've worked a normal day since I started. On the whole though, I do put in more hours than I'm paid for, which is one reason Nicole tolerates my many unscheduled comings and goings. She knows that my guilt-driven conscience will force me to work extra time to compensate. Another reason she puts up with me is that my work is exemplary, even if my work habits are not.

When I set out for the salon, the air had mostly cleared and the opaque cloud cover had become luminescent as pearl. The scene was already being set for a romantic resolution that night with Rafik. I arrived at Snips and found Nicole free, so I invited her into my office for coffee, where I planned to recount the recent troubling events. The first change I noticed was the presence of a new item—a dainty barrel chair executed in pink wicker and cushioned in seafoam green chintz. Nicole caught my appraising glance at it. Without a word I set about making the coffee.

"Well?" she inquired.

"I didn't know Talbots sold furniture."

Nicole plunked her ample hips into my leather throne and patted her palm on the cushions of the delicate newcomer. "It's quite comfortable, darling. See for yourself."

"Comfortable for a Nantucket dwarf. What happened to the other one?"

Nicole smiled brightly and fairly chirped. "I gave it to Ramon. Poor thing is having such a time setting up his new apartment."

"He's in over his head," I replied. Ramon had recently moved into a huge two-bedroom place with a balcony and an unobstructed river view. It was far beyond his means, at least the ones he earned in traditional ways.

Nicole asked scornfully, "Haven't you ever been in over your head?"

"Only with love, doll. Never with money."

While the coffee brewed I told Nicole about all that had transpired, from last night's party to this morning's horrible discovery of Max Harkey's body.

"Not again," she said when I'd finished. "Don't you dare get involved. You know it only leads to trouble."

"Don't worry, Nikki. I have enough to do keeping my ship of love afloat. That comes first now. As for this killing, I'll cooperate with the police, but my Nancy Drew road show is closed forever."

"Good. Now when is Rafik moving in?"

"Nikki, I told you that's not the solution for us."

"Then what do you intend to do? You can't go on like this, Stanley, living apart and expecting him to accept that. He's the kind of man who wants a home."

"And a wife."

"It could be worse."

"Would you do it?"

Nicole paused before answering. "Why not, if the sex was good or he was threatening to leave me."

"Well, doll, the sex is nil right now. And Rafik doesn't threaten, he takes action."

"Stanley, don't lose him."

"Is that mine to decide?"

"Yes, it is. You must stand by your man."

"Do I hear a song coming on, doll? What about my man standing by me?"

"He needs you now. You've admitted as much. He's under a lot of stress. Is it so much for you to be a source of comfort for him now, for someone who adores you?"

"It seems unfair somehow, that I have to nurture him but I don't get any nurturing back."

"Darling, you sound like those ridiculous people who negotiate every aspect of their lives. This is love. Love is simple. Here, just answer me yes or no. Don't think now, just answer me. Do you want Rafik in your life?"

"Yes."

"Do you want to help him now?"

"Yes, of course."

"Is there anything to prevent it? I mean something real, like an ocean or a disability or money."

I squirmed. "No."

"Then you must do whatever it takes to help him."

"But what if I get nothing back?"

"What is there to get back? Stanley, if your idea of love is to get something back, then you should give it all up and study financial planning."

The coffee maker puffed out its last shot of hot water, which meant it was java time. I stirred the pot to mix the denser stuff on the bottom with the more dilute stuff on top, then poured us both a mugful. Nicole took out her cigarette case and opened it, displaying a row of pastel-colored and gold-tipped shafts, custom blended at a local tobacconist. With all my futile attempts at smoking, she knew enough not to offer me one, but she lit hers and inhaled that first deep lungful with a glazed look of pleasure. For my treat I chose a triangular slab of raspberry-filled shortbread from the box of pastry sent by my mom. Nicole waggled a finger at me.

"Calories, darling. Five hundred at least."

"Love me, love my hips, doll."

The telephone on my desk beeped. It was the front desk announcing someone for me, one Lieutenant Branco of the Boston Police Department. I told the receptionist I'd be right out.

"Gotta go, doll. Mr. Mediterraneo is here."

Nicole looked at me quizzically.

"The cop, doll. Lieutenant Branco. Tall, dark, handsome, single. Remember him?"

Nicole replied with sudden animation. "Do I!" she said. Then, though she is not one to waste good tobacco, Nicole fastidiously rolled the small ember off the cigarette she'd just lit and tamped it out carefully. She never extinguished a cigarette by crushing it, which usually bent or broke the shaft and left a crumpled, charred stump. Even the debris in Nicole's ashtray showed her artful approach to smoking.

She stood up and walked briskly to the office door. "Let's go then, darling," she said impatiently.

We went back out onto the shop floor together. I looked out above all the hustle-bustle, beyond the shampoo sinks and the styling chairs, the snips and the clips, and focused my gaze on the reception desk near the front entrance. Sure enough, Lieutenant Branco was waiting there in all his Italian-stallion glory. He looked almost bewildered by the activity in the salon, as though his beauty was so natural he couldn't comprehend a place where it had to be created and applied to the lesser human forms. Did he realize how he'd been blessed by the architects and sculptors of bodily fate? How could he not?

Nicole was traveling fast, and I had some trouble keeping up with her without breaking into a trot.

"Got the old runway strut going again, eh doll?"

"I don't like to keep the police waiting."

"Uh, Nikki, I think he wants to question me, not you."

"I'm just going to say hello."

"Then what's that leg-hold trap for?"

Nicole arrived in front of Lieutenant Branco a few seconds before I did, which was just enough time for her to greet him first.

"You've been a stranger, Lieutenant," she said, and thrust out her hand.

"I've been pretty busy . . . Miss Albright, right?" Branco took Nicole's hand and gave it a light shake.

"That's right, Lieutenant. But please call me Nicole."

"This is business," replied the cop.

"Business with Stanley, yes. But surely I'm not involved?"

"Not at all, ma'am."

"Then please, Lieutenant, call me Nicole."

Branco's eyes brightened. "Another time, certainly. I'd like to talk to Stan now."

Hearing him say my name caused a little twist around my heart, just the way it had those other times. If Branco was using my first name, perhaps I was more to him than just another witness or suspect to help his case along. Sometimes I wondered what it would be like to have a closer connection to him, beyond the straight cop–gay hairdresser relationship, which had obvious limits. But today I was satisfied enough to hear him call me Stan again.

Nicole continued, "He's all yours, Lieutenant. Don't leave without saying good-bye." Her inflection and the subdued girlish giggle that followed meant that Nicole was up to no good.

As she walked past me I muttered sotto voce, "Your skirt is in your face, doll."

She moved off with sure-footed grace in every step, despite the four-inch heels. I noticed some extra oomph in the sway of her firm, ample hips too. Then I saw Branco watching her departure with keen interest, as though this renewed connection with Nicole was appealing to him in some unbusinesslike way.

"We can talk in my office, Lieutenant," I said, breaking the spell.

"That's fine."

I led us back to my office, where I offered him some coffee. The freshly brewed stuff had filled the small room with a welcoming aroma, but Branco declined my offer. From the tired look on his face I suspected he wanted and needed a cup badly. But his accepting any small hospitality from me might have softened the serious nature of his visit, which was after all a police interrogation.

Branco suggested we sit, but he left no choice about our places. He settled himself on my desktop, with one long leg braced against the floor and the other one hanging freely over the edge. The knife-edge crease of his slacks could hardly conceal the fullness of his calves beneath the fabric. And his black loafers, buffed to a metallic sheen and warmed by his feet within, gave off an inviting leathery aroma. Branco's stance blocked any use of my comfy desk chair, so I resigned myself to the new fragile wicker thing that posed as a seat. It squeaked and flexed to accommodate my healthy backside, and even after I had settled into it, it sagged and swayed unsteadily. I hoped it wouldn't collapse. Our mutual positions put Branco above me, with my line of sight right around his belt level. The seat might have been tight, but the view couldn't have been better.

"I assume you've talked to your friend," he said.

"Which one, Lieutenant?"

"Your lover. The one who found the body this morning."

"You mean Rafik? I talk to him often."

"Then you know that he's involved in this thing."

"That's not what he told me."

Branco grunted, then said flatly, "Well, he is."

"What do you want from me?"

"I want you to tell me what you know about it."

"Lieutenant, I know nothing."

"Just talk then. Tell me a story. You'd be surprised what might come out."

"Any story?"

"Start with this morning. How did you end up at the Harkey residence?"

"Rafik called me."

"When was that?"

"Six-thirty."

"So you weren't together?"

I moved slightly and the chair squeaked. "No," I said.

"Were you expecting the call?"

"No."

"Does he often call you at that hour?"

"Never."

"See?" Branco said with triumph. "Already you've told me things I didn't know."

I wondered what I'd said that was so important.

He went on. "Did you know Rafik was with Toni di Natale when he called?"

"He told me only that Max Harkey was dead and the police were there."

"So you didn't know he was with that woman, the conductor?"

"No."

Branco paused as if to breathe in the aroma of the coffee. Then he asked, "Why didn't you spend the night together?"

"Lieutenant, what does that have to do with anything?"

"Just answer me. It's a simple, direct question. Why didn't you spend last night with Rafik Panossian?"

I didn't see the relevance of it, but I also had nothing to hide. In fact, I almost wanted to tell Branco everything about my whole life, including my love troubles.

"Okay, Lieutenant. I'm sure you already know all this, but here goes. I was at a dinner party with Rafik last night. It was at Max Harkey's place. Rafik was flirting with Toni di Natale. It got serious and I got jealous. Very jealous. I drank too much, and I kept on drinking. I made a fool of myself, which probably embarrassed or amused everybody else. Then I stumbled home and spent the rest of the night alone."

Branco grunted again.

I said, "You might want to add that I cried myself to sleep too. I haven't done that for a long time. It might have some bearing on the case."

"I'll make a note of it," said the cop. Then he sniffed at the air again and said, "Maybe I will take a cup of that coffee if it's not too much trouble."

"Not at all," I said. But when I tried to get up from the chair, I found myself caught in its wicker grip. I had to push against the sides to spread them open. The flimsy strands of woven wood gave a slight groan, then made a crackling sound as they fought against the pressure I applied. Finally I was released. Once out of the nasty chair I gave it a sharp kick, just to show it who was boss. I caught a smile on Branco's face. Gay clown performs for straight cop. Was his look ridicule or genuine amusement?

I poured him a mugful of coffee. Just as I was about to ask him how he liked it, he said, "Black is fine." I handed him the mug, and then it happened: His fingers brushed against mine. It was nothing, completely unintentional, an accident. But what surprised me was how warm his fingers were, even during that briefest, lightest touch. And what else surprised me was the familiar little rush I felt, the tingling lively sensation that I had assumed was Rafik's exclusive domain.

"Mind if I take my jacket off?" said the cop.

"It gets kind of warm in here sometimes," I replied, then I pushed open one of the windows. Meanwhile Branco removed his sport coat and draped it over the big leather chair. The small office quickly filled with his scent, a heady blend of wild balsam and clean starched cotton. It went well with the coffee.

I sat myself on the desktop facing Branco—enough was enough with that ridiculous wicker chair—and I struck a pose parallel to his. He drank some of his coffee and nodded approvingly. I felt like a good boy. Then he went back to being a cop.

"Did you know your lover spent the night with Toni di Natale?"

I paused while my stomach knotted itself.

Branco said, "I can see from your face that you didn't know. Sorry it came out this way."

"It doesn't matter," I said with the words of a rational mind and a lying heart.

"You admitted earlier that you were extremely jealous."

"That was different."

"How so?"

"That was about love. I don't see how any of this relates to Max Harkey's death."

"It may not. But you may have been lying about your jealousy, even though you're convincing enough right now."

"Excuse me for having feelings."

"See, I think there's nothing to be jealous about. I think that maybe Toni di Natale planned this killing and is using your lover as an alibi."

"That's absurd, Lieutenant."

"I'm just trying to determine the extent of your involvement with the murder."

"I had nothing to do with it."

"But if your lover is an accessory, common sense tells me you'd be involved too."

"Then why don't you book us both?"

Branco sipped at his coffee. "Good stuff," he said. Then he gazed directly into my eyes and spoke. "The reason I'm not booking you or your lover, Kraychik, is that I can't find a shred of evidence on either of you."

So I was Kraychik now, strictly man-to-man business.

"So what was Toni di Natale's motive?"

"That's not clear yet. We do know that Harkey had just broken off his relations with her."

So they *had* been involved. I recalled the brief but nasty exchange between Toni di Natale and Alissa Kortland at Max Harkey's table that night, and all the allusions to sex.

Branco went on. "But what doesn't play for me is that she spent the entire night with your friend."

"Thanks for repeating headline news, Lieutenant." Did he enjoy tormenting me?

Branco continued, "See, it's got to be a phony alibi. Why else would a sexy woman spend the night with a gay man? It sounds—I don't know—fake. And you say you're not jealous about it. I find that strange. You said you were jealous last night at the party. In fact you claim you put on a real show, a first-class performance. Even have witnesses to back it up. But it doesn't make sense to be jealous at night and then not be jealous the next day. Do you get what I mean?"

My jealousy aside, Branco had no business assuming that women did not find Rafik attractive, no matter whether he was gay or not. Part of my dilemma was the very likelihood that Rafik and Toni di Natale *had* spent the night together, and in pleasure no less. Now Branco was trying to tell me the whole thing was planned as an alibi to protect them—and me!—from suspicion of Max Harkey's murder. It was crazy. What was Branco trying to prove? What was he after? Then I realized with sudden and painful certainty what had been happening in my little office. Lieutenant Branco had been manipulating me, toying with me, the same way Rafik often did. I felt my face redden. Both men had the same power over me, the power to make me forget who I was and become something useful, like a pawn, or diversionary, like a plaything, but always obedient and disposable. I hated myself for being so weak. I recognized the game and it enraged me. I recalled the odd pleasure on Branco's face when he arrested Toni that morning. It was time to tell him how I saw things, and it wasn't going to be pretty.

"Lieutenant, I think you might have the story wrong. But here's a version you can think about. Maybe you booked Toni di Natale because it gave you a boner to do it. And now you're afraid she may have slept with a gay man. And where would that put you?"

Branco's face froze. For long silent moments nothing in the small room moved. Neither of us breathed. Neither one blinked. The distant sounds of traffic through the open window seemed to be roaring now. Then, as though marking a dramatic beat, the coffee maker released a final noisy puff of steam. It was Branco's cue to speak.

"It's never good news to learn that you're not everything to the person you love."

His remark made me regret what I'd said. I'd meant to return his insult, to defend myself against his attack. But he had seen through my juvenile ranting. He had perceived the real message behind my words, that the news of Rafik's infidelity had hurt me to the core.

Branco finished his coffee then stood up. "I'll be talking to you again," he said. He put on his sport coat and opened the door. He turned back to me and said, "Good cup of coffee." Then he walked out of my office and left the shop.

6

You Don't Know What Love Is

Originally I had planned to make Rafik one of his favorite dishes for dinner: chicken breasts braised in butter and olive oil with fresh rosemary and chopped tomato, topped with a thin slice of Montrachet cheese. Yes, I was resorting to food as a way to reconcile us. But I'd planned that meal before I had learned of Rafik's *nuit d'amour* with Toni di Natale. Now it was easy to settle on frozen appetizers and a three-cheese calzone from the local pizzeria. The food would be good enough, but it paled in comparison to my first menu, the one inspired by love. And the prefab meal would be a drastic comedown from the culinary experience at Max Harkey's place only twenty-four hours earlier. At one juncture I even considered serving everything at room temperature, especially after hearing my aunt Letta's counsel in my mind.

"You don't give a man a hot meal when he has been with another woman. Never!"

Who would have thought a gay man would be contending with that kind of conjugal logic? But my heart softened while I was puttering around the kitchen, laying out the frozen appetizers on a cookie sheet and preparing my battle plan. It happened when I took a new look at my the refrigerator door. It's covered with photos and postcards and magnets—some erotic, some silly, all little scraps of things that delight me. The collection had become invisible to me, as things on refrigerator doors tend to do, especially those little signs that say, "Are you really hungry?" or the more direct "NO!"

What got to me was the snapshot of Rafik and me during our first honeymoon vacation. We had spent a weekend in Maine, and the photo showed us both on the beach. A passing hunk had snapped it for us. As different as Rafik and I were physically, the photo could have been used as state's evidence that we belonged together. There we were, embracing like young buddies in the sudsy white surf. We appeared so animated that I could almost hear the waves again, and feel the cold droplets of ocean water falling from Rafik onto me, and taste the sun and the salt on his forearm, the one he'd wrapped around my neck. It was a cliché, a snapshot of two men stupidly in love at the beach. Every person who's ever had a lover must have some version of this photo. I almost resented the effect it had on me. But I also knew that I wanted *that* again. I wanted those joyous times again, when being together was so easy because we were enchanted with each other's minds and bodies.

As I prepared the salad greens I wondered how life might be if things didn't work out, if we ended up separating. With a sinking feeling I recalled my life before Rafik, how I'd made myself strong to withstand the loneliness. Sure, I had tried practical ways to fill the void—placing and answering personal ads, accepting blind dates arranged by "married" friends, taking up country-western dancing and joining bridge clubs and attending bingo parties—but they usually resulted in dire incompatibility or else outright rejection. The idea of creating a social life for myself had seemed a reasonable solution, but in practice it was as romantic as driving a dump truck. So, to handle the ever growing frustration, I had cultivated a peculiar vision, one that focused however narrowly on the bright side of life: Happy thoughts only, head up, move forward, he travels fastest who travels alone, cha-cha-cha. The only question then was, With all my speedy, independent, positive, forward-moving activity, where exactly was I going?

Then Rafik appeared with his halo of danger and possessed me at once. Every second with him sent some piece of my former life into the archives of memory or else to oblivion. And whatever I lost made room for something new—some new emotion, sensation, elation, or doubt. But the anticipation of these thrilling new experiences also had the odd effect of diminishing that old independence, that self-reliance that had become my strength. Occasionally I even found myself hoping that Rafik would confidently chart the course for our life together in the same magical way he had solved the pain of my body's needs. I knew there were plenty of terms that described this submissive condition—transference, codependence, dysfunction, sadomasochism, love—but in my heart I also knew that the subjugation of one's self to another person has been around a lot longer than either classical or New Age psychologies and their attendant labels. Just take a look at grand opera if you don't believe me. So for whatever reason, whether conscious choice or inescapable destiny, Rafik's life and mine had become intertwined, and there was no turning back.

The door buzzer startled me out of my grim reverie. I took stock of what I'd been doing. All was perfect except for the onion. I'd intended to slice paper-thin rings to lay on top of the salad, but instead I'd reduced it all to mushy particles smaller than rice grains. No wonder the tears were running down my cheeks.

Stay alert, I told myself, or he will charm you into agreeing that he slept with Toni di Natale as a favor to you, and then he'll expect the favor to be returned. Become Strong Stanley. But my attempts at self-bolstering withered when I opened the door and saw him standing there. As if the vision of him in the flesh weren't enough—tired from work, posture a bit slack, smile wan, yet those eyes ever eager—as if all that weren't enough to undo me, the bastard had even brought me flowers, and my favorites no less—an armful of Rubrum lilies. What chance did I have? How could I be angry when he'd entered like that?

He stepped inside and we held each other. I sensed that he needed tenderness from me, the very thing I had neglected to give him earlier that day. I'd been through police stress like that myself, and if I'd had a lover at the time, I would have wanted him to comfort me, to help me forget it all. I certainly hadn't done that for Rafik. I told myself to forgive and forget any mistakes either of us had committed recently. Then I realized I was thinking like a Sunday school teacher.

I spoke into his ear. "You smell good."

Rafik said, "I showered at the studio." He sniffed at the air. "Something is baking."

So he did want a wife after all! Well, what else was I going to do with my life?

"I left the shop too late to make a real dinner," I said, "but I've got some stuff in the oven." I was careful not to apologize, not to yield, but I did feel a twinge of guilt for not preparing him a full meal with my own hands.

Sugar Baby greeted him enthusiastically, as she usually did, by wrapping both her forepaws around one of his legs and nuzzling him with her cheeks. Rafik released me and knelt down to face her at her level. He held his hand out palm down in front of her, about half a foot off the floor, and she promptly leaped over it. He raised his hand an inch, and she jumped again. This continued until his hand was too high for Sugar to negotiate the jump, at which point she simply flopped herself down and squirmed about on the carpet while he tickled her silky underside. Rafik had taught her the trick just after we had met, and Sugar Baby still did it only for him.

We had cocktails in the living room, so I guess it was a special occasion after all, though I didn't realize yet to what extent. I served the hot appetizers, small turnovers filled variously with minced mushrooms, chopped spinach, and herbed cheese. In Armenian they are called *beoreg*—pronounced, approximately, "burr-reg," with lots of roll on the "r"s. Rafik bit into one happily, and golden buttery flakes of phyllo pastry fluttered from his lips onto his plate.

"It is good," he said. "But yours are better."

"You taught me how," I replied with a modest shrug.

Step by step, domestic harmony was being reinstated. So, like the devoted wife who is ever watchful over her husband's career, I brought up something I'd neglected to tell Rafik so far.

"Last night at Max Harkey's I overheard an argument I think you ought to know about."

"Between which people?" he said, and took another *beoreg*.

"Max Harkey and Marshall Zander."

"Hmmmm . . ."

"It was about your new work."

"Oh? Tell me then."

"Max sounded adamant about taking it off the program."

"What you mean, 'adamant'?"

"Determined. Unyielding."

"Adamant," he said with a French accent. Then he shrugged and sighed. "What does it matter now? It will not happen."

"Not so, dearly beloved. Marshall Zander sounded just as adamant about keeping your new work on the program."

"Hah!" said Rafik. "Then why did he tell the police those things about me? He tells them I killed Max Harkey because my new work will not be shown. So the police ask me if that is true."

"So you knew about it?"

"From the police, yes. But why does Marshall lie to them about me? Why does he hate me?"

Possibly not hate, thought I, but its polar opposite.

"Fortunately, Rafik, the police didn't believe him. They did book Toni, not you." But I also recalled Branco using the word "accessory" that afternoon at the shop.

Rafik said, "The police know that Max left her for somebody else. So they think she kills him for that." He shook his head in dismay.

"Marshall Zander told me that you and Toni were in the bedroom together when the police arrived."

Rafik looked at me sadly. "We did not know what to do about Max. We arrive there, we find him like that. We were scared."

I got up to check on the calzone in the oven. As I was leaving the living room I said, "I sure hope you're not involved in this thing."

Rafik joined me in the kitchen. "Something makes you not trust me, Stani."

I was kneeling at the open oven. "It's nothing," I said.

"What happened?"

"Nothing, I told you. I didn't mean to mention it."

"Did someone say something?"

I closed the oven door and stood up to face him. "It was the police."

"What did they say?"

"It was about you and Toni."

"What?" he said with a beguiling and boyish smile, and with his hands open toward me, raised in supplication. Perhaps if he hadn't affected humility and innocence, I could have let the matter go. But Rafik's sudden theatricality raised a red flag to me, and I sensed that he was hiding something.

"Okay then, love. Tell me what you did last night after the party."

"I went home, of course."

"Of course you did. Were you alone?"

Rafik paused. "Why do you ask this?"

"Just answer me, light of my soul. Did you sleep alone last night?"

"Yes, I did," he said flatly.

I got the plates from the cupboard, and made sure to slam the door closed. Then I set the dishes down on the counter with a heavy clunk. But selecting the flatware was the high point. Do you know how much noise you can make getting knives and forks out of a cutlery tray? I figured, if I was about to face the showdown I'd been avoiding, I wanted the whole kitchen vibrating with the energy of my anger.

"Rafik, the police told me that you and Toni spent the night together, that you are her alibi."

"So?" he said coolly. "Have you never spent a night with a woman?"

Sly bastard. "Not when I already had a lover. And you just said you slept alone."

"I did. It is not what you think. We did not sleep together."

"Rafik, I know your room. There's a bed and a chair and a table."

"Stani, believe me. I only talk with her. She has a broken heart from Max. You know I cannot ignore a broken heart. What if I ignored you? Where would we be now?"

Be alert! Clear your mind! Pay no heed to the sexy man in your kitchen saying things to confuse you. But then I thought of Clark Gable and Claudette Colbert, and of the hanging blanket that had maintained chastity in a tiny motel room, and I wondered if Rafik was telling the truth after all.

Rafik continued, "I see from your eyes that you want to believe me."

"Let's just say I don't want to disbelieve you."

I turned off the oven and we returned to the living room to finish our cocktails. Sugar Baby leaped onto Rafik's lap and nudged his hand for affection. My own pet's allegiance had been swayed. I watched her shamelessly beg him for love. She was enraptured by Rafik. Perhaps there was a simple lesson there.

Rafik said, "Maybe you should go with other men so you will be at peace with me."

Suddenly my heart was racing and my belly was a knot.

"I don't want other men."

"Maybe you are lying to yourself."

"I may be confused about a lot of things, Rafik, but on that point I'm sure. I don't want other men." Yet as soon as I'd said it I recalled the thrill I'd had earlier that day in my small office with Lieutenant Branco, how his touch and his scent had caused an unexpected response in me.

"Stani, I will talk serious to you now."

I felt myself begin to tremble. "No, Rafik. It's not necessary."

But he held up his hand to silence me. "It is time to talk. I am thinking about this a lot. I know that my work often makes a problem between us. So I am thinking that perhaps you should go from me."

"No!"

"I do not want it, but you are so unhappy."

"I'm not unhappy. This is the way I am."

It was shocking to hear Rafik talk about our connection, our love, as though it was something that could be turned on and off at will. So what was I supposed to do now? Did he want me out of his life? These kinds of hurdles in the realm of love seemed too complex for me, too fabricated. But then, I'm only a hairdresser. Rafik was a murder suspect when we met.

"Rafik, this is absurd. I don't want to leave you."

"Then we should live together," he said with a satisfied grin.

"I told you I can't live with you until there is no reason not to."

"We should be together."

"I don't know you well enough."

"How can you say that? It is more than one year."

"Okay then. Say we move in together, and then you get this uncontrollable urge to stay out with someone else while I'm waiting for you at home. Or even worse, what if you brought him home to our bed while I was out, and then I smelled him on the sheets. That's why I can't live with you."

For a few moments after my harangue the only sound in the living room was Sugar Baby's loud rhythmic purring from Rafik's lap. She always did respond to high energy.

Rafik said quietly, "I do not want sex from anyone else."

"How long will that notion last? It's bound to wear off. You'll tire of me and go roving. And then what happens?"

"What do you mean 'roving'?"

"Having sex with other men."

He kicked the edge of the coffee table sharply and jostled everything on it. The noise startled Sugar Baby and she jumped off his lap and scampered out of the living room.

"I tell you, Stani, I will not do that!"

"You did with Danny."

"That was different."

"It was the same thing you want now—two men living together who claim to love each other."

"Danny did not love me. I was a decoration for him to show to everyone else."

Was that how I perceived Rafik? Was my idolatry just another version of decoration? I knew that wasn't true.

"Rafik, I want us to live together. It's a beautiful dream I have every day. I just couldn't face the pain if it didn't work out." I felt my eyes fill with tears, but there was no way I was going to cry out loud, not with Rafik present.

"It will work, Stani. I will always be here for you."

"The last man who said that to me went off with someone else two days after our first disagreement."

"Then he was a weak man."

"He blamed me for everything."

"I will never blame you for anything."

"He lied to me, beautiful lies that I believed."

"I will never lie to you."

"He said that, too."

"Stani, you must believe me."

"I want to, Rafik."

"How can I prove it to you?"

I shrugged hopelessly. "I don't know. What I do know is that I want you in my life for as long as any cell of mine is conscious. But I have to believe you want the same thing. It's easy to say 'I love you, I love you, I love you' and it's just as easy to forget someone's name."

"I will make you believe me."

The kitchen timer went off. I looked at Rafik. His eyes were gazing warmly at me, and his face was calm and smiling. Why did his emotions always come off so assured, so comfortable, so masculine, while mine loomed volcanic and larger than life. Yet for all my passionate noise, I felt the lesser person.

"Let's eat," I said.

In the small dining room we ate the calzone and the salad. For a long time we didn't speak, as though we were both afraid to talk any more about Max Harkey's murder and Toni di Natale. But then what else was disrupting our lives right now? Certainly not Bloomingdale's kitchen sale.

Rafik spoke first. "Toni could not do such a thing as the police say."

"Why not?"

"She is a fine artist. She could not kill anyone."

"If I recall, Floria Tosca lived for art and love, and she did a pretty good job carving up Scarpia."

"That is opera," he said.

Was it my place to remind Rafik that so was his life?

"What more can be done?" I said. "Toni has a good lawyer."

Rafik put his hand over mine and focused his sweet caramel-brown eyes on me. "Maybe you can help her?"

"What?"

"You remember how you help me before?"

"I don't want to get involved again."

"What if you did not help me then? I might be in jail."

"Rafik, I can't do anything for her."

"If you love me, Stani, you will help her."

Nice ultimatum. Then I recalled Nicole's words from that morning: Stand by your man. So what do you do when the two closest people in your life tell you how to live it? A whirlwind started in my head, and the big question was, Why does Rafik care so much about that woman? Was this the kind of stimulation I need to feel alive, to be strong, to be my best self again? I thought romance and security were the driving forces in my life, but apparently, it was bloodlust that spurred me on. Maybe I was more macho than I'd suspected.

Once I'd faced the demon head on, the answer came quickly and easily: I would help. But it would not be as a favor to Rafik. I wasn't so selfless. I had my own motivation. I would do it all for my own peace of mind, for with Toni di Natale free of guilt, and Rafik free to choose, I would finally know whether his love for me was true or transient, and what he really wanted—a man or a woman.

"Okay," I said. "I'll do whatever I can."

"Oh, Stani, *merci, merci!*"

"Don't kiss my hands, just tell me something."

"Anything. Whatever you want."

"Are you willing to lose me?"

Even in the candlelight I could see his face go pale.

"It will not happen! I will protect you."

"Rafik, I appreciate your chivalry, but I'm not talking about physical danger." Yet as I said the words I realized with a small shudder that the whole ridiculous mission could become fatal at any juncture. After all, the killer was still free.

"I mean," I said with a dry gulp, "if Toni is set free, your relationship with her may grow to preclude me."

Rafik looked confused. "I do not understand."

"You might leave me, Rafik."

He said the next word like a sacred oath.

"Never."

My heart pounded, my ears rang slightly, I felt pressure in my neck and head, and I saw spots in the warm light.

"Until death," he added.

Perhaps Rafik had meant to galvanize my trust, but somehow, with the sharp angles of his face in the flickering light and the solemnity of his words, he'd caused instead an unexpected tremor of fright.

"Do you want some dessert?" I asked. Food, food, food. It was always food to the rescue at a bad moment. Just like the Brits and their damn tea.

Rafik shook his head no. "Let's go to bed."

When we entered the bedroom, Sugar Baby had already enthroned herself among the pillows at the head of the bed. Rafik pushed me down onto the fluffy duvet.

"Now I will show you how much I love you," he said.

"Let's get our clothes off."

"No," he said. "You will lie quietly, and I will love you."

"But—?"

"Shhhhh . . ."

And so he began.

He unbuttoned my shirt and put his face inside, licked my skin with his tongue, nestled his way into an armpit, pulled at the hair with his lips. (That's why you *must* find alternatives to toxic deodorants.) All the while his clever hands were undoing other buttons and buckles. My shirt still on, he nuzzled his way back across my chest, pausing to chew awhile on a nipple, then strayed lower, where the pleasant pastures lie.

With his stalwart nose, Rafik invaded my briefs and rooted around in there for a while. When he backed out I felt him grasp my briefs and trouser tops with his teeth. Then, shaking his head like an animal, he pulled and yanked with his jaws until he had peeled pants and panties down off me, never once using his hands. Oh, the relief of cool air on my body!

Phase two started at my feet, where he paid great respect with tongue and lips to all ten piggies, and then traced elaborate designs with his pointy tongue on every surface of my feet, especially along the soles. (What relief that I'd showered earlier.) Then Rafik moved further up and lingered around my calves for an extended chew. At the same time he curled his body so that his erection could continue playing around on my feet, even working itself between my toes, thrusting like a minifuck. How can a penis be so smart?

Eventually Rafik's tongue made its way up to my thighs, where he settled in for a while. Lips and tongue and teeth conversed freely with the tender flesh on the inner side of my thighs, while his hard member toyed with my tootsies. He licked and chewed and pinched within millimeters of paydirt, breathed his hot breath on it, teased it all plenty, but never made contact with the external center of my sex. The torture made my rod pulse and drool in wild anticipation, ever ready and eager for his lips and tongue, ready for what it seemed would never happen.

I wondered, Is this how an accessory to murder makes love? Then I wondered, Why is it so easy to believe him guilty of something, instead of innocent? But finally I surrendered to the pure simplicity of what he was doing, what he was saying, talking without guile to some deep lost part of me with some bold and present part of himself—a hand, a lip, a shoulder, a thigh, what did it matter? I was being recharged with zings of electricity, small sparks that grew and intensified into small jolts and caused my muscles to tremble rapidly, then to vibrate, and then to fibrillate wildly out of control. And once Rafik had got my body into that state of electroshock, he played with it, improvised, navigated his way through the surges and eddies of pleasure, and coaxed from my lungs cascades of whimpers and tremulous wails of astonishment and delight. I heard myself saying, "You do love me. You do love me." And just before I left the earth, I realized I'd stolen the line.

Nine days later, or so it seemed, when the drama had run its course and I'd regained consciousness, Rafik was stroking my belly gently with a towel. Physically I was completely spent, yet I sensed something odd with my body, a vague feeling of fullness, of being more than I was before the sex. I supposed it was the afterglow. Then I realized that despite Rafik's Olympic-class ministrations, I had not let off. And though he had drenched my abdomen with his release, my usual copious climax had been internalized and contained. Well, superb as the sex had been, that's not exactly the way men come, and it troubled me for a moment. Was Rafik now robbing me of genital pleasure too? What was next? No erection? Or had he finally transported me far beyond the meager sensations afforded by a dangling attachment, transported me to the more elevated ecstasies of the soul?

"I did nothing for you," I said.

"You let me do this," answered Rafik, as though ravishing my body was pleasure enough for him. "And you already make love to me when you promise to help Toni."

In the warmth of his presence and the rumbling purr of Sugar Baby, who was lying at our heads, I asked myself, Was that love?

Later that night I awoke calmly. In the moonlight I could see Rafik and Sugar Baby breathing together, two of hers to one of his. I wondered how Rafik had managed to change the occasional horrors of life into a creative force. How could anyone make love the way he had after a day like his? He had been inspired, not exhausted in his lovemaking. There was something disturbingly divine about how he could transform the mundane debris he was dealt every day. Maybe that's what ultimately separated the artist from the ordinary mortal: The normal person resists or ignores or flies from the circumstances at hand, while the artist grapples them and seeks to create something from them, no matter what they are.

I resolved to use my artist lover as an example. I would accept the circumstances of Max Harkey's death as an opportunity to apply myself body and mind until I found the killer. That would be my particular piece of creation. For the moment, with that decision, I was at peace.

7

For the One I Love

The next morning Rafik was scheduled to teach company class at the ballet, so we were both up early. While he showered and filled the apartment with the steamy scent of wild fern, I fixed our breakfast to the strains of an old Fanny Brice song about the very scene of domestic bliss we were depicting at that moment. The big difference was that I wasn't making "hot-meal" for Rafik, but French toast. As I moved about the small kitchen, singing along and swinging my hips and shoulders to the lively beat of the music, Sugar Baby watched me warily from atop one of the tall stools.

I'd placed everything on the kitchen counter when Rafik came into the kitchen, all ruddy and moist and cleanly shaven, wearing a white cotton T-shirt hanging outside his khaki chinos and bulky white socks on his feet. (Rafik never came to the table bare-chested.) With his eagle's beak of a nose he surveyed the kitchen air, which I had managed to fill with the happy morning smells of coffee and browned butter and crusty grilled bread.

"Delicious," he said after a deep breath.

But to *my* nose the real treat was the scent that Rafik had brought into the kitchen with his scrubbed skin and his damp hair redolent of wild forest greenery. I opened my arms to him and we embraced like two virgins who had just spent their first night together.

Sugar Baby watched us wrapped in each other's arms. She cocked her feline face one way then the other, then said, "Gwow?" Though my girl's vocabulary may be limited, the message is always clear: When are you going to feed me?

Over breakfast I told Rafik that I needed to talk with people at the Boston City Ballet studios, especially the ones who'd been at Max Harkey's dinner the other night, if I was going to make any headway in getting Toni di Natale out of jail. Rafik agreed to help me any way he could. But then he added, "You will show discretion, of course." I promised that I would . . . try, that is. We finished eating and Rafik departed for the BCB. Ever the dutiful spouse, I cleaned up the dishes, then got myself ready to face the day—after feeding my favorite cat.

When I got to Snips I took Nicole into my office and related the turn of events to her. As usual, her response was blunt.

"I disapprove."

I shrugged. "I've got to do it, doll."

"How can you think that meddling in a murder case is going to solve your romantic problems—the ones you've created yourself, I might add?"

"It's the only way I can be sure of Rafik's love."

She shook her head in disdain.

I went on, "Last night we had sex, Nikki."

"So?"

"It was strange, almost troubling."

Nicole said, "Maybe you should consult a newspaper columnist about it. Everyone else seems to."

"No, Nikki. It was different this time. I felt more than I ever have before."

"Bosh! Felt what?"

"I can't explain. Some kind of shift."

"Stanley, what are you talking about? A shift where?"

"Everywhere. Nowhere."

She shook her head ruefully. "Dear boy, you should be happy that your lover is still finding ways to thrill you instead of trying to analyze what's happening."

"Doll, I'm telling you, this was different. I didn't even come, at least not in the usual way. It was as though it all happened inside me, but not physically."

"Are you telling me that you now understand the way a woman feels?"

"Not since women have been learning how to ejaculate. What I'm questioning is whether Rafik and I have finally transcended our bodies to experience a more elevated kind of sex, one borne in the soul. Have we finally surpassed the limits of physical love?"

Nicole took a few sips of her cream-laced coffee.

"Darling, you'll forgive me, but I have no idea what you're talking about. If you're not sure how you feel about Rafik, maybe you should look for the answer within yourself rather than setting up this test between him and that woman. You're basing your whole future with him on whether he passes or fails this arbitrary little quiz you've invented."

"It's not like that, Nikki. I have to know if Rafik wants me for love—for who I am myself—unconditionally. Or am I just a plaything? I know I'm not perfect. I'm not even intelligent most of the time. But this feels like one of those small opportunities to discover some bit of truth about my life."

"It sounds like a house of cards to me."

"It may be," I replied with a sad little sigh. "But just for the record, I promise to stack the deck in Rafik's favor."

Disregarding my bad pun Nicole said, "And just for the record, Stanley, I think you're courting disaster."

"So be it."

"What about your work here at the salon?"

"I already do a lot of the office work after hours."

"So you've worked everything out."

"Hardly," I said.

Nicole finished her coffee, then got up and went toward the door. She turned back to me and said, "I suppose as a friend I ought to offer you any help I can in your quest for the Grail."

"Thanks, doll."

She shook her head dubiously. "Good luck, then," she said, and closed the door.

I finished some of the urgent business I had on my desk, then left the salon a few hours later.

When I got to the studios of the Boston City Ballet I saw that the police were finishing up their own work and were just leaving the building. I entered through the main doorway where Lieutenant Branco saw me and waved me over to him.

"You're looking lively today," he said. "Things must be back on track at home." Then he raised one eyebrow as if to end his simple statement with a question mark.

"Things are just fine, Lieutenant," I replied with a caustic edge on my voice to counter Branco's presumptuous attitude and his bull's-eye accuracy about my personal life.

He said, "I'd like to have a little talk with you at the station when you have a chance."

A casual invitation to questioning by a cop is not exactly standard procedure, so I wondered what was on his mind.

"I've got some time now," I said.

Branco replied, "But I don't. It can wait, but do it soon." Then he left the building, the last cop to walk out the door.

I headed up the broad staircase to the main reception area, taking the steps two at a time with my strong Slavic legs. Up there I found small groups of dancers and company staff milling about in the expansive skylit area. Through the general hum of voices I heard one penetrate through all the rest with its unmistakable shrill staccato. Then I saw Madame Rubinskaya chattering nervously to a young man in sweat-dampened workout clothes, seated on the floor, drinking coffee and eating a hard-boiled egg—obviously a dancer.

"*Bozhe!*" muttered the old woman to him. "They are asking too many questions. Too much. Too much."

Madame Rubinskaya's magpie complaining must have wearied the young man because he glanced up at me with eyes full of hope, as though I might rescue him from humoring the old woman any longer. Madame had sensed my presence as well, either from the young man's look toward me or from the physical energy of my approach, for she turned and faced me with her watery pale-blue eyes.

"Finally you are coming," she said with great relief. "Rafik says you will help us, *tank God.*"

"I hope I can," I said.

"You must," she said, raising her voice to a henlike squawk. "The police are making many questions but giving not one answer. I want to know who did that to Maxi. Who can be such a monster?" Madame

then threw her head back and raised her wrist to her forehead, eyes closed and mouth agape in cliché pantomime from nineteenth-century melodrama. She moaned in a quietly descending glissando that ended with a slight gasp. I don't know what she intended by the gestures, but they elicited neither sympathy nor even a suppressed smile in me. Instead they produced an unsettling sense of deception, and I wondered what she was hiding. I recalled the night of the dinner party, when she and Max Harkey had openly disagreed on some programming change that he had proposed in connection with her young niece. Madame had left the party immediately after that episode. She had claimed to be tired, but she was clearly more angry than spent. Could that small disagreement, which so many people had witnessed, have motivated the old woman to kill Max Harkey? It seemed unlikely. It wasn't important enough. Her voice broke into my meandering thoughts.

"So," she said. I saw that she had recovered her composure, probably because her antiquated acting had had so little effect on me. "Rafik is rehearsing now." She pointed toward a wide, carpeted corridor off the main lobby. "You will find him there." I was about to explain that I hadn't been looking for Rafik at all, but she had turned and was walking away in the opposite direction. I stood there stupidly wondering how to get her back, but no ideas came. Nancy Drew had had a lobotomy.

Though I hadn't intended to visit Rafik, I headed in the direction Madame Rubinskaya had indicated. Perhaps the sight of my beloved would inspire me to more successful investigative techniques, to emulate my true hero, Perry Mason. Besides, if I lay low I might even catch a glimpse of the new choreography Rafik was being so secretive about. Sure enough, one of the curtains that usually closed off the long viewing windows of the rehearsal studio had been left partially open. A six-inch gap allowed me to spy unseen by anyone inside.

Rafik was demonstrating some elaborate movements to Scott Molloy and Alissa Kortland. The two dancers were in leotards and tights, while Rafik was in his T-shirt and khaki chinos. I watched him shape the air with his strong arms and legs and torso, mold it with the same love and conviction as a master sculptor. Every line and gesture he made seemed to push beyond the confines of his body and extend outward to infinity. Inspired by his dream world, he moved; then forced by the limits of the real world he would freeze the movement and clarify his intention to the two dancers. They nodded in assent while they imitated Rafik's moves in miniature. Then Rafik would return to the ethereal realm and once again redefine the space around him, only to stop mid-pose and explain some more. Creating art seemed to be a cosmic version of Simon Says, alternating between divine force and mundane response.

The mundane had its intriguing elements though—Scott Molloy's body, for example. Since he was in his early twenties, his soft-tissue structures—muscles, tendons, and ligaments—were all at the peak of elasticity for an adult. No matter how high he soared in a jump or how many tours he completed in a pirouette, when he finished the move and returned to earth he made no vibration, no sound beyond that of his kidskin slippers flexing through his pliable feet back onto the floor. Next to the younger man, Rafik's physical maturity was more evident. His muscularity had filled out with the proportions of a man, while Scott Molloy retained the slight imbalance of extremely developed calves and thighs and buttocks supporting a slender, boyish torso. It gave him an odd vulnerability, as though he hadn't grown up yet, but was expected to do adult things with his body. And when Rafik told Scott Molloy what to do, he obeyed unflinchingly.

Alissa Kortland's face was beautiful but inexpressive, as if cut from marble. It was at once captivating and disturbing. Her body was neither girlish nor womanly; by some aberration of genetics it resembled an exotic asexual humanoid that had been trained to perform ballet. When she stood at rest watching Rafik, she appeared ungainly and almost grotesque. But when Alissa Kortland put her body into motion or into a pose, she became a piece of living sculpture, breathtaking and mesmerizing, the lines of which no ordinary mortal could ever assume. She was a ballerina-machine of which Rafik was the virtuoso operator.

Watching Rafik create his art on these two rare specimens of *Homo sapiens* I wondered about my own work in the salon. Though in pursuit of another kind of beauty, it seemed pedestrian compared to Rafik's attempts at pure expression. I've tried to accept these vast differences in our work, yet I can't comprehend why any act of creation has to exact such a heavy toll from the person doing it. My work is creative, but a major project for me means a few hours of concentrated work, and then it's over. I'm happy, the client is happy, and it's on to the next one. For Rafik though, creating a piece of

choreography can take months—often many long, moody months—
yet the finished work might be a series of movements and poses that,
however grandly eloquent or playfully lighthearted, might last only
ten or twelve minutes on stage. And the emotional distance that
appears during those dark months of creation might trouble me
gravely, especially since Rafik the creator is such a contrast to other
side of him—the generous, mischievous lover, the man who, a patriot
to the end, once hummed the national anthem on the Fourth of July
while juggling my testicles within his cheeks.

With that fond memory, I turned away from the rehearsal studio
and went back to the main lobby. Returning by a different corridor
I made an unlikely discovery along the way: The new studios now
housed a fully equipped workout room complete with stair climbers,
ski simulators, and stationary bicycles; barbells, dumbbells, and cam-
driven weight machines; and the requisite walls of mirrors. I wondered, Would the visions that possessed artists like Rafik ultimately
be vanquished by the health-club mentality? Would balletic ideals of
form and motion evolve into nothing more than the athletic prowess
of a jock, a superrefined exhibitionist produced in the name of art?
That the workout facility was vacant offered some hope that art
might yet exist outside the gym.

I was passing through the main lobby on my way out the building,
already discouraged by the my lack of progress, when I heard a voice
call out to me, "Hello there!"

It was Marshall Zander.

"How are you doing today?" he said.

"As well as anybody after a day like yesterday."

He nodded as though he understood me completely. "It's hard to
believe it happened at all." He appeared relaxed and rested, and I
commented on that. He smiled broadly and replied, "It's an illusion.
I'm on medication. It's the only way I could face this catastrophe.
When the time is right I'll confront my grief."

"Sometimes it's best to yield to emotions as they happen."

"I don't think I could survive it," he said with a jocular laugh.

Whatever his doctor had prescribed was certainly effective. Far
from the weepy hysteria and accusatory outbursts of yesterday morning, Marshall Zander today was as carefree as a vacationer returning
from an island paradise. Either that, or perhaps this man had no
feelings to confront, or surrender to, or survive.

He asked me, "Are you here to see Rafik?"

"No," I said. "I'm trying to find out more about Max's death."

He narrowed his eyes momentarily, then blinked twice as if to expel a mote of worry that even his drugs couldn't block.

"Are you working for the police, then?" he said with a small vague laugh.

"Not for, not against," I said. "In addition to."

"I see," he said with an approving nod. "Good luck then. Sorry I can't talk any longer—board of directors meeting—kind of an emergency. Maybe we'll meet again."

"I'm sure we will," I said.

Marshall Zander was about to leave me, but then he added, "By the way, about yesterday . . . ?"

"Yes?"

"I'm afraid I behaved badly toward you and said some things I didn't mean."

"It happens sometimes in extreme situations."

"Still, I didn't mean to implicate Rafik. He is devoted you."

"I hope so."

"I don't really believe he's involved with Antonia. You know who I mean?"

I nodded.

He said. "It was probably just panic and confusion."

I nodded again.

"I mean, I didn't actually see them doing anything, though they did look guilty when I arrived. Then again, I probably imagined everything."

"Except for Max's body," I said, hoping to break through Marshall Zander's drug-induced vacuity. I wanted to challenge him, to make him face the death of his friend instead of running from it. Aren't there moments in life when grief should be met head-on and not avoided? Yet we invent fantastic psychic machinery to protect ourselves from such horrors as finding a person we claim to love laid open and bled to death.

Marshall Zander shuddered. Then I saw on his face a sorrow that no narcotic short of a sledgehammer could suppress. I guess I'd succeeded in putting him in touch with his feelings, for whatever good it did either of us.

Just then Scott Molloy came into the lobby. He'd put on extra-tight

blue jeans and an oversized shirt of brushed cotton twill unbuttoned
down the front to show the top part of his leotard, still wet with the
exertions of Rafik's rehearsal. The snug denim covering his legs and
haunches, and the loose cotton shirt around his torso tended to
reproportion his boyish physique. Now he looked like a young man,
a very desirable young man. Seeing Scott, Marshall Zander quickly
recovered his composure.

"There's someone I'd watch out for," he said with a mistrustful
look toward Scott.

"He's a nice dancer," I replied flatly, hoping my feigned lack of
interest might encourage him to elaborate on his comment. It worked.

"Scott would never admit he was in love with Max," he said. "And
it was so obvious to both Max and myself that it often amused us—for
very different reasons, obviously."

"Meaning?" I ventured.

Marshall Zander smiled a melancholy little smile. "Max was
heterosexual. I am not. And Scott is entangled in his own precarious
and moralistic doubts. It's too bad when people do that. It creates
trouble for everyone around them."

I felt myself redden with embarrassment. Marshall Zander's words
reminded me of my own appalling insecurities, and his simple insight
made me wonder if there was more to him than the bumbling nebbish.

"I've got that meeting," he said abruptly. And he was off.

Again I stood as though stuck in mud, watching Marshall Zander
depart in one direction and Scott Molloy in the other. I seized the
moment and followed the young dancer's tightly clad buttocks out
into the early-afternoon sunlight.

8

Dancing for Daddy

I caught up with Scott Molloy and walked alongside him.
"Can I buy you a cup of coffee?" I asked.
"I don't drink coffee," he said with a scowl that looked alien on his creamy-skinned young face.

I sensed his pace quicken.

"Tea, then," I offered. "Milk, punch, whiskey, whatever."

He stopped abruptly and faced me.

"What do you want from me?" he said.

My eyes drank up the sight of his compact muscular body, enhanced by the snug jeans and the loose-fitting shirt. Once again I couldn't help noticing how basically similar were our body types, though we hardly matched in any specific measurement. Did Rafik perceive that essential likeness as well?

"You knew Max Harkey," I said after a few seconds.

"So did a lot of people."

"But I'm trying to help."

He sneered. "Help who? Why don't you mind your own business?"

I felt no urge to correct his grammar, having abandoned my mission to teach the proper use of case to the huddled muddled masses. What intrigued me was the young dancer's portrayal of the world's first angry man. I presumed that his hostility, like most, was driven by fear. But fear of what? Me? Gay men in general? Or was it something deeper? Fear of discovery? If I was going to get him to talk to me, I'd have to show more empathy.

"I watched you in rehearsal," I said. "I really admire your dancing."

He narrowed his eyes in a tough, defensive squint. "I don't need your opinions about my dancing."

"But I mean it," I continued. "Whether or not you like *me*, I like the way you move."

That seemed to disarm him a bit.

"And so does Rafik," I added, even though he'd never said it.

"Really?" replied Scott Molloy.

"Isn't it obvious? You're featured in his new work."

I could see that my words were creating hairline fractures in his resistance to me. The mean squint was already relaxing, a sure sign that he wanted to be receptive, that despite his antagonism he wanted to hear me talk about him.

He said, "Rafik never tells me what he thinks."

"That's his way," I replied. "But he respects you a lot. And I ought to know." The unctuous lies felt like drool on my lips, and I had the urge to wipe my mouth.

Then, as though confessing something, Scott Molloy admitted quietly, "Rafik is hard to work for."

I concurred with a warm and understanding look. "Nothing less than perfection for him."

Scott attempted a small smile. "It must be really hard for you, too." Then as if to clarify, he added awkwardly, "I mean, being with him and all . . ." His voice trailed off.

"He is a constant challenge," I said. This time I wasn't lying.

Scott said, "Are you still offering that coffee?" His cool detachment failed to conceal his eagerness to hear any other accolades I might bestow—or else invent.

"Sure," I said, trying to hide my small sense of victory at winning him over for the time being.

We strolled to an outdoor café around the corner from the studios and took a table under a big colorful umbrella. You'd think with the arrival of warm weather we Boston natives would be eager to sit in the sun, but Scott and I, both being fair-skinned, opted for the protective shade. I ordered a double espresso and Scott took steamed milk flavored with almond syrup.

"When did you start dancing?" I asked, further pursuing his trust by asking about his career. Dancers, like most performers, love to talk about their favorite subject—themselves.

Scott Molloy tried another self-effacing smile and failed again, but he deserved an A for effort. Then he looked outward, as though into the far distance, and began the story of "How I Became a Dancer."

"I was twelve," he said. "But my life was already a mess. My father was gone. My mother worked two jobs. I was pretty independent, but I had a lot of time to kill and I didn't mix with the other kids." He glanced across the table at me with sincere eyes. "I had a girlfriend though," he added. "She used to take ballet lessons and one day she invited me to go along with her, so I did. And that's when everything changed."

"Meaning?"

"I know this sounds weird, but I knew from the second I went into that ballet school that I wanted to spend all my time there. My girlfriend's teacher must have seen it too, because she told me right off that I could take lessons for free, 'on the house,' she said. I was back there the next day."

"And the rest is history," I added.

Our beverages arrived and Scott went on.

"The ballet studio was like another home, a place where I could play make-believe and do beautiful things and not be called a sissy for it." He feigned another innocent smile. "And I could hang around with girls too."

"Not to mention what the training did for your body."

His smile grew to an open grin. "It did turn out pretty well, didn't it?" he said, finally brandishing his immodesty outright. "Funny thing is," he went on, "I discovered a lot of the girls were tough, not soft, the way I thought dancers would be. And then I liked them even more."

And what fabulous role models for a closet case!

I'd heard similar accounts of a dancer's beginnings from friends of mine. Of all the artistic disciplines, dance seems to attract the highest number of social outcasts. Maybe it's the group aspect of dance class that appeals to those sensitive lonely souls. Dance is usually learned with other people around, which creates a kind of community, a surrogate family that continues to function in spite of a tragedy in its midst. Father died yesterday; rehearsal today at noon.

"So you're happy," I said, not quite sure what I meant.

Scott answered, "I guess so. I wouldn't mind having more expo-sure, bigger roles. Max kept me pretty limited." He paused, then said, "I guess I shouldn't talk that way about him."

"Death doesn't make anyone better or worse than they were alive," said Pontifical Stanley.

"At least I have that big part in Rafik's ballet, and that's a sure thing now." He paused again, and this time his face flushed with color. He took a deep breath and recollected himself. "Well," he said, "it sure beats selling ties at Filene's." He chuckled. "I never did that though. Dancing is all I've ever done. I don't know what I'd do if I had to stop."

For all its human interest, Scott Molloy's autobiography sounded like a prearranged script, a sad story that he'd dreamed up long ago to be recited on suitable occasions. And it was also a socially accept-able shield to hide behind. But I had the feeling that Scott Molloy was using that shield as a decoy to distract me while he subtly turned the tables so that he could study me. For all his sincere efforts at direct eye contact, I found his glance always darting about me, as though he was taking a geological survey of my body's terrain. Here I had intended to find out about him, and instead I found myself feeling scrutinized. Self-consciously I rotated my cup on the tabletop using my thumbs and middle fingers. Scott Molloy proved my suspicions by analyzing the gesture and then mimicking it exactly, as though he was in rehearsal practicing how to be me.

I asked him directly, "Who do you think killed Max Harkey?"

The young dancer bristled. "Is that what this is about? Not me or my dancing, but Max?"

I nodded. "I told you that right off."

He made a sour face. "Max Harkey forevermore," he said.

"Maybe you feel more for him than you're admitting."

Scott laughed—guffawed—at my remark.

"If you want the faggot, go after Marshall Zander. He's the one who chased Max around the world all his life. I wasn't even born when they met."

"That doesn't preclude you from the chase."

He gave his mug of steamed milk a sudden and violent shove and spilled some onto the tabletop. He wiped it up with his napkin, then said, "I know how I feel about Max Harkey, or any other man. I don't know where you got the idea that I'm gay, but you shouldn't believe everything people tell you."

"Including you?"

"Look, I don't know who killed Max, but if you're looking for motives, maybe you ought to talk to Alissa."

"Isn't she your partner?"

He grimaced. "She's my partner all right, but onstage only. She saved the rest for Max."

With my questioning eyes I encouraged him to continue.

He smiled cynically. "She was his mistress. Don't tell me you didn't know. She snared him as soon as she arrived here, the golden-haired nymphet from Southern California."

"You sound like a jilted suitor."

Scott Molloy thrust his jaw forward. "I know it's hard for you to believe, but some men really prefer women."

I ignored his taunt and pressed him further.

"Do you think Alissa was involved with the killing?"

At first Scott appeared to shrug my question off, as if he wanted to do the right thing and not implicate Alissa Kortland. But his urge to acquit himself won out. He leaned forward in his chair and put his forearms up on the edge of the café table. He spoke in a whisper, like a secret sharer.

"Alissa is a devouring bitch. She takes all her strength from the people around her."

That condemnation didn't exactly fit the young woman Scott Molloy had giggled and flirted with the night of Max Harkey's dinner.

He went on. "When we're working together she pulls all the energy out of me. She makes it hard to dance. Sometimes I think being straight means being attracted to someone like Alissa, and then being used up and dropped."

It was odd to hear him tallying his sexual drives with cool logic.

He continued, "Sometimes I wonder if straight men should have sex with other men, just to keep their masculinity." He lingered on the word and relished it. "I mean," he said, "every time I have sex with a woman, I feel like I identify with her a little bit. I wonder what she's experiencing with me, what it's like to have a man inside you. And as long as that happens there'll always be a part of me that's exactly like the woman I'm with. But with a man it would always be one hundred percent male."

The young dancer's words recalled my own obsessive concern with Rafik's bisexuality. Then again, Scott Molloy's perverse theory appealed to the part of me that has always been more intrigued with why people do things rather than what they actually do.

"You sound unsure of yourself," I offered.

"Oh, I'm sure," he said quickly. "It's women for me all the way. I just think about it sometimes, what it might be like with a man."

My place in the realm of sexuality was obviously with male-male connections, and I found myself relieved that whatever sexual frustration I might have endured before meeting Rafik, at least I had never cowered behind a façade of heterosexuality while wondering about the alternatives. But recent rejection had turned Scott Molloy against the woman he claims to have wanted. It hadn't been enough for him to base their relationship on complementary ballet techniques and body lines. He'd had to prove himself by possessing her sexually, and he'd failed. I wondered how much of his anger was strictly the result of losing Alissa Kortland to Max Harkey and how much might have come from his blindness, purposeful or not, to his own suppressed urges.

"And the pisser is," he continued, "the only reason Alissa seduced Max in the first place was for her career. I know she hated him."

Terms from my old Freudian primer flew through my mind: repression, projection, transference.

I checked my wristwatch. "Thanks a lot," I said. "You've been really helpful."

"Don't you want to hear any more?" he asked, as crestfallen as if his shrink had announced that the time was up.

"I'd love to, but I have to get back to work."

It was the second time that morning I'd told him the truth. Fortified with caffeine, sugar, and prospective leads, I got up from the table and headed back to Snips.

As I set out I realized I was only a few blocks away from Station D, police headquarters. I recalled that Lieutenant Branco had wanted to talk to me, and though he'd asked me to call first, I decided to drop in unannounced.

Branco's police home used to be a smaller station deep in the South End. But that granite structure, small and perfect, became

one of the city's crown jewels of gentrification. It had been so lovingly and authentically renovated that it was promptly named a
historic landmark and appropriated for police administration only.
That way it could retain its new cleanness. There'd be no more
criminals with their dirt and their bugs traversing the hallowed
halls of old Station E.

At headquarters luck was with me, or so I thought. Branco was not
only there but free. I pushed against the heavy oak door with the
frosted-glass panel that bore his name. His office was small and
compulsively neat. He greeted me with a question.

"Things all right at home?"

"So far," I answered.

"That's good. Sit down. Coffee?"

Though the recent *espresso doppio* was already sending gigavolts of
energy through my nervous system and causing the kind of high-
tension cerebral activity that distorts even a great artist's eye-to-hand
coordination—the kind of hyperenergy that can turn a client's request for a "light shaping" into a total restyle the likes of which are
rarely seen outside a prison camp—despite that kind of rush, I could
hardly refuse Branco's atypical hospitality.

"Sure," I said. Then, hoping to buffer my stomach from the on-
slaught of another dose of caffeine, I asked, "Do you have cream?"

"You'll have to take it straight," said the cop as he filled a paper
cup with brown sludge and handed it to me. No delicately roasted
and cautiously brewed Arabica for that guy. This stuff had come from
a supermarket can and had cooked and reduced for at least an hour
on the hot plate.

"I've been thinking," said Branco. "I know we don't see eye-to-eye
on very much."

I swirled the paper cup as if to cool down the steaming muck
inside. I had no desire to taste it.

"But this time I'm not going to fence you in," he said.

"When did you ever, Lieutenant?"

He cocked his head slightly. "In the past I've ordered you to keep
out of these things, not that you ever listened to me."

I bobbed my head and shoulders slightly as though I was enjoying
some cool Latin music, audible only to me.

"But this time I'm going to give you the go-ahead. You can meddle
away to your heart's content."

"Did I ever need your permission?"

"Not really. I just wanted to tell you where I stand."

"Is that what you wanted to talk to me about?"

Branco nodded.

And I didn't trust him for a second.

"Why?" I said.

"Isn't it obvious?"

The Latin rhythm in my head was changing to something more percussive, more like the sacrificial drums from *The Rite of Spring.*

Branco continued, "In the past you've always taken an opposing stance to mine. And in spite of whatever happened between us, it never hurt the final outcome of the case."

"Lieutenant, are you asking for my help?"

"Absolutely not. But I'm not putting any limits on you either."

Reflexively I raised the paper cup to my mouth and let the murky liquid touch my lips. It was bitter and burnt but strangely not loathesome. I caught Branco watching my reaction.

"It's not as good as yours," he said.

"You're right," I replied with a smirk. "And since we're being so buddy-buddy today, can I ask you something?"

Branco wavered for an instant as if fearing what secret I might dare to know, but he quickly regained his cool machismo.

"What?" he said, braving my impending query with manly composure.

"Can I see your file on Toni di Natale?"

Palpable relief showed on the cop's face.

"Officially, no. But I can tell you what's in it."

"Shoot, then," I said.

Branco twisted his big sensuous mouth into a smile.

"You like to provoke me, Kraychik?"

"Don't flatter yourself, Lieutenant. I do it to my cat too."

The virile Italian frowned, obviously displeased at being conjoined with other household pets.

"So?" I said. "What's your take on Toni di Natale?"

"Care to tell me why you're so interested?"

"I'm trying to settle a domestic score."

Branco pulled one corner of his mouth up into a wry smile. Then he leaned back in his chair, put his hands behind his head, and stretched his torso luxuriously, like a big contented tiger about to engage in a playful bout of get-the-gazelle.

"We suspect that Ms. di Natale committed the crime to protect herself from defamation."

"By whom?"

Branco smiled. "We figure that Max Harkey was in love with her, but she was involved with someone else, possibly even your friend."

"You think she killed Max Harkey because he was in love with her, but she's really after Rafik?"

Branco held up one of his big hands. "Do you want to hear this or not?"

"Sorry," I said. "Sorry." I shrank back dutifully. But I did recall Toni di Natale's open flirtation with Rafik the night of the dinner. Yet Max Harkey had appeared unmoved by it. Had that been good acting on his part, or had he truly not cared?

Branco went on. "A man like Max Harkey couldn't accept that kind of humiliation. He'd take revenge. So he planned to cancel her contract with the ballet company—an extremely lucrative contract— and also to defame her throughout the arts world so that she'd probably never work again."

I felt as though Branco should have finished with a question to me: What's wrong with this theory?

"Lieutenant, first off, Max Harkey was incapable of being humiliated. He was the kind of person who used people up and then discarded them. It was very simple with him."

"Sometimes those big important people can be pretty fragile underneath."

"Sometimes, yes. But from what I know of Max Harkey, there was nothing about him that was fragile, least of all his ego. And beyond that, from what little I know of Toni di Natale she's too smart to kill somebody over money."

"What else could she do?" asked Branco.

"She'd work it out another way, maybe seduce Max Harkey into some kind of amiable settlement. But she wouldn't kill the guy."

"How do you know that?"

I almost told him, "Because Rafik says so," but figured that wouldn't convince Branco. Instead I said, "I guess because she's an artist. An artist just wouldn't do a thing like that." When Rafik had expressed that very idea to me, I had denied it as nonsense. Now here I was spouting it to Branco, who sat there silent as stone.

"If it's possible," I said, "I'd like to see her."

"That's no problem," he said.

"You'll arrange it, then?"

"No need to. We released her half an hour ago."

"You what!"

Branco's mouth spread open to a full grin. "She's out," he said. "Free as the breeze."

"But you were holding her for murder. Who paid the bail?"

"No bail," he replied. "We were holding her for questioning. We don't have sufficient grounds for a charge, not yet."

"You led me on!"

"I told you the facts as I know them. You inferred what you wanted."

"Do you know where she is?"

"You'd know that better than me."

Damn his wrong usage! I relinquished my cup of coffee to Branco's desktop. It was still full, though now tepid, with an oily rainbow-hued slick forming on its surface. I stood up.

"I guess that puts things between us back the way they've always been."

"That may change soon," he said enigmatically.

When I left his office one question persisted: Why had Branco been so friendly yet so deceitful?

I telephoned Nicole at the shop and explained that I was on my way back there. When I told her I'd just seen Branco she said brightly, "Oh, how is he today?"

"Odd," I replied before pondering the very oddness of her question.

"That's good," she said.

Then, as is Nicole's wont, she hung up without saying good-bye. I hope someday to uncover the root of that strange habit. But for now the question persisted: Why hadn't she scolded me for my truancy?

I was returning to Snips along the same route I'd come, and once again I passed by the outdoor café near the ballet company studios. I was surprised to see Scott Molloy still sitting at the table where we'd spoken. But now Alissa Kortland was with him. They appeared trapped and miserable in each other's company. Scott happened to catch sight of me approaching them. Within seconds he stood up and fled from the table. Not a subtle exit. When I got there I asked Alissa Kortland if I could join her.

"Suit yourself," she said, hiding behind huge opaque sunglasses and a wide-brimmed hat of starched linen. Her blond hair was mostly tucked up underneath the hat, but from what I could see, the rare and uniform platinum hue was all natural.

"Scott was telling me what you've been up to," she said. "So why don't I save you the bother of asking questions and just tell you my side of everything."

"Thanks," I said. But I knew that easy cooperation like hers was not to be trusted. A waiter appeared at our table. Alissa ordered "another" and the waiter dutifully verified her café Borgia. After my earlier dose of caffeine a glass of lemonade would have been a wise choice, but it might have cast me as a delicate creature, oversensitive to legal drugs. So I ordered a real man's drink—another double espresso.

Then Alissa Kortland lit a cigarette and, like the best of storytellers, began her tale in medias res.

"I was Max Harkey's mistress, but it didn't last long."

"What ended it?"

"What usually does? Another person."

"Toni di Natale?"

"So it would seem," she said.

"Were you hurt?"

"I wasn't in it for love."

"Then were you angry?"

She allowed a tiny smile, but her eyes were concealed by the dark lenses of her sunglasses.

"I was hoping," she said, "for something from his estate, some appreciation for services rendered if nothing else."

"What about the way he treated you as a dancer?"

"What about it? I was a vehicle for his creative whims. That's all we ever are. The audience sees a ballerina as a fairy-tale figure, a princess from an enchanted world. But really we're nothing more than neurotic, emaciated athletes—contortionists actually—who jump and spin and perform circus tricks on our toes."

"Is it like that with Rafik, too?"

Another smile, more playful this time, but no reply. Our coffee arrived. Her café Borgia was extravagant with the scent of orange liqueur and bitter chocolate capped with a layer of *crème fraîche*. My espresso was straight, uncut, and aromatic. As I said earlier, a manly drink.

I said, "You make dancing sound horribly grim."

She took a sip of her coffee. Then, demure as a damsel, blotted a hairline of cream from her lip with a gauzy handkerchief. I'd bet she'd rehearsed that gesture a lot.

"The illusion of glamour is worth all the pain," she said.

"What about your relationship to Scott Molloy?"

"He deserves the gold medal for Most Earnest Closet Case in the Ballet World."

She waited for my reaction, which I held in check. Two could play the game of cool.

She went on. "After years of Scott trying to get Max's attention, I arrived in town and Max took me as his mistress at once. All hell broke loose with Scott. He accused Max of treating him unfairly—and he did it in front of the other dancers, right there in class."

"How did they react?"

Alissa shrugged. "Ballet isn't democratic. Everyone else knew enough to keep quiet. But Scott went on and on, even threatening Max if he wouldn't start treating his dancers equally. It was shocking, I think most of all for Max. He never suspected that Scott had any feelings for anyone, least of all for him, and suddenly Scott was threatening to hurt Max unless he loved him back."

"Was it that blatant? Did Scott really demand that Max Harkey love him?"

"Of course not." She sipped at her coffee, then said, "You're almost as sappy as he is."

"You don't much like Scott, do you?"

"He's silly. He has no goals for his life. He wanted Max to be his father. I find that mildly disgusting. I think it's better to be independent of everybody, including father figures. They're useful for getting started, but it's better to learn to get ahead without them."

"If you dislike Scott so much, why do you stay friendly with him?"

She turned her head as though she wanted me to admire her profile instead of asking stupid questions. She *was* beautiful.

"Scott helps me keep my own weaknesses in check, like a barometer for character flaws." She turned her face back to me. "Are you surprised that I can admit I'm not perfect? Well, I don't delude myself about anything, including my shortcomings. Scott is a mirror that tells me when I'm thinking or behaving in a weak way."

Alissa Kortland portrayed emotional honesty so well it was almost convincing. No wonder the critics loved her. But I took her cool logic one step further and realized that she had a vested interest in keeping Scott Molloy in her power, in sustaining his heterosexual delusions. Through him she could artificially enhance her own strength. Scott had admitted to me that as a dance partner, Alissa drained the energy from him, like a succubus.

"Doesn't anything affect you?" I asked, unable to control the tinge of moralism in my voice.

As if on cue, she removed her sunglasses.

"I got my fill of that warm-and-fuzzy-feel-good stuff from my family. Everything they do, everything they stand for—environment, health, love of mankind, all the New Age clichés—it's all crap. There's nothing before or after this. It's all now. And I want big helpings of everything. That's why I left the tyranny of California."

Ask for the world and end up in Boston, Massachusetts.

However different the circumstances, Alissa Kortland's "escape from tyranny" very much resembled Scott Molloy's.

I gulped the rest of my espresso and stood up.

"I've got to get back to work," I said. "Maybe we can continue this another time."

As Scott Molloy had done earlier, Alissa Kortland looked astonished that I could end our open hearted discussion about art and life and love and *her* so lightly, for something so mundane as my job.

9

The Czarina Manquée

By the time I flew back into Snips Salon—neurons all misfiring from the caffeine overdose—it was after three. Fortunately I had only one customer on the books, and that was later on, just before closing time. By then my eyeballs and my fingers would have returned to a more normal state of hyperactivity. Until then I could catch up on the other work I'd neglected because of my afternoon capers. I prepared myself to explain all this to Nicole, to defend my errant behavior, but she seemed strangely indifferent to my absence most of that day.

When she came by my office, I related everything that had happened earlier. I concluded the long explication with a dose of dramatic irony.

"And so, doll, the upshot of all my running around was to find out that Toni di Natale was already free."

"Is that so?" said Nicole, hardly interested.

"Branco released her this afternoon."

Nicole corrected me. "You mean Lieutenant Branco."

"The same one," I replied. "So now that Toni is free, I guess I can go back to fretting about home and hearth instead of Max Harkey's murder."

"Yes, I suppose so," she said absently. Then she got up and gathered her coat and purse. "I'm leaving early today, Stanley. I want to run a few errands before I go home."

"Big date tonight, doll?"

Nicole smiled enigmatically. "That's right, dear."

"Do tell."

"You take care of business here, darling. I'll see you tomorrow."

Nicole was almost out the front door when she turned back to me and said, "And would you open tomorrow? I may be late."

"Sure, doll." Then I added with a smirk, "Enjoy yourself."

"Oh, I will."

Later on my client Garrett Wade arrived. Garrett had achieved brilliant if limited celebrity as a cabaret performer under the name Miss Doll. These days though, he doffed the sequins and pumps for pinstripes and wingtips, and his stage was more likely the courtroom, where he was quickly building a reputation as an effective if outrageous defense attorney. Garrett conversed like a talk-show hostess, a parody of a woman who can't count to two without unbuttoning her blouse. I'd asked him once how the court judges reacted to his strategic use of dramatic, often campy devices to sway that gravest of audiences, the jury.

Garrett had replied with a squeal, "They remind me to cross-examine and not cross-dress!"

The question remained, Was he serious?

I set him up at my station and began his monthly color adjustment. Ever alert to litigation, Garrett already knew about Max Harkey's murder and had quickly made the connection to Rafik.

"Is that hot lover of yours involved?"

"Not criminally," I replied.

"If he needs representation I'm available."

"Let's hope it doesn't come to *that.*"

Garrett's animated face paused uncertainly in the mirror, not sure whether I meant his litigious talents or the fate of my lover. An awkward silence followed, much like the unsettling hiatus when the wind shifts direction. Then Garrett quickly resumed the conversation all-ahead-full on an entirely different tack.

"So how is married life?"

"Hardly married," I said.

"Why not?"

"We're not ready," I lied.

Garrett dismissed my remark with a downward flap of his wrist. "Oh girl, when I get like that I just dump the hunk and start dating again. There are too many men around to spend your life trying to understand just one of them."

I replied, "I wasn't very successful at dating." Besides, I thought, what would Garrett Wade, the reigning queen of the weekend romance, know about relationships? Once Miss Doll's stud picked his nose or wore the wrong accessory he was history. And knowing what I did about about Garrett's matriarchal lineage—the numerous marriages, divorces, alimonies, and flings—one thing was certain: He was his mother's daughter. But whatever his quirks, Garrett always created effervescence around him, a lot of fun and frolic, and for that alone he was welcome company. In addition to that, all things being relative, he made me feel extremely masculine.

Which was exactly what I needed, since at that moment Rafik rushed into the shop urgent and troubled.

"Stani," he exclaimed breathlessly. "Someone has made an attack on Madame!"

Around the salon the few late-working stylists halted their scissors while they and their customers eavesdropped in morbid curiosity. When someone grabs center stage you listen.

"It happened one hour ago," Rafik continued excitedly.

"Was she hurt?" I said.

"Non. The police are there now."

"Where did it happen?" I said.

"In the entrance to her building."

Garrett Wade chimed in. "Did you scare the attacker off?"

"Eh?" replied Rafik.

"Did you rescue the victim, you big strong man?"

Rafik's brow wrinkled. "Who is this?" he asked me impatiently, as though he didn't really want an answer.

I attempted an introduction, but Rafik grabbed my arm and pulled me away from my station and back toward my office. Once inside he spoke bluntly, like a military officer during a crisis.

"You must help. Madame is afraid for her life."

"Rafik, this is a matter for the police, not me."

"They do not believe her. I can see by their faces and their questions. They think Madame is imagining the attack."

"It couldn't have happened at a worse time."

"What do you mean?"

I pursed my lips, then told him, "Toni was released this afternoon."

"Oh! That is good news, no?"

"Not really."

Rafik's dark eyes, full of pleading just seconds ago, now smoldered. "Why not?" he said.

"She could have been the one who attacked Madame," I said.

"Not possible." The fires within him were already kindled. "Tell me exactly what happened."

"Madame was unlocking the front door. Someone grabbed her purse and knocked her down."

"Did she see who it was?"

"She was too . . . how you say? . . . started?"

"Startled."

"Startled, yes."

"So she saw nothing?"

"No."

"Rafik, I still think this is for the police. I agreed to help get Toni out of jail, but now I have other things on my mind."

"What things?"

"You and me. I want to spend time on us."

"But Madame is my family."

"Not mine," I said.

He aimed his fiery eyes at me.

"So you will not help her?"

"Not when there's danger."

"You are afraid, then?"

"I'm trying to be sensible."

"You are the only person who can help me."

"The police can handle it."

"Please, Stani. Can you talk to her? Just talk? It will help her. It will help me."

I heaved a sigh. Love, lover, lovest. "Rafik, what can I possibly say or do that can't be done by somebody in authority?"

"You can bring peace. Madame Rubi likes you. She trust you."

Flattery again. It worked on others and it worked on me.

"Okay, dear heart. I'll talk to her, for whatever good it does."

Suddenly Rafik grabbed me and pulled me into a strong embrace.

With our heads pressed against each other he said, "I knew you will help."

"I'll go see her after work. Tell me where she lives."

"She is in the same building with Max Harkey."

"The Appleton?" I said, pulling my head back slightly to face him.

"Oh yes. Madame lives downstairs. She is his neighbor."

"Why didn't I know that?"

Rafik shrugged. "She always lives there."

That was a curious fact.

I nuzzled my face against my lover's neck. "Since I'm doing this favor will you stay tonight?"

"Oh . . ." He wavered. "I am so tired."

Was it really tiredness? Or was it Toni di Natale's new availability?

"I understand," I said. "It's no wonder you're dead on your feet. I saw how hard you work in rehearsal."

At once Rafik pulled away from me. "When?" he demanded.

"Today, just after noontime."

"You watch me?"

"Yes. It was wonderful."

"How dare you to watch me?"

"Dare? I watched you because I love you."

"I tell you before, do not watch my rehearsal."

"I didn't plan it. It just happened. You were so beautiful showing the dancers what to do. I fell in love with you again."

At this Rafik softened a bit. Once more I asked him to stay the night with me. Once more he claimed to be tired.

"Be tired with me," I said, despising the begging sound in my voice.

"Non. I will go home."

"Shall I call you after I see Madame?"

He nodded. "If you like. Probably I will be sleeping."

In whose arms? I wondered.

"Rafik, I'm tired too. But still you expect me . . . ask me . . . to do another favor for you. I'm supposed to soothe Madame Rubinskaya's troubled mind and heart. And I agreed to do it . . . for you. Well now, what about me?"

"Stani, you have a strong spirit. You must help others. I am too weak now. My work takes all my strength."

One last time I offered myself. "Why don't we spend the night together so I can help *you?*"

"You will help me if you talk to Madame."

Rafik embraced me again, kissed my neck, my cheek, my mouth. Then he left the shop.

Back at my styling station Garrett Wade remarked, "What was that all about?"

"That," I replied, while trying to conceal the gnawing in my heart, "that was about love."

"It's no wonder you hang on to him."

"It is?"

I finished applying the magic mud that would transform Garrett Wade's roots to a state of absolute blondness. As I brushed the color on, I wondered aloud, "Why should I run another mission of mercy?"

"Do you want my opinion?" Garrett said.

"Sure," I said, catching his eyes in the mirror.

"If you don't do it, what will happen?"

"Nothing."

"There's your answer, girl."

"Didn't you just tell me to dump him and start dating again?"

"Not him. Any other ol' hunk. But not *him.*"

Garrett Wade had obviously been vanquished by Rafik's charm.

I finished his hair and sent him away humming. The renewed color and cut would surely impress tomorrow's jury.

After that I was planning to do some office work and then go home, but Garrett's words nagged me. If I didn't do what Rafik had asked— visit Madame Rubinskaya—then it was certain that nothing more would happen regarding Max Harkey's murder, at least nothing provoked by me. But if I did do it, if I did pay the old woman a visit and meddle a bit, what then?

Arriving in front of the Appleton I realized an odd conflict of facts and events. If Max Harkey had had the presence of mind to call Rafik, Marshall Zander, the police, and God knows who else after being attacked, then why had he not identified his attacker to anyone? Had he been protecting someone? Also strange was the lack of any evidence that suggested he had tried to stop the bleeding. Had he been too consumed by panic? Or had Max Harkey realized that his wounds were fatal and that nothing could save him? Or perhaps—why hadn't

I seen this before?—perhaps Max Harkey had not phoned anyone. Perhaps he had been unconscious through the entire horrific episode. Except for an exquisitely staged suicide, how else could a person sustain those efficient, deliberate wounds?

I rang Madame's apartment and identified myself to her. She buzzed me in, and I saw that the front door latch had been repaired already. Upstairs, I pressed the button outside Madame's apartment door, when a dog started barking noisily within.

"Verushka! Verushka!" squawked the old woman on the other side of the door.

With my innate fear of dogs, I had a feeling that Verushka and I were not going to be best of friends.

Madame Rubinskaya opened the door and the dog rushed out past her. Given Madame's Russian heritage I'd expected to see a borzoi or an Afghan hound. But Verushka was just a mongrel bitch. She wagged her tail excitedly and ran her snout up and down my trousers, then raced back and forth through the hallway, yipping and yapping and sniffing everywhere. Madame Rubinskaya stood in the open doorway admiring her pet's antics.

"I save her," she said. "She is good girl, my little czarina." Madame stooped down slightly and clapped her hands. "Inside now, Rushka. Inside!"

The dog barked—two short, sharp barks—then obeyed her mistress instantly and charged back into the apartment. I followed Madame Rubinskaya into a large sitting room of decayed imperial elegance.

"Rafik sends you?" she asked.

"Yes," I replied.

"Good. You wait here. I will bring *chai*."

"*Chai?*" I asked.

The old woman grinned. "*Tea,*" she said emphatically, then turned and left me alone in the room.

The sitting room was a historian's dream but a designer's nightmare, a hodgepodge of furniture and other possessions with no discernible theme, no link, save that of age. The furniture looked European and from the postwar period during which modernity was adopted at the expense of good design. The collection of odd table lamps barely illuminated the gloom of the dark-papered walls and the heavy window drapery. An ancient Byzantine icon with eyes saddened by the weight of the world gazed down from a high corner. On one side of the room sat a grand piano enshrouded by a musty-smelling jacquard fabric edged with long fringe. A few musical scores lay on the music rack. I leafed through one and I saw that it had been autographed to Madame Rubinskaya by the composer. On the piano top were many framed photos. One in particular caught my eye. It was a sepia-tone print of a young male dancer, a god actually, taken in half profile from behind. The man was naked. I picked up the photo and studied the finely honed muscles of the subject's backside. Here was a piece of work that engaged me. Just then I felt Verushka sniffing at my shoe. She did it gently, as if to apologize for her boorish greeting when I arrived. Without a pedigree, like me, she was at odds with the artifacts in Madame Rubinskaya's flat.

Madame arrived with a tray laden with plates of food and a tall copper urn, a samovar. I felt my face redden, since she had caught me in a prurient moment with the photo of a young naked man in my hand.

"Is Maxi," she said as she laid down the tray. I put the photo back on the piano and went to help her.

She served the *chai* in a tall glass. It was strong—pungent and sweet and floral. Along with the *chai* she served cold veal sandwiches on hearty dark rye bread, accompanied with Polish pickled mushrooms and potato-egg salad. We ate quietly for a while. I was about to ask her about the attack when she put her plate down and stole the moment from me.

"I tell you story about Maxi," she began. "You see from that picture how beautiful was his body. When Maxi was dancer in Monte Carlo, I was *régisseuse*. That is rehearsal director, you know?"

I nodded and glanced at her finely wrought ankles and her high insteps, which seemed constrained by the vamp of her shoes.

Madame Rubinskaya continued her tale. "One time after class I am closing studio and I hear noises in girls' dressing room. I ask myself, What is this? Someone is in here? So like cat I go to dressing room. Quiet, quiet, soft steps I make. Slowly I move curtain to see inside. And what is in there?"

She paused theatrically, and I knew to say nothing. Then she smiled at me with her whole face. Even her eyes shone through the gloomy atmosphere of her sitting room.

She whispered, "Maxi is making love to young ballerina." Madame then placed her glass of tea on the table and exclaimed, *"Bobze!"*

Her story was a reversal of the classic primal scene. And as if reading my thoughts, Madame said, "That is when I know I love Maxi forever. After that he is like son to me." She sighed and shook her head, then let her breath out slowly and finished with a sad little moan.

At intermission she offered me a tray of small flat pastries redolent of baked apples. I took one and bit it. It crumbled in my mouth, creating a cloud of spiced fruit and buttery caramel.

"You like?" Madame Rubinskaya asked.

"It's delicious," I replied honestly.

She smiled contentedly, pleased with her excellent culinary skills. "Is simple," she said. "Just butter and cream cheese, and a little flour to hold it."

The luscious mélange teased at my tongue so playfully that I went to olfactory heaven. Then I recalled all too clearly the mission from which Madame Rubinskaya had cleverly distracted me with food and drink and fable. I scolded myself for being thrown so easily off the track, which is probably what accounted for my next remark, a zenith of non sequitur.

"Did you lose anything valuable?"

Madame Rubinskaya looked at me as though I had just spoken a line from high church liturgy.

"The mugging," I continued. "Did the attacker take anything?"

The startling shift in Madame Rubinskaya's deportment would have required a lesser actress to undergo lengthy sessions in coaching and makeup, though I suppose I had provided her with a superb motivation. She made the change from nurturing "baba" to victimized senior citizen—slumped shoulders, sagging cheeks, pinched lips, wary eyes—in less time than it took to say "Action."

"Ach!" she exclaimed. "From nowhere he came."

"So it was a man?"

"Of course it was man."

"Did you see him?"

A sly glance from her clever eyes.

"No," she said. "It all happen too fast."

"Then how do you know—"

"I know it was man!"

"Of course," I said. I became the concerned therapist, the persona I had used when I was training at the psych clinic. "It must have been terrible for you," I said, forcing warmth into my eyes.

Always acting, always hiding something, now the two of us were at an impasse. She was obviously faking hysteria and I was just as obviously faking sympathy. The real question was, if there had really been an attack, who did it and why? And if not, why had the old woman invented the episode? It was time for some charm.

"Forgive me," I said. "I should have been more understanding."

Her face remained fixed on me.

I said, "Tell me about your dancing career."

That finally broke through her resistance.

"Ah, so much to tell. What you want to know?"

I shrugged. "What did you like best?"

She took a deep breath and looked out into the room, as though putting herself in a trance. Some stage people seem to forget when they're not onstage. "I like best to watch my grandmother. She was beautiful dancer. *Assoluta.* She was favorite of the czar."

She'd used the phrase before and I suspected that recalling her family's past glory was Madame's way of ensuring her own worthiness.

She went on. "I was never prima ballerina like my mother. Who is family ballerina now is Mireille. She will be *assoluta* someday. Beautiful dancer. Like my grandmother."

"Mireille is your niece, right?"

Madame Rubinskaya corrected me. "She is great-niece."

Grand-niece, I thought.

I asked, "Did you ever dance the famous roles? Odette-Odile? Aurora? Juliet?"

The old woman scowled. "I was character dancer. I had big passion, big fire, big technique, but I was never pretty young girl on stage. So I do my dance and the audience love me. I did *tours en l'air* like man. Big jumps too. Very strong."

"It must have been wonderful," I said admiringly.

She basked in a brief moment of former glory. Then her eyes became mischievous and she leaned toward me. "Shall I tell you secret now? Big secret?"

"By all means."

She grinned broadly. "This is—how you say?—my deep dark secret." She wanted to milk the moment for suspense, but she also wanted very badly to tell me the secret. In a hushed voice she said, "I never like stage. I never like performance."

I gave her my best anticipatory look.

She continued. "I like only rehearsal and class. That is where ballet is serious. Sometimes on stage is like circus. But in studio it is always . . ." She paused to reflect, to choose the next word carefully, even though I was certain she'd divulged this secret often. "In studio," she said, and added one more interminable pause. "Studio is like church."

Well, I thought, Brava! Point finally made.

She added quickly, "So I am content to be *maîtresse de ballet*, to serve my art and also my beloved Maxi."

At his name her eyes became watery again. It was time for me to pounce.

"Can I ask you a question about him?" I said. "About Max?"

Her left eyelid twitched.

"If it help," she said, faintly displeased to have me ruin the effect of her solemn confession.

I knew my question was going to smell of accusation. I was there, after all, supposedly to comfort her, not to provoke her. So I launched forward uncertainly.

"The night that Max was . . . The night it all happened? Did he call you for help?"

"What you are saying?" she answered sharply. "Maxi call out for help? I hear nothing here. You see is almost soundproof." Her face was still rigid, defensive.

"Madame, did he *telephone* you?"

"Oh," she said, as if she had finally understood my question, though I was certain she knew perfectly well what I was asking. With a little more charm on my part, she might even tell me.

After a lengthy pause, during which Verushka sneezed twice and then resettled herself at Madame Rubinskaya's feet, the old woman said simply, "I don't know."

"Did you hear the telephone ring?"

She lifted her hands as though surrendering. "I cannot answer your question because I was not here." Her voice had now acquired a feminine softness which became more obvious and almost intrusive as she continued. "I was staying at ballet studios that night."

"But you were at the dinner party. Why would you go to the studios?"

"After I come home, I was taking walk with Verushka."

"Was that safe so late at night?"

"I am not afraid. In Russia, *there* is to be afraid. Here is nothing to be afraid. Even now I am not afraid."

I couldn't agree with her one hundred percent, but I wasn't there to discuss domestic politics.

She added, "You must never be afraid."

I nodded in faux gratitude for her advice.

She continued her diversionary tale. "So, Verushka and I are walking, and we come to ballet studios that night, and I decide to stay there."

"But why not just stay here at home?"

She gave me a condescending smile, as though only a great and venerable artist could understand why she had done it.

"Maxi hurt me very much that night. He break my heart. He gives that role for *The Phoenix* to young girl Alissa. It should go to my dear Mireille. It is for her. So I am hurt and I am angry and I want to be far away from him. So I don't stay at home."

An alibi that limp needed all the hairspray in Boston to hold it up. Yet I could almost empathize with her reasoning, with wanting suddenly to be far away from someone who has just hurt you. But my empathy stemmed from lover's misunderstandings. What had been the real relationship between Max Harkey and Madame Rubinskaya? One thing was certain: For someone who claimed to dislike the stage so much, Madame sure put on a good show.

I thanked her for her hospitality and prepared to leave. Verushka stirred and then roused herself for my departure. At the door, while I bade good night to Madame Rubinskaya, Verushka sniffed gently at my hand. I pulled away reflexively and the dog cowered at my sudden movement. Madame Rubinskaya laughed.

"She will not hurt you. She is good girl."

Verushka looked up at me with big, sorry eyes.

Maybe some dogs really don't bite.

Life on the domestic front offered an extra challenge that night. Once home I faced my other dearly beloved, Sugar Baby. Under veterinary advice I was to clean her teeth on a regular basis. I know it sounds simple, but have you ever tried to brush a cat's teeth? Cats, for all their enigmatic charm, are basically jaws and claws. To brush the teeth of such a creature is pure folly. But I had a scheme to get my girl to cooperate with me, thus saving me many dollars and sparing her a round of prophylaxis under general anesthesia. Once I'd ensnared her, I was ready to administer the implement of torture: a kitty toothbrush dipped in crabmeat juice. It worked. Sugar Baby let me brush her teeth. In fact, she tried to help, as cats are wont to do when you least desire it. She licked her chops as soon as a drop of juice hit her tongue, then poked at me with her paw for more. It made brushing a bit more difficult, but I accomplished the entire procedure miraculously scratch-free. And I wondered about the market potential for other crab-scented cat-care products.

I rewarded Sugar Baby's courage with a leisurely comb-out afterwards. Hell, with Rafik absent that night any fur person would do. During the purr-filled session with my girl, I indulged in a generous martini—mogul martinis, I believe they're called when they're that big. And in my solitude I recalled some advice a businessman client had once given me: When in doubt, organize. If nothing else, I was certainly in doubt. So, to allay the doubt, I mentally organized the list of people I'd spoken to recently, the supposed suspects and their possible motives for killing Max Harkey.

There was Marshall Zander, the wealthy nebbish who financed the Boston City Ballet. Since I couldn't determine his motive, I invented one, the most obvious one to me: sexual jealousy. I imagined that Max Harkey had always rejected Marshall's love on the grounds that he was straight. When Max Harkey fell in love with Toni di Natale, perhaps Marshall Zander killed him in an uncontrolled moment. I had no evidence for any of it, but I liked the melodrama.

Scott Molloy, the defensive young dancer with the nice legs and haunches, might also have killed Max Harkey out of jealousy. Not only had his girlfriend been Max's mistress, but there was also the rumor that Scott's feelings for Max had gone beyond professional adulation. Unrequited love is always a decent motive for murder.

As for Alissa Kortland, she might have been seeking professional revenge for the limitations Max was putting on her career despite her submission to his sexual demands.

For another talented sex object, Toni di Natale, I could determine neither motive nor opportunity. Perhaps her entanglement with Rafik put her too close to see objectively.

And where was her fiancé, Jason Sears? Where had he gone? Was he really on tour?

My most recent exchange had been with Madame Rubinskaya, and she had certainly acted erratic and suspicious. But how could anyone who baked so well be a villain?

And last but not least, dangerous only to the heart, was my errant lover, Rafik.

Every person on the list had had an opportunity to kill Max Harkey, and none of them had a good alibi for their whereabouts that night. But someone was missing. Someone's face had not yet appeared in my catalog. Then, like random computer garbage, my brain suddenly recalled the musical score on Max Harkey's piano, the score with the hand-painted cover. Perhaps it was seeing similar old scores on Madame Rubinskaya's piano that had jogged that bit of information from my sluggish data bank. But I couldn't remember seeing that score when I was at Max Harkey's place on the morning of the murder. Then again, I had been quite loaded the night before, so my memory could easily have been supplanted by my imagination. But I knew who might have the answer, and he was also the missing name on my mental list.

Tomorrow I would find Rico, Max Harkey's devilishly cute houseboy.

10

She Could Have Danced All Night

Next morning I was at Snips catching up on the previous day's neglected office work. It was a vague relief to be using the left side of my brain. The drudgery of paperwork seemed to put order in my life, unlike my fumbling murder investigation.

Nicole breezed into the salon around ten o'clock. I heard her cheery good-mornings as she made her way through the shop to my office in back. She appeared in the open doorway at full attention, bosom lifted high and neckline drawn taut.

"Good morning!" she exclaimed as though all was well with the world. She entered, poured herself a cup of coffee, and sat down comfortably in the new side chair.

"Sex therapy is working, eh doll?" I said and focused myself on the paperwork.

"Put that aside for a moment, darling. Let's talk."

"You're telling me to stop working?"

"Just for a little while. Did you see the sky?"

"The sky?"

"It's gorgeous this morning. The clouds are so white against that azure blue. It's almost like the Mediterranean."

"You're effluviating, doll."

"Oh, Stanley. Boston can be so beautiful!"

That did it. I slammed the ledger closed and swiveled my chair to face her.

"Who and how?" I asked.

Nicole sipped her coffee demurely and batted her long eyelashes at me. "You know I never tell," she said.

"Do I know him?"

"I should say so," she replied with a unnatural giggle.

"I need a clue."

"No, you don't," she said coyly.

"Then it must be Branco," I joked.

But instead of refuting my guess, Nicole blushed.

Amazed, I asked, "Did you bed Branco?"

She said nothing and cast her eyes toward the open window.

"Spill it," I demanded.

Nicole made no reply.

"Does that mean there's nothing to spill?" I went on.

Silence and a cool stare were her answers.

"Or maybe nothing *got* spilled, eh doll? Sometimes those younger men lack experience."

"The lieutenant is hardly a younger man," Nicole replied bluntly.

"He's younger than you, doll, but then—"

"Stanley, some experiences are too elevated for vulgar conversation."

"Look who's getting ritzy."

"Don't bare your claws, young man. You tend to your work. I'll tend to the lieutenant."

"And how."

But I knew that Nikki had intended to provoke me. She and the lieutenant couldn't have done it, could they? Really? Coupled? I knew she had a fairly active sex life, but Branco? Was such a thing possible? Given his machismo charismo, instantaneous lust was the typical human response to him. But performing mundane sexual acts with that Olympic god of the Mediterranean seemed improbable, too common—too vulgar, as Nikki had said. Lieutenant Branco was the kind of person who appeared to be on reserve, waiting for his complement, the singular star-crossed partner, the matching goddess who could never materialize in an ordinary world, and certainly not in the embodiment of Nicole Albright. No, more likely their evening together had been a sexual bust, and Nikki was concealing her disappointment under the guise of secrecy.

Suddenly, Ramon the shampoo boy stuck his head in the partly open doorway. "Walk-in request for Stanley," he said, adding with a smug grin, "It's a man." Then he vanished.

At this stage of my career, a walk-in request is nearly always a referral from one of my exclusive clients, so the new customer, though a stranger, is primed to be pleased and to pay.

"Duty calls," I said.

"You mean money," replied Nicole. "We'll continue this later."

I took a gulp of coffee and went out to the shop floor. Standing in the reception area was Marshall Zander, and he didn't need a haircut.

"I hope it's not presumptuous to arrive without an appointment," he said. "It was such a beautiful day that I went walking, and I thought I'd stop in."

"I have some time," I said coolly.

"How fortunate for me! I'd like a shampoo and condition and a trim," he said. Then he laughed heartily and added, "The works." His attempt at cleverness made me feel more like a utility-company employee than an exclusive stylist. But I can play the dutiful proletarian when necessary.

I gave Marshall Zander a smock to protect his clothes. After he changed and came out of the dressing room, I noticed a faint but unpleasant odor about him, something like rotting fruit. Perhaps it was all the mood-lifting drugs he was taking.

I led him to the shampoo sinks. Ramon, keeper of that fief, grinned broadly as if to say, "Mr. Bigshot still gets some pretty ugly walk-ins." Dear Ramon didn't recognize my opportunity to do some PI work. I knew perfectly well that Marshall Zander had come to Snips for something other than hair work. My simple challenge was to find out exactly what he wanted to know without telling him anything from my side of the styling chair.

I applied a dollop of moisturizing shampoo to his coarse brown hair and worked up a creamy, sudsy mousse. As I massaged his scalp, he closed his eyes and moaned quietly in pleasure. That particular response to my able hands is not uncommon, but I wasn't too eager to get so cozy with Marshall Zander. I nipped his moment of bliss with a not-so-accidental burst of icy water from the spray nozzle. He flinched but then smiled, and I saw that he had enjoyed the jolt of surprise, however uncomfortable.

I said, "You seem to be holding up well with all this nasty business."

"It's thanks to my pills," he said. "I've been sleeping better too. How are you doing? Have you come up with anything new?"

"Regarding what?"

"You've been talking to people around the ballet company."

"Talk is cheap."

"Whom do you suspect?"

I didn't reply, though I was impressed with his grammar.

He went on with a light tone. "Do you suspect me?"

"I don't really have the right to suspect anyone."

"Forget about your rights. What about your logic? At whom does your ratiocination point its accusing finger?"

That was a big word from the man with the big bankroll.

I was about to answer him when I felt the rustle of a familiar energy behind me. I turned around to see Rafik standing there with a gigantic floral bouquet in his arms. With what mixed emotion did my heartbeat accelerate?

Rafik couldn't see whose head was in the sink, and Marshall Zander couldn't see Rafik behind me. My intuition told me it was better left that way. I sent Rafik a silent kiss shaped with my lips, then nodded my head toward the office in back where he and I could commune in privacy. First though, I squirted a massive dose of conditioner into Marshall Zander's hair.

"Don't move," I ordered.

"I'm not going anywhere," he said obediently.

Fortunately Nikki had already left my office, so Rafik and I could be alone. Once inside he closed the door with his foot and then, suddenly, we were grappling at each other. The flowers fell to the floor. We swooned, we tripped over my chair and tumbled into it together, entangled in a passionate embrace. My guy.

He spoke first. "Forgive me."

"For what?" I replied, as though there was nothing to forgive.

Rafik spoke haltingly. "Last night. I was the *jerque*."

"No, beloved. 'Twas I in my jealous frenzy who was, is, and always will be *le jerque*."

Please sign here.

"So you are not angry?" he said.

"Dubious perhaps, but not angry."

More insistent hugs and kisses followed—two people too much in love.

When we finally came up for air Rafik said, "Toni wants to talk to you."

That wasn't exactly the sweet love line I was hoping to hear.

I spotted the flowers lying on the floor. Now they seemed something more than a generous gift from my lover. They were a distraction from Rafik's renewed infidelities. And with that observation I sensed we were at it again, dancing our schizophrenic tango.

Forgive me.

Trust me.

Help me.

Here are flowers.

I love you.

Go away.

Da capo.

"What does she want?" I said.

"She has the idea who killed Max Harkey."

"She should tell the police."

"No, Stani. They do not believe her."

I stared into Rafik's eyes. His were not the kind of eyes to be refused easily, if at all. I already knew I was going to do what he wanted. I was going to chase down Toni di Natale and talk to her solely because she had asked it of my lover. But this time I intended to extract something in return, something to equalize the deal with Rafik. I already knew what that was, and in the most nonchalant tone I could manage, I asked for it.

"Do you know where I can find Rico?"

Rafik's eyes flared in sudden anger.

"Why?"

"Because he is the one person at that dinner party I haven't spoken to yet."

"That is all you want from him?"

"I want from him what you want from Toni di Natale."

He narrowed his eyes, but the fire still came through.

"You do not know who I am with her."

"I'm trying to make you understand how I feel."

He turned his head away as though my feelings were the most repulsive things in the universe. I suppose sometimes they were.

"If you want Rico," he said angrily, "you should ask Marshall Zander. Rico lives with him now."

Max Harkey's former houseboy seemed to be moving faster than ever.

"I only want to question him, Rafik. And in return I'll talk with Toni. Fair is fair. Where is she now?"

Rafik's eyes burned. "She is staying with me."

Silence again. Now I *was* the flowers on the floor, something innocent that had been used to perpetrate a lie. I'd thought we were different, Rafik and I, stronger, truer, above this kind of mawkish scene. The more fool I. Oh, I know I'd set it up from the beginning, pitting my provincial love against the sophistication of Toni di Natale. But now Rafik had made his choice. And it was an odd surprise, the quietness of it, that he would choose her over me. I should have been generous and thanked him for the thrill of novelty, of being left for a woman. But I could say nothing.

He turned quietly and left me alone.

Maybe we could still be friends.

And maybe someday I'd be married with children.

A few minutes later I regained my bearings, or so I thought, and returned to the shop floor. Marshall Zander was still at the shampoo sink where I'd left him with a load of conditioner in his hair. With that stuff penetrating his hair shafts all that time, Mr. Zander was going to be extremely fluffy when he left Snips Salon today. No extra charge.

As I rinsed his hair he asked, "Is everything all right?"

He sounded so earnest that I almost burst into tears, even though his concern for me resembled the witless devotion of a big stupid dog.

"Nothing time won't fix," I said ruefully.

I wrapped a towel around his head and led him to my station.

Once he settled in there he reminded me, "Just a trim."

"Only the tips," I said and began my work. It was more combing than anything else. He didn't need cutting at all, and once again I wondered why he'd come to see me. Well, he could keep his secret for all I cared. I just wanted to get to Rico, who was now staying with him.

"You live in town, don't you?" I asked.

He raised an eyebrow. "I have a place here, yes."

"Close by?"

He made a small frown.

I added quickly, "I thought you might want to be on my mailing list."

"That's not necessary. I know where you are."

I shrugged. "Sometimes we have special offers for our better customers, and we let them know by mail."

He wouldn't even nibble. How was I going to break through this guy's defensive torpor and get his address? By the time I finished faking his trim, the disgusting answer came to me in a flash of voluptuous glory: Use sex. Hell, it wasn't working as an expression of love, so why not use it as a bargaining chip?

I caressed Marshall Zander's scalp extra tenderly and leaned toward him, putting my head near his and murmuring into his ear.

"If you live close by, well . . . I might drop in sometime."

Of course I'd never do it, even though I was technically a free agent as of ten minutes ago.

Marshall Zander turned his head toward me.

"Do you mean that?" he said.

"Why not?" I replied.

His eyes were swampy with desire. "I keep a suite at the Copley Palace. Just give my name to the concierge."

He winked and my stomach turned. Sure, I'd got the information I wanted, but I was horrified at how easily it had come once I'd found the key. Even worse, I realized that this was probably how a lot of people were getting what they wanted from each other.

The hair work finished, I removed the protective cape. Marshall Zander stood up and put out his hand. I accepted it but recoiled at its rough dryness. Yet he held onto me and spoke as though reciting a carefully prepared statement.

"It was a difficult decision for me to come here today, but I can tell you the truth now. I was concerned about the things I said to you the other morning, about you and your lover. I regret it very much. I'm still quite distraught, but thanks to the tranquilizers I'm functioning well. But beyond all that, my point is . . . well, I like you. And I was worried that I had offended you the other day. But just now you've proven to me that everything is all right between us. You've put my mind at peace. I hope you'll come by sometime soon."

Oh. God. No. A date with him was not what I wanted, but I had to forge ahead. "Thank you," I said in the most neutral voice I could muster. Then, solely to find out when he would *not* be there, I ventured, "Will you be around today?"

"I'm afraid not. I've got appointments all afternoon."

"Another time then," I said, utterly relieved and straining to conceal it.

"Soon," he said with a hungry leer.

I extricated my hand from his. He turned and went toward the reception desk, making his way there with a noticeable spring in his step, a ridiculous bounce that made him look like an absurd motor-driven toy. I knew that my flirtation had caused it and I was disheartened. I fled to the solace of my little chamber in back. Minutes later Nicole joined me there.

"Somebody likes you a lot," she said.

"He's not my type, doll."

"Not to mention that you are already betrothed."

I grunted in reply, the way Branco might have.

Nicole placed a crisp fifty-dollar bill on top of my desk.

"From Mr. Zander," she said with a raised eyebrow.

"See what I mean? Rich and crass."

"Is everything all right with Rafik?"

"Why?"

"Your shoulders are drooping."

I pulled myself up straight. "Everything is exactly the same, except I think we just broke up."

"Stanley, what have you done now!"

"Hardly my fault alone."

"Oh," she exclaimed with exasperation. "I give up. Why can't you just—"

"Because I can't!" I shouted in a sudden burst of frustration. "I just can't, Nikki. I want to be strong and understanding. I want to accept everything calmly. I want to be the rock of stability. But I just can't do it. I can't accept him wanting to be involved with . . . with *that* woman—with any woman. It feminizes me."

Nicole waited for the air to settle down, then she said faintly, "What a pity. He loves you so much."

"That's an illusion."

"No, darling. Your denial is the illusion, and one of your own creation."

"Nikki, how can a man like Rafik love me? Look at me. The only secondary sex characteristic I have is my mustache. The rest of me is as pink and smooth as a girl."

"But you have that nice square jaw. And those strong legs."

"So does my aunt Letta."

"Darling, the fact is, when Rafik wants a woman he goes to a woman. And when he wants a man, he comes to you."

"You haven't seen us in bed, doll."

Nicole grimaced. "I meant your kind of masculinity. You're confusing sex and love again."

"Don't you think I know that? If anything, I'm *too* integrated. Believe me, Nikki, if I could disconnect my body from my heart and my mind I would do it."

"You analyze your feelings instead of enjoying them. Then you try to control them, just the way you try to control Rafik."

"It's my nature."

"Nonsense. It's a bad habit."

"This is foolish," I muttered. "I've got things to do." I got up and went to the door. "I'll be back later."

"Where are you going now?" she asked with an edge.

"To create my own reality," I said flatly.

"You'd do better to face your destiny," she replied.

I departed through the back door, which opened onto the alley that led to Berkeley Street. One block farther on, at Boylston Street, I was about to head up toward Copley Square to the newly erected Copley Palace, where I would find Rico the houseboy. But instead I continued along Berkeley Street, which led directly to Station D, where I intended to verify some dubious data with Lieutenant Branco.

On the way there I had the odd sensation that I was moving through time and space solely on reflex, undirected by any conscious thought. I recalled one fact only: Rafik had walked out. And one consequence: I felt nothing—no love, no loss, no hatred—just pure cold objectivity. I was a locomotive robot devoid of sensation.

I stopped at a café and bought two cappuccinos to go. I couldn't face Branco's coffee again, not today. Perhaps there was hope for my emotional recovery if I could still worry about good coffee. And getting one for Branco proved that I was still aware and considerate of others. And I could even recall the year it was and the name of the President. Optimism surged.

Fortunately Branco was in. When I gave him the cappuccino he accepted it graciously, like a contented mortal, like a guy who'd had a good time the night before.

"Don't care for my coffee, eh?" he said good-naturedly.

"I'm just a desperate and lonely man bartering for friendship."

"How is Miss Albright today?"

Once again my mind raced with images of Branco and Nicole joined together at the pelvis. It was as grotesque as imagining your parents copulating. It just didn't parse, even though the evidence might have indicated otherwise.

"Just ducky," I said.

I searched for a sign from Branco regarding his night with Nicole, but the cop divulged nothing either. He pried the lid off his coffee cup and gave an approving nod to the contents. But I kept wondering, What had happened between them? And why now? Branco and Nicole had met before. What new catalyst had appeared to conjoin them now? Was it the presence of the luscious Toni di Natale? Maybe that she-beast had not only won my lover's heart, but had also got this cop's juices bubbling to the point where he needed a mortal release, poor thing. And Nicole provided a safe and comfortable haven. She was a known entity and she wasn't a suspect, which eliminated the unpleasant possibility of a conflict of interest. Someone like Branco would choose his sex partners like that, rationally and sensibly, like a lawyer.

"Lieutenant how about instead of friendship, I settle for some information?"

"Like what?"

"Did your crew find a big musical score with a hand-tinted cover at Max Harkey's apartment?"

Branco pondered awhile.

I added, "I remember seeing it on the piano the night before."

The cop pulled his lips back tightly and shook his head no.

"I don't recall anything like that in our reports. Are you sure about it?"

"I admit I was loaded that night, but the image is clear in my mind. I know that score was there, and the next morning it wasn't."

As if lost in thought or else bored with me, Branco focused on his coffee. Maybe he was really enjoying it. Love does enhance the senses. If he and Nikki had done the job right last night, today's cup of coffee would be a whole new experience for him.

I went on to tell him that I'd spoken to Madame Rubinskaya and that I wanted to verify her farfetched story.

"Can I see her statement?" I said.

Branco held the coffee under his nose as if intoxicated by its aroma. Again he shook his head gently no. "But it's all there," he said, "pretty much how she told it to you. We thought it was odd too, but she really did spend the night at the ballet studios. We have the security guard's records to corroborate it. She arrived there well before Max Harkey's death."

"Neat alibi," I said, "as far as it goes. But those records could have been fudged. Madame Rubinskaya lives in the same building as Max Harkey. She could have killed him and then gone to the studios, only a few minutes' walk away."

"You sound like you suspect her," said Branco.

"Don't you?"

He took a big gulp of coffee and smiled. "The old woman arrived at the studios around twelve-thirty and stayed there. We figure Max Harkey was attacked after five that morning."

"How do you know?"

"Body temperature," replied Branco. "When we got to him he was still warm. And with the nature of the wounds and his excellent physical condition, Max Harkey wouldn't have lasted more than five minutes."

"What about the phone calls?"

Branco arched an eyebrow. "Which phone calls?"

"I, uh, heard that Max Harkey phoned for help that morning."

"Including the call to your friend Rafik," said the cop.

"Yeah, well, the question is, with everyone else he called, did Harkey ever phone the police? Doesn't it seem strange that a man is bleeding to death and—"

Branco cut me off. "As a matter of fact, we got a 911 call from Max Harkey at five-fifteen that morning, and another one shortly after that from Marshall Zander."

"How shortly after?"

"Four minutes," replied the cop.

"So Max Harkey was alive at five-fifteen."

"If you use arithmetic, yes."

"Did you trace the calls?"

Branco's full lips made a little smile.

"The first one originated from Max Harkey's apartment, and the second one from one of Marshall Zander's private lines." Then Branco almost snickered. "What's strange is that Rafik never called us to report the crime, even though he claims that Harkey called him for help too."

"I think that's easy to explain, Lieutenant. Rafik told me that Max Harkey said he'd already called the police."

"Right," said Branco. "That's what he told us too. So *your* two stories agree just fine." His voice oozed with insinuation.

"Well," I said, grasping defensively, "I'm sure Rafik just wanted to get to Max as fast as possible."

"Or away from him," said Branco.

"What do you mean, Lieutenant?"

Branco sat back in his chair and seemed to be relishing some morsel of classified information.

"Well?" I said. "Do you have something on Rafik?"

"Not exactly," replied the cop, extending the words provocatively. "There is some evidence, but we haven't determined its exact bearing on the case."

"What is it?"

Branco's face went rigid, like a portrait cast in bronze.

"Max Harkey had reached a sexual climax shortly before his death," he said. "But we found no evidence of semen anywhere outside his body."

"Maybe he was a clean freak and flushed everything away."

Branco frowned at my attempt at levity.

"So, Lieutenant, it appears we have the delicate mission of identifying Max Harkey's sex partner that night."

Branco hedged. "Possibly."

I continued, "But even then it might not be his killer. It could have been anybody."

"Except for the old woman," said Branco.

"Why not? Just because a security guard said so?"

Branco snapped. "Because I can't imagine it, that's why not!"

"So your lack of sexual imagination means she's innocent?"

"Look you," said Branco, "I'm running this case, and until I'm convinced otherwise, what I say goes."

"Fine, Lieutenant. I'll just go ask the suspects if they had sex with Max Harkey that night."

"I'd advise you not to," he said.

"I'll be discreet about it. We hairdressers know how to get people to talk about sex. In fact, I plan to grill someone this afternoon on his sexual technique. I'm on my way there now."

Branco said, "Then you'd better get going."

I stood up. "I thought you said we'd be working together this time."

"Did I?" he said.

I headed toward the door.

"Thanks for the coffee," he said.

I grumbled back, "Anytime."

As I opened the door he said, "Please give my regards to Miss Albright."

"Sure thing, Lieutenant."

I left Station D and headed to the Copley Palace. Maybe Rico the houseboy held the keys to more than the front door of his new master's abode.

11
So Danso Samba

In the main lobby of the Copley Palace numerous posters announced a special performance by the famous stage and film actress Sharleen McChannel. Sharleen had embarked on a new career as a psychic channeler and seer, and apparently she was wrapping up a nationwide tour to promote her latest book of personal knowledge, *Up in a Tree*. Her easy publishing success made me wonder about writing a book myself, something about the mystique and romance of salon life, a runaway bestseller called *Hair Today, Gone Tomorrow*.

But fleeting dreams of fame and fortune could not distract me from the mission at hand. I went to the main desk and asked for Marshall Zander's suite number. It seemed a simple enough request, yet they referred me to the concierge, exactly as Marshall Zander had suggested in the first place. I sensed that he was being protected from the public for some reason, and since I wanted to get to his suite to see Rico, I was going to have to confront Monsieur le Concierge, which meant sacrificing my anonymity. Concierges are usually clever, observant, prying individuals. I couldn't just ask him to ring the suite directly, because if Marshall Zander was home I'd have to invent a reason for *not* going up, which might attract suspicion: "Oh, he's home? Never mind." Yet if Marshall Zander *wasn't* there, which is what I was hoping, I *did* want to get in to see Rico. I devised a simple scheme to get the concierge to cooperate, then approached his desk and began my spiel.

"I have a rather delicate mission concerning a Mr. Zander, who is staying here." My formal tone caused an insolent twitch from the man's fastidiously groomed pencil-line mustache.

"Is Mr. Zander expecting you?"

"Not today," I said. "But I must speak with his attendant, Rico."

The concierge's eyebrows went up. Like his mustache, they had been compulsively plucked and trimmed. Dragons at the gate came in many guises.

"On what business?" he asked suspiciously.

"I'm a caterer. I'm here to confirm the plans for a small reception, a surprise for Mr. Zander. So I'd like to see Rico, but only if Mr. Zander isn't in. I don't want to spoil the surprise for him."

The concierge gave a little snort of disbelief, as though my story was a common excerpt from *The Hustler's Handbook*.

"I see. So if Mr. Zander is home, you do *not* want to go up. Is that correct?"

"That's right," I said, but my bravado was crumbling fast.

"And if Rico is there alone, you *do* want to go up."

"Yes," I said guiltily.

"Your name?" he said.

"Just say it's the caterer."

"Will Rico know who you are?" he said suggestively.

"If he's alone, you can tell him it's Stan."

"Just Stan?"

I nodded. "You can describe me to him. I'm sure he'll remember me."

"Yes," said the concierge. "I'm certain he will."

I nodded.

With the efficiency of a Prussian officer the concierge punched the magic sequence of buttons that connected to Marshall Zander's secret domain. I wondered what all the mystery was about. Maybe Marshall Zander was a drama queen who required intrigue and tragic overtones in every aspect of his life.

After a brief and extremely hushed telephone conversation, of which I could not discern one word, the concierge regained his obsequious propriety. He pronounced the message like a verdict.

"You may go up. *Rico* is expecting you."

I felt like the oldest call boy in the world.

Then I got to witness the further securities protecting Marshall Zander's living quarters. The special elevator to his suite required a key to operate it. Once the concierge inserted the key, the control panel inside the elevator lit up and provided a simple choice of destination: up or down. I began to suspect that the domicile at the other end of the elevator shaft was no mere suite of rooms.

After an express ride into the ionosphere, the elevator door opened onto a large rectangular foyer about the size of a good hotel room. At one end a large window looked out over Boston. I could actually see part of the harbor, and from this high up the water's natural beauty was affecting, especially since the pollution and debris were imperceptible. At the other end of the foyer was a set of massive double doors, which, when I turned away from my momentary enjoyment of the view, framed the small but classically proportioned form of Rico, Brazilian houseboy to the late Max Harkey.

"Hi," he said with a wide grin. His mouth was big, almost too big for his face, but his lips had been so lovingly formed by their creator that their slight coarseness was forgivable, even attractive. "I didn't think I'd see you again," he added coyly.

"Bloodhound Kraychik always finds his man."

To my surprise my silly comment destroyed the flirtatious web he'd already begun to spin.

"What do you want, then?" he asked firmly, as though addressing the butcher's delivery boy, one minion to another.

"To talk about Max Harkey."

Rico stared at me as though trying to decipher my real intentions. And he seemed distracted too, perhaps by a lingering sadness over his master's death. Yet I wanted information from him. But how could I state it so baldly? After all, he might talk more openly if he thought he could earn a pleasant reward. Was this *moi*, trading sex for facts?

"You'd better come in," he said.

I stepped through the double doorway and immediately recalled Marshall Zander's words: "I keep a suite." He'd said it offhandedly, as if we both came from the same class of decent fellows who keep a suite of rooms in all their favorite cities. But Marshall Zander's modest appraisal of his downtown residence had been duplicitous. "I keep a suite," he'd said, when in truth he lived in a modern-day palace. And though the late Max Harkey's penthouse was splendid, when compared to the floor plan of this place it was a mere prototype, a quarter-size model for the vast expanse of space and light that housed a single man atop a forty-five-story hotel. The excess of it all was vaguely sickening. The place reeked of a designer's heavy hand, yet it reflected nothing about its inhabitant except for the lordly sums of money available. There was no sign of emotion, no accident of hue or line, no betrayal of passion. Marshall Zander's castle in the sky was a testimony to sterile correctness. Even the stately concert grand piano had been positioned for visual effect against a wall of glass windows that provided a background panorama of the Boston skyline. The instrument would have preferred the acoustic advantage of a location far away from any walls, especially glass ones.

I spoke under my breath. "How do people live like this?"

Rico overheard me and answered easily. "He owns it."

"He owns this?"

"The hotel."

That tidbit challenged my New Jersey working-class values. To me an extravagant real estate holding is something along the lines of an old beach house or a musty lakeside cabin, not a bloody high-rise hotel. Oh well, someone had to own the grand hotels of the world. It certainly wasn't going to be the likes of me, not outside a game of Monopoly.

"It's quite a view," I said, determined to cover my awe that one person, any person could live with so much floor space so far above the surface of the earth.

Rico showed me the balcony that faced west. It was torn up, as if under reconstruction, with pipes and broken slabs of marble scattered everywhere. I asked him why.

"Mr. Zander is afraid of heights," he explained. "He couldn't go out there alone, so now he's installing railings everywhere. That way he'll always have something to hold onto when he gets dizzy."

It was another case of treasures and pleasures hoarded by someone who couldn't really enjoy them.

Rico continued, "He's going to install bright lights too, but for now it's still dark at night. Sometimes I go out there just to get away from him. He never follows me."

I recalled the classic condition where extremely high places could actually lure a person to throw his or her body over the edge.

As if reading my mind Rico said, "That's why the piano is blocking the sliding doors. I think Mr. Zander is afraid he's going to run out there some night and just jump off."

I noticed that the doors that opened onto the west balcony were directly behind the long flat side of the piano. You had to go out of your way, literally underneath the piano, to get to the balcony through those doors.

"Are you happy here?" I asked.

"I'm happy to have the job, even if Mr. Zander isn't paying me as much as Mr. Harkey did. The view is worth it."

"Did Max Harkey come here often?"

"I don't know. I never went places with him."

"Did Marshall ever visit Max's place?"

He nodded. "Every few days," he said. Then he added, "I never noticed it before, but now that I work for him I do. He smells bad."

"What do you mean?"

"The worst is when he takes off his jacket. I think he gets nervous. In Brazil we have a saying, 'Like two goats on a hot day.' That's what it's like."

That partly explained the unpleasant odor around Marshall Zander at Snips earlier that day. What relief that I'd been spared the full olfactory assault. I cleansed my nasal memory with happy thoughts of Rafik and Lieutenant Branco, both hirsute men yet both always attended by appealing scents, as though their bodies were incapable of any form of grossness.

Again Rico showed his psychic talent and remarked, "Mr. Harkey always smelled good too."

He led me to the main sitting area. As I followed him, I asked, "What part of Brazil are you from?"

"Where do you think?" he said with a flirtatious smile. "Rio. I come from Rio de Janeiro."

That explained the built-in samba of his hips, that hypnotic archetypal swaying of the ocean and the palm trees. Rico's body once again stirred up pleasant memories of my short-lived affair with a young Balinese. It had been a shallow kind of love based on mutual provocation as much as physical compatibility. Yet it had been so easy. Neither of us had had questions or expectations of the other. I had never analyzed a single moment I'd spent with that young man. I had simply enjoyed them all. And then followed the complex and often disturbing relationship I shared with Rafik. It was futile to resist the

obvious: I knew that I wanted him in my life forever. Today's separation was only temporary. Our connection was too strong for me to
imagine living without him. Yet nothing was ever simple with him.
Even the physical aspect of our love seemed too complicated these
days, too full of meaning and consequence. And here was Rico now,
the boy from Ipanema, offering me another chance for plain old
ordinary pleasure.

We sat facing each other on opposite ends of a long dove-gray
leather sofa. He put his legs up on the plump squeaky cushions. I had
the urge to do the same, but reminded myself I was there on business.

"Rico, do you know what happened to the music that was on Max
Harkey's piano the night of the dinner party?"

"Which one?" he asked guardedly. "There were so many."

"The big score with the hand-tinted cover. I remember seeing it
that night, but it wasn't there the next morning."

Again the young man stared at me as though trying to go beyond
my words to some truer message on my face. "Is it a clue?"

"That's what I'm trying to find out."

His eyes wandered nervously, avoiding me and the room and the
grand vista behind me. "It was there when I . . . went out . . . after the
party."

"Didn't you live with Max Harkey?"

"Yes."

"Then why did you go out?"

Silence. Then I realized my blunder.

"I'm sorry," I said. "That's none of my business."

His eyes engaged mine with an instant and powerful magic.

"But it is!" he said. "It is your business."

"I don't understand."

"Don't you?" he said.

I shook my head no.

"You Americans have no heart," he said disdainfully. "Can't you
see?"

"I'm sorry, Rico. I don't—"

"I wanted you! That night I wanted you and you went home and
left me."

"But I was with Rafik."

"I know, but I didn't want to marry you. It was just for one night.
I was lonely. And you are a nice person." He paused. We both caught

our breath while the air settled from his surge of high energy. Then Rico said, "Besides, your lover was being rude to you. If you stayed with me he would appreciate you more. That's how some men are." Such labyrinths a PI must traverse just to verify a fact or two.

"So that made you go out?" I said.

"I told you," he replied, almost pleading with me, "I was lonely. And you left me." He stalled, then went on, "So I found someone else that night."

"And before you went out you saw that musical score still on the piano?"

"Yes," he said coolly. "It was there."

And since Branco had just told me that the police did not find the score, it had obviously vanished sometime that night. The simplest assumption was that Max Harkey's killer had taken it.

I went on. "Did you tell the police about this?"

Rico answered, "They didn't ask me."

Stonehearted Stanley continued, "What about your alibi?"

The young man glowered. "It isn't an alibi and I didn't do anything wrong. Mr. Harkey was like my father, not my lover. He even left me some money and all the kitchen equipment."

"Has the will been released already?"

"That's what Mr. Zander said. He told me that Mr. Harkey left me fifty thousand dollars and all the kitchen things."

With morbid curiosity I wondered about the rest of the estate—the penthouse and all the art and sculpture and that magnificent piano within.

Rico continued, "I'm going to send some of the money back to my family in Brazil, and the rest I'm saving for my *marido.*" He winked at me.

"You'd better make a will for yourself, then," I said.

"Why?" he asked with eyes full of temerity and the youthful presumption of life everlasting.

I told him the harsh truth. "In case anything happens to you, the stuff and money will go where you want it to."

He considered my sobering advice. "I'll take care of it this afternoon," he said. "Let's not talk about it anymore. Do you want some lunch?"

No sooner had he said it than my stomach growled and grumbled. Rico laughed at the raucous sounds.

"I guess I do," I said.

"Let's order from room service."

"Can you do that?"

"Sure. Mr. Zander owns the hotel. I'm sure they don't send him a bill." Rico laughed. "He's so rich he probably doesn't even know how much money he has."

There was a certain irony in that.

And so, since lunch was being paid by some anonymous dime, we ordered lavishly: a bottle of gin for me; a bottle of rum for Rico, along with a liter of cola and some lime; and for eats, one each of the hotel chef's daily specials and one each of every dessert available. The meal arrived on two carts.

After a few drinks and too much of the fine food—including some crunchy-crusted sourdough baguettes flown in fresh daily from San Francisco, one of which reminded me of an altar boy who had long ago initiated me into the high art of self-abuse—I found myself facing the very situation I'd been accusing Rafik of lately: easy sex with no strings. I wondered if having sex with this attractive young Brazilian would affect how I felt about Rafik. A part of me said, "Do it! It's not a sin. It doesn't matter. Release yourself from the confining spell of love." But another part protested, "If you do this, then some aspect of your emotional connection with Rafik will be changed forever." The answer came in a horrible pun, at the exact moment I was sliding Rico's white cotton briefs over his ankles and hoisting his honey-brown limbs over my shoulders: My emotional connection to my lover was as magnetically potent and consuming as a cosmic black hole. I chuckled aloud, and Rico asked me what was funny.

"I just thought of my lover," I said without guile.

My truthful remark had the odd effect of stoking Rico's fires even more, much the way a married man's appeal can be heightened by his loyalty to wife and children. Rico pulled me close to him and clutched me with his thighs. Much squirming and rolling and wrestling on the cool smooth leather sofa eventually caused our mutual release, achieved through the safety of external friction rather than unprotected penetration.

Later, spent and nestled in my arms, Rico told me that on the morning of Max Harkey's murder, there was a particular item he couldn't find at the penthouse after the police had been there.

"His diary was missing," he said softly. "That was the only thing

I wanted. I wanted to know how Mr. Harkey really felt. I wanted to know his secrets."

"Did you ever read it?"

Rico looked at me with imploringly honest eyes.

"No," he said.

Hearing this intimate confession, especially after *coitus externalis*, I felt like Mata Hari. I reminded myself to ask Lieutenant Branco about the diary.

"Rico, do you still have the key to Max Harkey's apartment?"

"I gave it to Mr. Zander," he said.

Like Cary Grant asking the same dangerous favor of Ingrid Bergman, I said, "Do you think you can get that key for me?"

"I'll try, but why do you want it?"

I said, "You never know what the killer may have forgotten."

We were lying quietly entwined when a shocking thought seized me: What if Marshall Zander should arrive home and find us reclining leg-over-leg on his leather sofa? Despite the urban panorama that served as our backdrop, it was not a pretty picture I saw. Panic ensued. I leaped from the sofa and dressed quickly. Rico watched me wide-eyed.

"I've got to go," I said.

"Will you come back again?"

"I don't know." I gave him one last affectionate smooch.

"Thank you," he said.

"Thank *you*," I replied.

"Your lover is very lucky."

"No," I said. "I'm really a subterranean monster, and you've let me come up for air."

"Maybe I can be your *tesão.*"

"What's that?"

"Your little stud," he said with a devilish smile.

"I'm not sure . . ."

"No marriage. Just like this. Easy. For fun."

I weighed the proposition. "Maybe," I said.

I felt his eyes glued to me as I got up from the sofa and made my way across the long open space to the double doors. I turned back for a last good-bye. Rico's small golden body was still folded cozily on the sofa. He waved to me and I let myself out.

12

Whose Lover Is She?

On the way back to Snips, I felt a renewed optimism and freedom within me, and as much as I denied it, I knew it was from the nooner with Rico. See, I'm atypical for a gay man. Before Rico I had never tricked while I was involved with someone else. Yet strangely I felt no guilt for doing it now, maybe because the pleasant episode hadn't been aimed at getting back at Rafik and his infidelities. I did it because the opportunity arrived and I found Rico attractive and likeable and willing. And in my perverse psychology, having sex with him had actually galvanized my connection to Rafik. I knew I would love *him* forever. Or was that the guilt talking now? No, no, and again no. The sex with Rico had simply been a novel way to get off with a young Brazilian on a spring afternoon. It had been my long-overdue initiation into "real" manhood, into enjoying sex for its own sake, without emotion and without engaging the heart. Sure.

I arrived at Snips and Nicole remarked, "You're all pink and flushed. What happened?"

"I guess I was walking fast, doll."

She gave me a suspicious look and said, "Then you'd better cool down before you get back to work."

"A customer?"

"Another walk-in request."

"Two in one day, and me in semi-retirement. This must be my

brief moment of fame." I glanced toward the waiting lounge, where all the chairs were empty. "So where is she?"

"Having a cocktail at the Ritz Bar. I'm to telephone there the moment you arrive."

"That really pushes the term 'full service.' Is she royalty?"

"She seems to think so."

While Nicole made the telephone call, I went to my office and started some fresh coffee. Within minutes Nicole joined me back there.

"How was your busy, busy day?" she said.

"Branco sends his regards."

"You mean Lieutenant Branco. I suspected that you'd seen him, the way you came in all flushed."

"That flush, doll, was from something else entirely."

"Was there any message from the lieutenant?"

"Yeah. He wants you to have his baby."

Nicole replied, "I don't think medical science is up to the challenge."

Five minutes later my walk-in arrived. It was Toni di Natale, looking somewhat haggard from her recent detention. Or was it from more recent exertions in Rafik's bed? Ah, now that I was an unfeeling sex device, what did any of that matter?

"I'm so glad you're able to see me," she said. "My hair . . . I can't get it clean. I think it's because of the police."

Or the bloody guilt of Lady Macbeth. Most people don't realize that emotional stress can cause havoc with their hair. As for blaming the police, didn't she know that a certain cop was so hot for her he was dating my best friend just to relieve the pressure? Did she even care?

"That Lieutenant Branco sure is something, eh?" I said, putting a litmus test to her.

"He's a fascist," she replied curtly.

Acid turns red.

"Not to some," I said with a glance toward Nicole.

Hell hath no fury like Nikki's eyes at that moment.

"The issue is," said Toni, "can you fix my hair?"

Now, in my vernacular, hair care is not what I'd categorize as an "issue." Issues, for me—at least the ones you're not giving birth to or receiving in your mailbox as part of a subscription—comprise the larger, more difficult questions of life, complex debatable topics like world population or domestic labor policy or the separation of church and state. Yet every day I hear people say things like, "I have issues about red meat," or "I'm working through my obesity issues," or "I have monogamy issues." But if Toni di Natale had no conscience about abusing language, I could make bad verbiage too.

"I'll do my best," I said examining and analyzing her hair with my knowing fingers. "But truth in the esthetic arts exists beyond the mundane. I own my limitations. I appeal to a higher power. I allow all the creative forces of the universe to flow through me. I give the hair permission to wave. I honor its integrity."

The trouble was, Toni de Natale seemed convinced by my peroration, or else she was humoring a New Age nutlet. And for all my invocations, I received not divine cosmetic assistance, but instead a dose of good old carnal jealousy. For as I shampooed Toni di Natale's auburn tresses I realized that this was the very hair and head that my beloved Rafik had recently held in his hands. As I worked up the creamy lather I wondered, How had he held her? Tenderly? Or fiercely? Had he slid his long tapered fingers langorously through this hair and gently caressed these temples and this forehead? Had he kissed these eyes? Had he murmured lip-against-lip how smooth and soft her body felt next to his? Or had he grabbed great fistfuls of this vibrant mane and pulled on it like the reins on some untamed animal he could vanquish only through his howls of ecstasy? For a brief and insane moment I was tempted to botch her hair and do something tasteless with it, like a severe frizz. But my artist's soul intervened, for Toni di Natale had my favorite type of hair for a woman: long, naturally wavy, and auburn with reddish highlights. I applied a dollop of conditioner to her wet hair. It was my own special formulation, an elixir that would coax the hidden highlights to blaze in all their mad Mars-red glory.

I rinsed Toni's hair and wrapped it in a towel. Then I led her to my station, where I would dry that hair lovingly under warm air while I charmed her with my version of a Perry Mason cross-examination.

I began, "Are you enjoying your time with Rafik?"

Her eyes shot toward my reflection in the mirror. Then her full mouth turned upward in a generous smile.

"I hope you understand it's all platonic," she said.

"I'm sure."

"Honest," she said, adding more conviction to her voice. "I just like to play with men."

" 'Play' has a lot of meanings," I said.

"I'm not having sex with him, or anything like that."

What else, I thought, is anything like sex?

"Were you having sex with Max Harkey?" I said.

She gasped. "You *are* blunt."

I shrugged and applied slightly more pressure to her scalp with my clever left hand. Then I sifted her hair through my fingers, lifting it and fanning it outward from her head into the warm stream of air coming from the dryer. My reflection in the mirror resembled a conjurer beckoning secrets from the depths of my client's dark heart.

Toni di Natale closed her eyes and spoke with a confessional tone. "At first I was just toying with Max. He was in Europe looking for a conductor, and rumor had it he was offering an obscenely lucrative contract for the spring ballet season here in Boston. I wanted that contract and I was willing to use sex to get it." Then her shoulders bounced slightly as she chuckled.

"The trouble is," she continued, "my flirtation backfired and I fell in love with him."

"Did he know?"

"I'm sure I was just another statistic for him."

"What about Jason Sears?" I asked. "Were you engaged to him then?"

She answered, "Jason is a dear friend, but I'm afraid I set him up as a smoke screen. We were never engaged. I wanted to make Max jealous, but it didn't work."

I recalled that night, and Max Harkey hadn't even been in the room when Toni announced the engagement. Perhaps she had told him earlier. Or perhaps it was all lies, even now.

"How did Jason feel about the hoax?" I said.

Toni snickered. "He was already in love with me. Isn't that typical? He wanted me exactly the same way I wanted Max. Sometimes I think love is pure accident. You start out so simply, as friends or colleagues, and the next thing you know you're hoping for something from the other person—some favor or special consideration or even sex. But the other person is oblivious or else unwilling to give you what you want. And then you start making demands, politely at first, but when that doesn't work you get hurt and then you get angry, and it all escalates until finally you've become a hateful monster."

"Is that what happened to you?" I ventured.

Her eyes flashed brightly at me. "I don't let it get that far out of hand any more. It's naive to think that desire and pressure will get me what I want."

"That's one theory," I said. "Where is Jason now?"

"Still on tour. His career always comes first. Even as a friend, Jason is never around when I need him most."

Sure, doll. We all just sit here on the face of the earth waiting on the whim of some principessa. I made a mental note to check with Lieutenant Branco on the whereabouts of Jason Sears. That and Max Harkey's diary.

"That's why I flirt with Rafik, too," she added, bringing me out of my thoughts. "That man is yours and yours alone."

"Everyone seems to know it except me."

"I confess that I did use him as a further test of Max's affection for me, but I didn't mean anything by it. I hope you don't hate me for it. It's all harmless. No one gets hurt."

Only dead.

She went on, "But as you saw that night, Max had absolutely no interest in me as a woman."

"Just professional respect."

"Oh, plenty of that," she said. "But it's still humiliating to hear the man you love respond to your desire so frankly. I can still hear him say it in that arrogant, erudite manner of his. 'But my dear, we are *friends*,' as though that precluded any sexual attraction. And to think I used to get wet just thinking about him."

That comment put Toni di Natale in the finals for the Snips Award for Unrequited Candor. But Max Harkey's collegial affection and admiration notwithstanding, I wondered if his rejection was motive enough for her to kill him. And beyond the other discards in her deck of usables, whom was Toni exploiting now? Me? Was she here at Snips solely to build a strong case against her own criminal guilt, so that I, along with Rafik, would perceive her as the divine and innocent angel of music? Was that her present use of Rafik as well? Or did it extend to his extension?

"Toni," I said, "do you remember that night when I was leaving I saw a musical score on the piano? I asked you about it."

"The score to *The Phoenix*," she said. "Of course I remember. It's extremely valuable—a hand-tinted cover."

"I know. But the next morning the score was gone. It wasn't on the music rack where it had been the night before."

"So?"

"So, when did it go away?"

An annoyed frown appeared on her face. "I'm sure I don't know." I shrugged casually. "I thought you might."

"No," she said flatly. "Maybe you should ask the police about it."

"I already did."

As I removed the protective cape from her shoulders, I put one last question to her.

"Did you know Max kept a diary?"

"No," she said with a blank look, and then with sudden brightness added, "But now that you've told me, I'd love to get my hands on it." She ran her fingers through her hair and gave me a satisfied smile. "You're very good," she said.

I gave her the "family discount" for the shampoo and blow-dry, which meant it was free. Maybe someday I'd get to collect it in personal service from my erstwhile lover.

Right after Toni left the salon, Nicole hauled me back to my office for what I assumed would be a down-home friendly chaw and a talk. Instead I heard, "Just what did you think you were doing?"

"Huh?"

"Talking about the lieutenant like that? His personal life is no-body's business, especially not hers—a suspect. And she dares to call him names!"

"What names?"

"You heard what she said."

"Nikki, we talked about everything *but* Branco."

"*Lieutenant* Branco!"

"Doll, are you jealous? I can't believe—"

"Don't be vulgar!"

"She said from her high horse."

"Stanley, you can ruin your own domestic life if you want, but please leave Lieutenant Branco out of it."

"So now it's domestic life and Branco in the same sentence."

"He is not Branco! Show more respect for the man."

"I need a pill."

"You need a spanking."

She walked out of my office and slammed the door.

There was no doubt now: Nicole and Branco had made it. The once cool and worldly Ms. Albright was about to become a silly young deb, a love thrall to a cop. Was such a thing possible? Was the ultimate driving force of the universe really male ejaculate? And contrary to satellite photos, was the earth's axis truly a cosmic-sized erection?

After work, I left the salon by the back door and headed home. Once safely in my apartment, I fed Miss Sugar and then poured myself a double shot of bourbon. Thus began the toboggan slide into self-imposed depair.

Later that night Rafik telephoned to thank me for doing Toni's hair. He even complimented my work, to which I responded, "Jesh shampoo."

"Are you drinking?" he asked.

"Little."

"What is wrong, Stani?"

"Nuthin'."

"I am sorry for our disagreement today."

Embarrassed by my own slurred speech, I didn't dare answer him. I wanted to maintain a light tone, as though our misunderstanding and separation earlier that day had never happened. I was just spending a relaxed night at home, just me and Jack Daniel's. In my sodden state of mind, if I tried to explain anything I'd lose all control and just blubber and wail in a torrent of tears. And that would only irritate the hypercontrolled man who was once my lover.

"Shall I come to you?" he said humbly.

But even through the fog I knew that he must have been feeling guilty too, especially with Toni de Natale as a houseguest in his one-room apartment. What good would be his coming to me now? What kind of resolution could two guilt-laden people achieve, especially with one of them verging on the sloppy boo-hoos? I struggled to gather what was left of my wits and then pronounced my verdict.

"I have to wash the cat," I said with perfect elocution. I sounded like a Junior Leaguer snubbing the town's most desirable bachelor.

Rafik responded the only way he could after hearing such a brazen lie.

"Is somebody there?"

How could I explain that I had already been as unfaithful as I suspected him of being?

"Stani?" he said.

I couldn't speak, suffocated by bathos.

"Why are you drinking?" he said.

Was the concern in his voice real?

Lunga pausa.

"Rafik," I managed to say. "We are all the same." And then I hung up before he could hear my sobbing.

13

Dancing in the Dark

I was lying face down on my bed watering the pillows when I heard the familiar pulse of a motorcycle pulling into the back alley. Rafik! He must have fixed Big Red. Ashamed of my condition, I ran to the kitchen and filled both hands with crushed ice and pressed it to my face and my tear-reddened eyes. I would not be seen like this.

He let himself into the apartment and I heard him go directly to the bedroom. He called from in there.

"Stani? Where are you?"

"In the kitchen."

Rafik entered, resplendent in high leather. A sullen gray cloud hovered over his brow, an accoutrement to his dark costume. From his shoulder hung a weighty hank of braided leather rope. I knew what that rope implied, and I wasn't in the mood for it, as if anyone is ever truly in the mood for ritualized discipline.

"Not tonight," I said.

Rafik replied, "You can do it to me."

"I don't want to," I said.

"But I do! I deserve it. You can do what you want."

So he wanted to be punished. Just as with any naughty boy who's never caught, guilt ultimately forces a surrender. But who was I to inflict a blow when, as Nicole had observed, I deserved a spanking myself?

Rafik held the hank of leather rope out to me.

"Please," he said. His eyes were pleading. "For me."

If I accepted his offer, I knew we'd have a heavy session, nothing like the playful time I'd spent with Rico that afternoon.

I took the leather and said, "For me too, then."

It was the Golden Rule of Sex: I'll do unto you what should be done to me.

Half an hour later he was lying belly-down on the bed, spread-eagle, each limb bound to a corner of the bed. The room was filled with the scent of his skin and the leather ropes that constrained him. I envisioned the harem boys of ages past. Had they begged for such formalized punishment too? In the flicker of candlelight I saw a moment of delicious fear in Rafik's eyes as I opened a straight razor and honed the edge on the leather chaps I'd peeled from his legs. I crouched close to him and ran the flat side of the razor lightly over the muscular terrain of his strong back. His skin bristled in a thousand bumps of fear and pleasure. I nibbled his butt and he clenched the muscles hard. I kneaded the cheeks with my free hand, worked the flesh like sculptor's clay, then began my work. I would mark my lover. I would shave the coarse short hair on his butt, selectively exposing the skin in the form of one large initial on each half, so that Rafik's meaty behind would show Toni di Natale and the rest of the world that Stan Kraychik had a claim to it, his chattel. The "S" was particularly difficult, but I maneuvered the razor with the precision of an eye surgeon. When I'd completed both letters, I went back and added serifs to them using the point of the blade. There was a momentary temptation to cut into the flesh and scar my lover, perhaps even drink his blood. But this delusion of power passed quickly. Rafik flinched when I slapped alcohol onto the freshly shaved areas. I wondered how I could have been so playful with Rico, and then so serious with Rafik. If sex was only biology, then why was the same basic act—engorgement and release—expressed so differently depending on the partners and the circumstances? Had Rafik only sought punishment for his misbehavior? Or did this submission mean something else? What was he trying to say to me? And what was I saying to him? Why couldn't we simply be tender with each other? Why did our sex always have to mean something?

After the slap-filled alcohol rub, I unbraided one end of a piece of leather cord and lashed lightly at Rafik's backside. As I increased the intensity of my strokes, his skin reddened in the soft light, and for a brief instant I thought I saw not Rafik but Max Harkey lying on my bed. I recognized my own subconscious attraction to the dead man—though it was more to his power than to his body. The feeling of that power got me hot. I scooped my arm under Rafik's hips and grabbed onto his member from behind. Then I thrust myself against the deep crevice of his butt. I saw myself as a muscular young dancer. I was Scott Molloy. Was this how sex felt to him? As Rafik released himself into my hand, I splattered his strong back with glistening droplets. At the final instant of climax, when the insides of my eyelids blazed like a fabulous kaleidoscope, I was visited by a host of uninvited images. If Rafik was Max Harkey, could I at that moment be any of the people who had desired the man? Toni di Natale? Alissa Kortland? Scott Molloy? And even the weak-willed Marshall Zander? The grotesque visions at first revulsed me, then intrigued me.

"Who was it?" I said aloud, as the last sticky drops fell into the furrow of his hard-muscled ass.

"Eh?" said Rafik below me. "What did you say?"

I collapsed on top of him. "Nothing."

I woke up a few hours later slightly chilled. Rafik was sound asleep under me, enjoying the sleep of the innocent, I guess. As I pulled the blankets over us, he stirred.

"Don't go," he said.

"I'm right here."

"Do you love me?"

"If there was a better word, Rafik, I'd still say yes."

He rolled over onto his back and faced me. Even in the darkness his eyes glittered with fire.

"No more jealousy?" he said.

"Now you're asking for the moon."

"What can I tell you, then? What secret do you want to know from me? I will confess everything."

"Okay, love. Did you ever see Max Harkey's diary?"

"Why do you care about that? Do you think I had a liaison with him?"

"No. I just wondered . . ."

"Everyone thinks that I am a sex machine," protested Rafik the sex machine. "Do they think I have no heart? I cannot help it how I look. Everyone thinks I am having sex with somebody else, even you. So then, tie me to your bed and let me die here. Then maybe you will believe that I love only you."

That was certainly one answer to my doubt-plagued heart. But what to do with the corpse? Did I dare tell Rafik what I was thinking at that moment? That whatever he had done before tonight or whatever he wanted to do tomorrow with anybody else didn't matter to me anymore, as long as he still wanted to do it with me sometimes. It was the primary compromise of a desperate lonely heart.

He pulled me down onto him again, then reached behind me to gather the blankets and cover us.

Then he whispered into my ear, "Let's go to sleep, eh?"

14

Corps de Ballet

Early the next morning, with my front side docked snugly against Rafik's back, we woke with the sun and with Sugar Baby's raspy tongue alternately scrubbing my cheek, then his. Rafik got up first, and while he showered I shuffled into the kitchen and performed the daily ritual with some Bourbon Santos coffee beans I'd picked up yesterday afternoon. Life was resuming an ordinary course, or so it seemed. I had just finished setting the breakfast table when Rafik appeared in the kitchen freshly showered and completely dressed, with his dance bag slung over one shoulder. He was ready to face the outside world.

"No coffee?" I asked.

"I have an important meeting at the studio."

A brief and urgent embrace followed, and he was gone, leaving me to breakfast with Sugar Baby. I poured myself a mugful of the rich Brazilian brew, then went to the bedroom to pick up after last night's party games. Rafik's leather duds lay on the floor, randomly strewn around the bed where they'd been dropped during the course of the night. I picked up one piece, a half-harness, and held it in my free hand. It comprised a strap of black leather about an inch wide, the two ends joined by a heavy chrome ring that was itself connected to the main belt by a second, narrower strap. When worn, the half-harness embraced the hips along the pelvic crest, the ring was a portal for the obvious, and the connecting strap ran deep within the body's main crevice. The cross-tensions among the parts caused a synergy of ecstasy in the loins. The half-harness was my favorite item in Rafik's collection, partly because of its functional simplicity and partly because of the sexy, flattering line it gave the hips, even mine. I sniffed at the leather and wondered again about its strange appeal. I caught Sugar Baby watching me.

I asked her, "Any regrets, doll?"

Ineffable as ever, Sugar replied, "Wowr."

"I agree," I said, and went to shower.

When I stopped by Snips I was surprised to find that Nicole hadn't arrived yet. Ramon told me that she'd called earlier to say she'd be in late. I grabbed the chance to do some more legwork on the Max Harkey case, and what better place to do it than the Boston City Ballet?

I arrived there just in time to watch the end of company class, the grand allegro that included the biggest jumps and the aerial tours. Madame Rubinskaya was teaching this morning, marshaling the dancers with a voice that rode high on the wild storm of piano music. From the open door of the studio came the warm moist air of a ballet class well in progress. At the far end of the studio ranks of ballerinas dragged their tired bodies into position, prepared themselves grimly, and then called upon unnatural energies to send their beings aloft, suddenly leaping and spinning like airborne furies. Row upon row of women executed and repeated the intricate combination, the *enchaînement*, while the music surged louder and stronger from the piano, cramming the air with intense sound as if to saturate and replenish the poor dancing creatures with sonic energy. On and on it went, until one final crashing chord declared an unquestioned completion of the exercise.

All was silent.

Then Madame Rubinskaya spoke with a practiced stage whisper, uttering a single word, a single syllable.

"Men."

The first quartet of male dancers silently took their places at the back of the studio and set themselves into preparatory positions. Among them was Scott Molloy in all his youthful, plump-muscled glory.

"Eeeeeeee!" screeched Madame Rubinskaya, and the piano responded with renewed vigor, with sonorous chords and driving rhythms even further beyond the torrents of sound it had produced for the women, as though the measures of music were now being expanded and filled to reflect the blunt potency of masculine strength. And accordingly the men launched themselves upward and lingered midair to execute their movements as if in slow motion, in brazen denial of gravity. Their sculpted, finely honed muscles defied such mundane limits as the earth's downward pull. And when their flight was spent, they descended from the heights without surrender, still arrogantly buoyant, eschewing a pedestrian thump for the feathery whisper of a leather slipper settling softly onto a wooden floor. Ballet, like other wonders of the world, seemed to define itself by contradicting nature. Yet watching these men and their feats of derring-do, I couldn't help wondering about the source of their machismo, the fierce energy that propelled them into the air, especially since I'd seen some of them in tulle skirts and *en pointe*.

Just about the time my attention was beginning to flag from the unceasing visual and aural stimulation, the men finished their grueling work. Then the entire company quickly arranged itself on the vast studio floor for the *révérence*, which is the traditional show of formal respect and gratitude to the teacher, the musician, and the art itself. Coming at the end of class, when the body's adrenaline and confidence are surging, the *révérence* was probably devised by some clever Russian ballet master to keep his dancers humble. It forces them to subvert that rush of power into the calmest, simplest movements. Times have changed though, and many dancers use the *révérence* to improvise extravagant curtain calls, some of which will never be taken on the stage.

After the final chords had faded, and the dancers' poses were placidly fixed, Madame Rubinskaya spoke humbly, as if addressing her own Muse.

"Tank you," she said.

Those two words caused an ovation from the dancers. The modest smile on Madame Rubinskaya's face proved that she still enjoyed the sound of applause.

The class dispersed and eventually Scott Molloy came out of the studio. I stepped up to him and said hello.

"What do you what?" he said brusquely.

"Just a few minutes with you."

"What now?"

"I want to ask you about Max Harkey."

"I thought we already did that."

I smiled an obsequious smile. "That was round one."

He said, "I don't have time today." He looked around the lobby nervously, as though he expected to see someone there, someone he really didn't want to see. Once again I was struck by the young dancer's complexion—the lack of any lines or pores—and by his slim hips. How could everything be so firmly defined? He began to walk away.

I said, "What was the last thing you said to Max Harkey?"

Scott Molloy turned back toward me, thought a moment, then said with a sardonic grin, "I said good night."

"Was that at the dinner party, or did you see him again that night?"

He narrowed his eyes but said nothing.

I pressed him. "I keep hearing that you were in love with Max."

"From who?"

"Quite a few people. Marshall Zander, Alissa Kortland, even Rafik."

"Especially Alissa," he said with an angry little snort. "She'd enjoy saying something like that."

"Is it true?" I said.

Our eyes connected long enough for me to sense that behind the façade of Scott Molloy's angry young man dwelt an extremely hurt and lonely little boy. Keeping my gaze directly focused into his eyes, I repeated my question with all the sympathetic fervor I could muster.

"Were you in love with Max?"

Something shifted in his face. Perhaps because I had asked the question so directly with so much applied warmth and concern, or perhaps because a gay man was asking it, or perhaps because Scott Molloy's defenses were down after the rigors of ballet class, or perhaps because this young man's moment of truth had finally arrived and I happened to be the catalyst for the event. Whatever the cause, I sensed that he wanted to open his heart at last, to break through the oppressive bonds of his past, to disclose the news of his truest self.

He said quietly, "Let's talk somewhere else."

He led me down a corridor and through a door that opened onto a stairwell. We ascended two flights of stairs to a door that led outside, onto the roof of the building. The sun was bright and the sky was clear. With all the old rooftops of the South End in view, we could have been in Europe. I half expected some kind of garden café up there, but there was nothing except the huge pebbled asphalt roof and numerous skylights. Scott was quite sweaty from ballet class, so we sat in the sun on the warm pebbles with our backs propped against one of the skylights.

He began, "I don't know why I'm telling you this," and then he paused.

I encouraged him. "Sometimes it helps to tell someone, especially someone who doesn't know you well. Like me."

"I guess," he said uncertainly. "But I don't know how to begin."

"Just say the things that want to be said. You know what they are."

He looked at me with those little-boy eyes.

"I wanted Max Harkey to be my father."

I nodded as if I understood and accepted his statement, though I wasn't sure if he meant father-and-son or daddy-and-boy.

"But I wanted more, too," he added, then looked away.

"Go on," I said. "Just talk. It's all right."

"I wanted him to love me back. I wanted to be his favorite dancer. I wanted him to choose me first of all the other men." Again he turned his eyes on me. "Isn't that disgusting? It sounds so weak when I hear myself say it."

"Not at all," I said. "We all want unconditional love and acceptance. It's a human need. Don't be ashamed of it." After all, didn't most organized religion exploit that very need?

Scott continued, "But it was in everything I did, everything I said and pretended to want. I did it all to please Max."

"That's part of love. It's okay," said the unauthorized expert on such matters.

"But he didn't notice me. He only wanted women. So I began dating women too. But even that was just to please Max, to make him accept me."

"Did it work?"

He shook his head. "But I didn't know what else to do. So I tried to give up on him, but it was all an act. No matter what I told myself, in my heart I still loved him. Then Max finally did something that really pissed me off. It changed everything."

Another long pause.

"Well?" I said.

"He chose another dancer, an obviously gay guy, for a big role that I should've got. I was perfect for the part, and instead this raging queen got it. And all that time I thought Max hated gay men. I was pretending to be straight, all for him, and it didn't even matter."

"So how did that change everything?"

Scott hesitated. "One day I went to see him at home to tell him finally how I felt about him. I told him everything, that I loved him, and then I asked him if he felt anything for me."

"And?"

"He laughed at me."

All became quiet around us. A slight breeze played with Scott Molloy's fine blond hair. Strands of it fluttered like golden threads in the bright sun. Max Harkey must have been genuinely straight, for how else could he have refused the proffered love and beauty of this dancer, who possessed all the natural grace and strength of a young palomino stallion?

"What happened after that, Scott?"

"I made a big scene. I was screaming at him, blaming him for making me pretend to be straight when it didn't make any difference to him. It was all for nothing."

"Worse, it may have worked against you," I said.

"What do you mean?"

"Sometimes people can accept others more easily when they're honest about themselves, rather than hiding who they really are."

"I think you're wrong. Most people hate the truth."

"Well, somebody always will," I said with a shrug.

He went on, "That's what happened with Max. After I told him everything, confessed to him, the next thing I knew the whole company was gossiping about how I was in love with him. First they talked behind my back, then right to my face."

I recalled Alissa Kortland's version of the same story, how Scott had confronted Max in front of the ballet company, not in private as he was telling me now.

I said, "It's too bad Max handled it that way. Telling the company, I mean."

"I guess I got what I deserved," he replied with vexation.

"That's not true, Scott. You had a dream of love, but it was one that could never materialize, at least with Max. The only mistake you made was to deny your own needs and try to become someone else to win him over. But the important thing is that you didn't run away in shame. You stayed with the company."

"I had no choice."

"You did have a choice, and you did the brave thing."

He laughed cynically. "I'm not brave. In fact, if this is what it's going to be like," he said, "I don't want to be gay. At least with women there's no punishment or shame. You don't have to hide anything. You can do what you want in public."

"And live a private lie," I said. "Is that why you're dating Alissa now?"

His young face tightened suddenly, then he admitted, "If I couldn't have the great Max Harkey, I could at least get his mistress."

I thought of myself and Rafik, how I was willing to accept the crumbs of his love by washing the hair of his girlfriend.

Scott added, "Max had already dumped her anyway."

"And so you swooped in to save her."

"You make it sound bad."

"No. Just desperate. Like me, in fact."

"But you have Rafik."

"That's a saga in itself," I replied.

"I know," he said.

"You do?"

His little-boy eyes were suddenly back in action again.

"Don't you know how much Rafik loves you?" he asked.

"Scott, so many people have been saying 'Rafik loves Stan' to me lately that it's beginning to sound like a household phrase. I guess my version of the story is a little different."

"Then you're in for a big surprise," he said, modulating his voice to give the cliché the weight of an irrefutable maxim.

I checked my watch. It was almost noontime.

"I've got to get to work." I gave him one of my business cards. "If you want to talk some more about this, call me. For some people coming out is the most difficult milestone they face. Just don't settle for the easy way, Scott, unless that's what you really want."

He pursed his lips, then drew them back into a smile.

"You know, I didn't like you at first," he said. "But I guess you're all right, maybe even kind of nice."

"More persistent than nice," I replied. I had, after all, got him to confide in me while I'd given little of my own self. My early shrink's training still came in handy.

We got up and went back inside the building. When we descended the stairs and re-entered the lobby outside the Grand Studio, I noticed a small group of police officers waiting in there. I also saw Alissa Kortland talking with them. She turned toward us, and after a moment's recognition gave a startled look.

"There he is!" she yelled to the police, and pointed at us.

Scott Molloy and I froze in our tracks. The police ran toward us and grabbed both of us, wrenching our arms behind our backs and shoving us up against the wall. In spite of my panic, I was hoping that Scott wasn't seeing this encounter with the cops as yet another punitive experience for a gay man.

"Which one of you is Scott Molloy?" said one officer.

Scott identified himself and was rewarded by having his arm pushed harder up toward his shoulders. The officer who was restraining me released me immediately. No apology. I watched the cops haul Scott away while Alissa followed them. Her face had a look of victory. The only thing I heard Scott say was, "I didn't lay a finger on her."

It was then that I finally realized that even though I had no idea about who had done what to whom—or why—during any of the events surrounding Max Harkey's death, I had already become too involved with the case and its attendant personalities to quit now. Anything half-done is not done at all. There was nothing to do but see this thing through to the end.

I was just leaving the ballet studios, heading toward the main door, when I was intercepted by Marshall Zander. He looked tired and his voice sounded weary and disillusioned. Apparently his tranquilizers were losing their effect.

"The police act in the most illogical way. Instead of finding Max's killer, they arrest a young dancer on charges of assault and battery of a young woman."

"Is that what happened?"

"According to Alissa," he said. "Apparently she and Scott had a big fight this morning and Scott threatened her."

"He seems incapable of violence like that."

"You can never tell," said Marshall Zander. "By the way," he added, "did you enjoy your lunch with Rico?" He punctuated his question with a sluggish wink, a failed attempt at camaraderie. Rico had assured me that Marshall would never find out about our extravagant room-service meal, yet he obviously had.

"It was very pleasant," I said. "Thank you for your generous hospitality."

"It doesn't cost me a thing. I own the hotel and everything in it, except of course Rico." He raised his voice when he added, "*He* was yours for the taking."

I scanned the lobby to see if anyone had heard him, especially if Rafik might be nearby. The coast was clear.

Then he continued speaking more discreetly. "Your friend Rafik will be receiving some good news regarding Max's will."

"You've seen the will, then?"

"I'm Max's executor," he replied.

"Then you must know what happened to his diary."

"If there was one, it would be with the rest of his belongings."

"It wasn't," I said.

"Maybe the police have it."

"They never found one."

"Then perhaps there never was a diary."

"Rico said there was."

"Rico fabricates," he said quickly. Then he chuckled and added, "I should think you would know about that."

I ignored his taunt. "Can I ask you one more thing?"

"By all means," he said agreeably. "I'll help you any way I can."

"Do people who support big arts organizations always spend so much time on the premises?"

"You sound suspicious of me. I'm sorry you feel that way, because as I've said before, I do like you. As for your question, I can give you an honest, direct answer. Some benefactors like to write a big check and have done with it. Then they show up for the gala events and opening nights. But I prefer to be actively engaged, to see where my money is going. Besides, I love ballet. I love everything about it—the rehearsals, the classes, the dancers, the choreographers. It's my only passion."

"I can understand that. And I apologize for sounding suspicious. I guess I suspect everyone at this point."

"That's to your credit as the unofficial investigator in this case.

Anyone who knew Max probably, at one time or another, wished him gone forever. I know I certainly did."

"You did?" I said, failing to conceal my astonishment.

"My dear boy," he said with a loud chortle. "I may have felt that way, but I would never act on such an impulse."

"Then the question remains," I said. "Who would?"

Marshall Zander forced a smile. "I'm sure you'll find the answer and put this horrible matter to rest. Just remember that I'm always available for *any* help you might need."

"Thanks," I said as I tried to suppress a slight shudder.

We went our ways, he to some important meeting and me back to Snips Salon. But once again I was stopped on my way out of the ballet studios, this time by Madame Rubinskaya.

"I thought I see you watching class," she said.

"It was impressive," I said. "Especially the men."

The old woman dismissed my comment with modest shrug.

"The dancers, they can do better. But they are young, and it is springtime. They have other things on their mind."

"Do you know what happened between Scott Molloy and Alissa Kortland?"

"Is a shame, no? Such beautiful young people and always fighting. They make too much tragedy. They don't know how to enjoy their life."

"The police can't help much with domestic squabbles."

"But he was hitting her."

"Is that true?" I said.

The old woman shrugged again. "Alissa says it, but who knows? She likes to live in big drama."

"Madame Rubinskaya," I ventured cautiously, "Do you know if Max Harkey kept a diary?"

"Maxi had diary? Maybe."

"Did you ever see it?"

After a lengthy pause, Madame Rubinskakya replied coolly, "I don't recall."

"Then do you recall the musical score to *The Phoenix?*"

"Why are you asking that to me?"

"Because it's missing."

"So?"

"I thought you might have some idea where it was."

"You are thinking now I took it?"

"Not at all."

"*Bozhe!* I thought you were fine young man, but I see you are rude."

"I don't mean to be rude, but the only way to find things out is to ask, and sometimes the words come out wrong. May I ask you just one more question?"

Wearied now, and huffing impatiently, Madame Rubinskaya said, "No. You are not very nice boy."

And having made her pronouncement, she walked off.

I thought to myself, Just because you say it doesn't make it so. So I quickly improvised a mantra to undo Madame Rubinskaya's harsh verdict of me: I am a nice boy. I am a nice boy. I am a nice boy.

But without the ruby slippers, nothing happened.

One more time I headed for the doorway. I wanted out of that place, but I'd just about taken two steps when I saw Rafik and Toni di Natale entering the main lobby. They were jabbering and laughing together. Toni saw me first and pulled Rafik along with her.

"There you are!" she said. "I love what you did with my hair. It absolutely glows in the sunlight."

Rafik grinned broadly. "You make her very beautiful."

He held her closely around the waist while she hung onto his shoulder.

"Thanks," I said. "Where are you all coming from?"

Toni replied, "We just had the longest, most luxurious breakfast in the world at the Copley Palace. Have you ever tried it?"

"Not yet," I said in stark opposition to her effusiveness.

"It's marvelous. You simply must do it."

Rafik added, "We were talking about music, and the time was flying by. It was very productive."

The two of them radiated positive, creative energy. They were utterly pleased with each other and with the rest of the world, with all things bright and beautiful. And once again I was struck by the broad range of Rafik's energy, and how I got to witness the other end of that spectrum, the polar opposite of what I was seeing now with Toni di Natale.

"What brings you here?" she asked me.

"Max Harkey's murder," I answered bluntly.

"You're working so hard on that," she said. "I'm sure you'll be the one who solves it. You'll be the hero."

"Yeah," I said. "Hold that thought."

Rafik was still grinning when he pulled Toni closer to him and put his other hand on my arm.

"We have rehearsal now," he said. "I see you later."

"I'll be at the shop," I said.

"Thank you again for my hair," said Toni. "It's too bad you can't sign you work."

Rafik and I exchanged knowing glances.

"Sometimes I do," I said.

They went off and I finally got to leave the studios of the Boston City Ballet. This time nobody stopped me. But then, who was left? I'd seen just about the whole cast that morning.

I set out for Snips. As I was passing through Copley Square I saw the Copley Palace and felt an strange urge in my body, a kind of undulation that began in my belly, then ran up to my head, and then down to my feet before settling again in my gut. Perhaps it was just hunger, a subliminal suggestion from the breakfast enjoyed by Rafik and Toni di Natale. But no, it wasn't breakfast or lunch that I craved. I stopped and looked at the massive structure of the hotel, so new and clean and austere next to the classical architecture around it. I stared at the modern building and let my eyes wander all the way up to the top, to the penthouse, where Rico was probably having a cup of coffee at that moment. And that strange, sensuous wave moved through my body again, and then I realized what it was. I wanted something that I hadn't identified before, and it was indeed a desire that Rafik had triggered, especially by the way he behaved with Toni di Natale. What I wanted was some lite sex. And I knew just where to get it.

15

Change Partners and Dance

The concierge at the Copley Palace recognized me from yesterday, but that didn't help at all. Neither his formality nor my attempt at propriety could counter the rush of lecherous energy I was feeling, and when I asked to see Rico, the man shook his head gravely.

"Young Mr. Rico is no longer employed by this establishment."

Strange, I thought, when just minutes ago Marshall Zander had been so cordial and hospitable about the expensive lunch Rico and I had shared, yet he had not mentioned Rico's departure.

The concierge continued, "Mr. Zander is not in, either, though as I recall, yesterday you specifically wished *not* to see him."

"Yes," I said with hesitation. "That is correct." Gonads agog over Rico, I'd carelessly assumed that Marshall Zander was still at the ballet studios, heedless that he might have returned home himself in the few intervening minutes. That would have been cute: me showing up all moist and hot for the houseboy, only to be greeted at the door by the lard-ass master of the manse.

"Is there any message?" interrupted the concierge.

"Do you know what happened?"

He raised his nose haughtily and spoke in clipped syllables.

"There was an unpleasant incident which I am not at liberty to divulge. However, the locks on Mr. Zander's suite are being changed presently, and at great expense."

"So what, if it's for the emperor?"

"I beg your pardon?"

"Doll, your haute drag doesn't cut it. Come back to earth."

I left the hotel troubled by the idea that Rico would steal anything from Marshall Zander. Sure, he was cute and charming and sexy, but I had a feeling he'd hustle with more class than a petty thief. The real question was, Did Rico leave or was he fired?

I walked one block along St. James Street to Berkeley Street. I'd make one more stop before reporting for duty at Snips. After this strange news of Rico's disappearance I wanted to consult with boss cop Branco. Luckily, the lieutenant was in. When I entered his office he was engrossed in a pile of papers on his desk. He whistled softly as he studied the documents—a peppy little tune, Italian I think. It was not typical of Branco to make music. After the polite formalities of greeting, I told him about my concern over Rico's sudden disappearance.

Branco remarked, "The coincidence is amazing, Stan. Either you've got a nose for this kind of thing, or else you're involved deeper in this situation than you admit."

"What happened?" I said.

"We got a report from Traffic Division this morning. Your young friend was on his motor scooter. Ran a red light. Bad accident."

"How bad?" I said with a shaky voice.

"I'm afraid he's gone."

I felt the blow, of all places, between my shoulder blades. Then, like a dull blade, it jagged and ripped its way diagonally through my chest toward my stomach. When I regained my focus, I was cold and sweaty.

"My *tesão,*" I said quietly.

"I'm sorry," said Branco.

I had to fight the pressure of tears and a tightness that was growing throughout my body. Everything in me wanted to wail. But not here, I told myself. Not in front of the cop.

"Is there anything I can do?" he said.

And the sudden, unexpected warmth in his voice opened a tiny hatchway in my resistance, and against my will I felt some quiet tears slipping out. The surge of intense emotion both startled and annoyed me. When I knew I could speak without blubbering, I asked Branco what had happened.

"The driver of the car claims the scooter came out of nowhere. He was really shook up about it, too—confessed everything was his fault and submitted to us without resistance, even offered to go straight to jail."

Branco stifled a small but inappropriate laugh. He'd probably have liked the whole world to be that submissive.

He continued, "Ordinarily we let a thing like this go through the regular channels, but since the young man was directly involved with the Max Harkey case, I've put Homicide on it. The lab is examining the scooter for any sign of foul play. The brakes might have been rigged to fail."

Branco's suspicions recalled an old movie with a similar setup. So who in this drama was the most like Lana Turner?

"Where's . . . Rico . . . now?" I asked. I'd started my question strongly, but my courage faded into a whispery croak.

"In the morgue. I can arrange it, but I don't suggest you see him. He's pretty banged up."

"No," I said feebly. "You know best."

"By the way, I just released Scott Molloy. Alissa Kortland's charges are insufficient to book him." Branco added angrily, "Damn kids."

"Do you think he could have killed Rico?"

"The two of them have very neat and complete alibis in each other, even if they are at odds right now."

"Then what about Marshall Zander?" I said.

"Mr. Moneybags?" said the cop.

"Rico lived with him. He'd have the perfect opportunity to rig the scooter."

"He doesn't impress me as being very mechanical," said Branco, adding a little grunt. "And what's his motive?"

"What's anyone's motive? Rico must have known something."

"If it was murder."

"Of course it was, Lieutenant! So we know it's got to be someone who understands motor scooters."

"Or motorcycles," said the cop. Then he added smugly, "Since you're so sure."

I felt my cheeks flush angrily.

"I was with Rafik all night," I said. "He couldn't have done it."

"What about this morning?"

I balked. Rafik *had* left the apartment early for his urgent meeting, which turned out to be a clandestine breakfast with Toni di Natale at the Copley Palace. Had he taken a few moments to make a fatal adjustment on Rico's scooter?

"Lieutenant, Rafik didn't rig that scooter."

"Does he know how you felt about Rico?"

"Even if he did—"

"It's okay, Stan." Branco halted me with his big raised hand. "I'm not going to book him. Your alibis will hold for now." Branco looked directly at me, and then I saw a smile creep across his strong mouth. "Besides," he said, now opening the smile to a glorious broad grin, "someday I might be in the same boat, with my date being my only alibi."

Was Branco relating the concept of a date to himself?

"You'd have to be a suspect first, Lieutenant."

He shrugged slightly. "Do you suspect me?" he said.

"Me?"

"Yes, you. Stan Kraychik. Do you suspect me?"

"Of what?"

"Of anything."

"What are you talking about, Lieutenant? What should I suspect you of?"

"I'm asking you," he said.

Now this was a switch I could not fathom.

Branco grinned victoriously and said, "You're afraid to be honest with me, aren't you?"

I wondered, Why this sudden urge for intimacy?

"Lieutenant, I think you're pushing the bounds of the cop-civilian dichotomy."

Branco replied, "And I think you're using big words."

What did he want to hear me say?

"I'm late for work, Lieutenant. Can I use you as my alibi?"

"Sure. Give my regards to Nicole."

So it was "Nicole" now, no more "Miss Albright."

He went on, "I'm really sorry about last night. I hope she's all right today."

"What happened?"

Branco faltered a bit as he tried to explain. "Nothing too serious. Just a stupid mistake I could have prevented."

So even bigshot cops occasionally blundered.

I said, "Shall I bear sad tidings from Lieutenant Branco? Or from Vito?"

"Either way she'll know," he replied.

"Either way," I repeated.

Back at the salon, Nicole was occupied with a client at her manicure table. As I passed by I was astonished to hear Nicole softly humming a tune while she worked. She paused in the music just long enough to greet me with an exaggerated smile.

"How nice of you to drop in today, Stanley."

Then, without missing a single stroke of the emery board, she resumed her humming.

Now one thing I do know about Nicole after all our years together is that she never sings. Ever. It's an activity unknown in her life. Yet here she was humming a frisky little tune, a dancy number I seemed to recognize. Italian, I think. Had she heard it on Branco's tape player? And what had they been doing? Celebrating the fertility and abundance of springtime?

"Vito sends kisses," I said.

"That's nice, darling," Nicole answered, and continued with her work.

"I'll be in my office," I said, as though I owned the place.

But all I heard from her manicure table was the sound of holiday merriment.

Half an hour later Nicole came by my office, holding out her empty Rosenthal coffee mug like a high-class beggar. I filled it with steaming fresh brew. When I was about to add the usual dollop of heavy cream, Nicole stopped me.

"Just plain."

"Watching the waistline?" I asked.

"No. I simply don't want cream today. Is that a crime?"

"No, doll." I handed her the hot mug. "Do you say no to Branco's cream too?"

Nicole glared at me.

"In your coffee, doll. Did I touch a nerve?"

"Sometimes you are so crude."

"Nikki, it's obvious that you and Branco are having a fling. I don't know why you try to hide it."

"It is not a fling, Stanley."

"Then what is it?"

"We are developing a very cordial relationship. You barely know the man, yet you're ready accuse him, and now me, of the same coarseness that you seem to crave so much."

"Whoa, doll. I'm not accusing."

"Then perhaps I should have said 'ridicule,' since that's what you really do. You ridicule people. For your information, Stanley, yes, Vito and I were together again. And I think it's wonderful. He's a perfect gentleman. There's a refinement about him that you'll never know because you always focus on the crotch end of your life."

"Straight men do that too."

"Don't hold that against him now."

"Doll, a penis is a penis."

"How deluded you are!"

"Excuse me. Branco's is a holy object."

"You are hateful."

"And you're acting superior when it's just a case of—"

At that instant I noticed a nasty bruise on the underside of Nicole's forearm.

"What's that, doll?"

She self-consciously pulled the sleeve of her blouse down to try to cover it.

"Nikki," I said. "Did he hurt you?"

Nicole was speechless.

I was speechless.

Had Branco been rough with her? Was it accidental? Or was it a secret part of being a "perfect gentleman"? How dare he hurt her? The games I played with Rafik were different, done in the name of love. Nicole didn't like that stuff. Or did she? Maybe it took the likes of Vito Branco to awaken that aspect of her desire. Well, well.

As if to halt my imaginings, Nicole said, "Vito has a very small kitchen, and one of the doors over the counter doesn't close properly, and I was reaching up—"

"You don't have to explain Nikki."

"I know I don't!"

"Just so long as it's your choice, and not just his."

"You don't understand anything, Stanley. You see only what you want."

Just then Rafik appeared in the open doorway to my office. He was out of breath, as though he'd sprinted there across town.

"I have good news!" he exclaimed.

"We could use some of that," said Nicole and I in unison.

Rafik spoke excitedly, like a child who has just won a big prize. "Max has left to me his magnificent piano."

"That's wonderful," said Nicole.

"It is," I added, knowing how much Rafik respected the musical side of Max Harkey's creativity. It was the perfect legacy from one artist to another.

"But," continued Rafik, "I have no place to put it. It is very big."

"I know," said I.

"Oh," said Nicole.

"So," said Rafik. "Now we must get an apartment together, Stani. It will be so beautiful. I always dream of a grand piano in our house. And now we have the one of Max Harkey."

Nicole said to me, "I think he loves you."

"First person plural always gives it away, doll."

Nicole got up. "I'll leave you two alone," she said, and took her coffee out of the office with her. I closed the door.

Rafik embraced me. "You will be happy to hear that Toni will soon be again with Jason Sears. He will arrive tonight. No more jealousy for you." He gave me a quick peck on the nose.

"That's good," I said. "Everyone will be happy now."

Rafik asked, "What is wrong, Stani? You sound so empty, like you lose something."

"I can't help it," I said. "Rico was killed this morning."

"Mais non!" he said. "How did it happen?"

I told him everything, except for the sex in the sandbox.

When I finished Rafik said ruefully, "So the trouble is not finished."

"Not at all."

"What will you do?" he said.

"You got me started. I guess I'll just have to keep poking and prodding until the answer comes out."

"Will you promise me one thing?"

"I'll be careful, Rafik."

"I already pray for that," he said. "But when everything is solved, then you and I will find a new place together, yes?"

I hesitated, bit my lip, yielded.

"Okay," I said. "If only for Max Harkey's piano."

Rafik gave me a big noisy smooch, then left by the back door. I went back out into the shop.

Nicole saw me and said, "Why so glum? You didn't fight again?"

"One thing I haven't told you, doll. Rico was killed this morning."

"Rico?"

"Max Harkey's houseboy."

"You never told me about him."

"I think he had a crush on me, or me on him."

"Is that why you're so irritable? I had no idea you'd lost a friend, or I wouldn't have been so brusque."

"I probably deserved it, as usual."

"It sounds like you've been having a horrible day. Any other time I'd send you home, but right now you have a customer."

I glanced to the waiting area where I saw a strange woman seated regally in one of the spacious leather chairs. She wore what appeared to be a costume, the rich theatrical attire of old European nobility. She had the aura of the Ages.

I looked at the woman more closely. "Doll, isn't that—?"

"Yes," replied Nicole. "But today she's a *duchessa.*"

It was Sharleen McChannel, the same celebrity whose poster had been all over the main lobby of the Copley Palace.

I greeted her and complimented her on the rave success of her new book, but Sharleen utterly denied any claim to being the person who had written it. She insisted that she was of Italian nobility, and called herself La Duchessa, complete with broken English and a heavy accent. She told me she wanted a simple wash-and-set, and that she had been referred to Snips and specifically to me by the desk clerk at the Ritz.

During the hair work she talked about her villa on Lake Como, and about Europe-this and Europe-that, and about her ancestors who had lived in the Doge's Palace. While I was drying her hair, La Duchessa made an odd disembodied sound.

"Is anything wrong?" I said.

"Wait," she replied. "Wait. Quiet. Please, everyone, quiet. I am receiving the message."

"Blowers off," I called out to the other stylists.

The salon went quiet except for the jazz music in the background and an occasional scissor snip. La Duchessa had closed her eyes and was making troubled little moans, as though wrestling with her inner demons. Some of the stylists moved toward my station to watch the show, which went on for about three minutes.

Then she came out of the trance and said, "I have returned."

"Resume your stations," I called out, and the salon once again was filled with the bustling sounds of beauty.

La Duchessa, or Sharleen McChannel—I wasn't sure which, at this point—said to me, "Very soon you will take a long trip."

Flippantly I asked, "And will I meet a handsome stranger?"

She smiled. "I believe you have already found the dark knight of your soul."

"How did you know?"

"They told me, of course."

Of course. Was it a lucky guess, or did this woman really have psychic powers?

I finished her hair and she was joyous about the results. I thought her reaction a mite extreme, even for someone whose life was spent seeking exalted experiences.

When it came time to pay however, Sharleen McChannel, a k a La Duchessa, had a little problem with a more mundane side of life. Nicole called me up front to the reception desk, where I found Sharleen rummaging nervously through her purse—a tooled-leather satchel from Venice that easily cost a month's tips. Finally exasperated and suddenly devoid of any Italian accent, Sharleen announced to me, "I don't seem to have any money with me. I don't know where my mind is today."

I was about to tell her where, but I felt the sharp heel of Nicole's calfskin pump pressing into my instep. What could I do? I couldn't very well create a scene with a superstar. To her credit, Sharleen La Duchessa did offer me her antique gold earrings, which she claimed were authentic heirlooms from her ancestors, the Medicis. Sure, doll. And I am Marie of Romania. Though at this rate she'd probably have claimed that she and Marie were best friends, exchanging quips about their respective courtiers. Still, I refused the offer of La Duchessa's costume jewelry, and contented myself with having another great story to tell my friends.

After the shop was closed and locked, Nicole and I sat in my office for a cocktail and her cigarette.

"Darling," she said once we had settled down, "You look so sad. Did Rico mean so much to you?"

"I'm not sure. Maybe all the events of the past few days are finally affecting me. Or maybe it's because Rafik wants to get a place together again."

"Then perhaps it's time to do it. You must be tired of finding reasons why you can't be satisfied with him. It might even help you get over Rico."

"You sound like those people who replace a dead pet immediately, before any real grief can settle in."

"Is that what he was to you? A pet?"

"I'm not sure. He was certainly playful. And after Rafik's seriousness, that was appealing. But now I seem to have found a new appreciation of Rafik."

"Perhaps because he's alive, darling."

"Still, Nikki. Living with someone—think of how it changes things. Would you move in with Branco?

She laughed. "Why ever would I do that?"

"Because you're dating him. It's the same reasoning you use for Rafik and me."

"Silly boy, it's not like that at all. Besides, you and Rafik have been together so long."

"What's the difference, Nikki? What's the real purpose of living together, anyway—to collect china and shop for furniture?"

"You already have all that, dear."

"I rest my case."

"So why don't you just enjoy it together?"

"I want something more, Nikki. I want an immutable connection of the soul."

"Oh, Stanley. You already have that too."

"I suppose I do," I said vaguely.

As if to mark the end of our futile debate, Nicole extinguished her cigarette barely half smoked.

"Cutting down?" I asked.

"Yes," she said, "along with the coffee cream."

"I sense a new you emerging."

"I'm not afraid of change," she said, getting up and putting on her light spring coat. She kissed me and left. Somehow, just the tiniest bit, Nicole seemed to be floating on air.

I was alone in the shop. It was blessedly quiet. My mind was blank. I was so tired I couldn't think, or even think about thinking. So I flipped mindlessly through a travel magazine that had arrived at the salon that day. At one point I found myself facing a full-page photo of Big Ben in London, and that photo activated a few dormant neurons. There was yet another character related to Max Harkey whom I had not met yet. Perhaps she held a key to the unanswered questions. It would be so simple. I would fly to London to find and question the ballerina Mireille Rubinskaya, grand-niece of Madame Rubinskaya.

I called my travel agent, Hanni, the only German expatriate who never flies her clients on the major German carrier. Fortunately she works late to be available for her West Coast clients. After a long wait with an electronic operator, I finally heard Hanni's real voice on the line. She always sounded as though she should have been singing *Carmen*.

"You're next on my list," she said.

I replied, "That sounds like a good title for a murder mystery."

Hanni laughed and said, "Where have you been, you bitch?"

"Hanni, I've got to get to London."

"I don't hear from you for two months and now you're going on vacation?"

"It's not a vacation," I said. "It's urgent."

I quickly explained the situation to her, and she, as usual, attacked the problem like a four-star general on the field.

"First question, Do you have a passport?"

"It's the one thing I always renew but never use."

"You never know when you'll have to leave the country," she said, and then jammed the local telephone lines with her vibrant laugh. Click-click-click went her keyboard. "I can book you on British Airways departing Logan in about two and a half hours. Can you make that?"

"I'll have to, Hanni."

"So it's a go?"

"Yes."

"Is this going on the plastic?"

"You mean it's going to cost me?"

"Stanislav, this is a full-fare round-trip ticket to London. I can give you a good deal, really good, but not a freebie. You know my expenses. The lease just went up, I have the alimony to my ex, the kids' school bills are due, both dogs were at the vet today, one of my nannies wants a raise, I have a new boyfriend, and—"

"Okay, okay, Hanni. How much?"

She quoted me a price so ghastly that I couldn't stop myself from asking, "What is that, first class?"

She laughed out loud. "That's the back of the bus!"

"What about my discount?"

"That is discounted. Look, Stanislav, your timing is awful. You're flying midweek, last-minute, open return. At least you'll get double miles."

"What I need is a double income."

"So you want me to book it?"

"Jeez, Hanni. Yeah. But my plastic won't handle that much. I'll have to call you from home with the financial arrangements."

"I won't cut the ticket until I hear from you."

I sprinted home on my strong Slavic legs. Once inside I called Nicole, but got her answering service.

"Ms. Albright is unavailable," they said.

I guessed where she was, and I had Branco's private number. Hell, this seemed enough of an emergency to use it. But his private phone had been routed back to the police station. I couldn't bring myself to leave a personal message for him there.

Rafik wasn't home either, but he had no ready cash or credit anyway.

Where were my friends when I needed them? Who was going to pay my way to London? I needed a goddam benefactor.

Then the answer came with startling directness.

Marshall Zander had offered his help to me. Would I be able to ask him? How would I bargain for the money? There was no time for moral debate. I called him and explained the situation, that I wanted to see Mireille Rubinskaya. He agreed easily, even after I told him how much the ticket was. Though he did say, "I'd rather be buying you a nice vacation instead of this kind of trip."

"I'll pay you back as soon as I can," I said.

"Don't worry about that. Your friendship is more important. Tell me whom to call."

I gave him Hanni's number.

Marshall said, "I'd come with you if I thought I could help."

"Paying for the ticket is help enough."

"Do you need a ride to the airport?"

"Thanks, no."

"Please let me take you. I like to drive people to the airport."

"You do?"

"I'm a person, too, beyond my money. Helping others makes me feel useful."

I almost said, "Then order me a limo." But instead I said, "It's really no trouble to get a cab."

"I insist. I am paying your way, after all. Tell me where you live."

I made more excuses, but finally yielded to his insistence and gave him the address. I did manage to keep my apartment number secret, explaining that the doorbell didn't work.

"Then I'll call you from my car phone when I get there."

We hung up and I set to packing madly.

What was I doing and at what cost? Every time my path crossed Marshall Zander's, there was the feeling of a deal, of a transaction, of trading something. Was this the same desperate innocence that drove the courtesans to live their way?

Sugar Baby watched my frenzied packing in wide-eyed bemusement. The phone rang. Was it Nicole or Rafik? I waited for the machine to pick up while I screened the call. I heard Hanni's voice and grabbed the receiver.

"Where did you find *him?*" she asked.

"His money is good. He owns the Copley Palace, among other things."

"I know that, but he's not your type. I could hear him drooling on the phone. You don't like him, do you?"

"Hanni, I was desperate and he was home."

"Just don't put out for him, not for a lousy plane ticket. You get some gold or some property first."

"I'll remember that when the courtship begins."

"Your ticket will be at the British Airways counter. And you'll be going first-class."

"Huh?"

"I convinced him you were worth it. I must be losing my mind. Hah! Anyway, you'll be more comfortable. First-class is wide open."

"So I've heard. I owe you, Hanni."

"No way," she said with her big laugh. "Do you know what my commission is on that kind of ticket? I owe *you*, Stanislav, so I booked you two nights at La Folie, prepaid at my rate. You're a travel agent now."

I felt more like a secret agent.

"Thanks, Hanni."

I finished packing, and just as I snapped the clasps on my luggage closed, I had a disquieting revelation: The cosmic predictions of Sharleen McChannel had begun to occur in real life. I was taking a long trip.

Quickly I changed Sugar Baby's water and doled out a whole can of food. The cat box would have to wait.

Marshall Zander arrived in his low-slung German coupé. I pushed my bag into the narrow compartment behind the two front seats and got in. He pressed his hand onto mine.

"Hi, there," he said.

His hand felt dry and rough and cool, much like a reptile's.

"Hi," I replied, pulling my hand away. And we were off.

On Storrow Drive I asked him why he had fired Rico.

"When did you hear that?" he said.

"I dropped by the hotel to see him today. The concierge told me Rico had been discharged."

"Well, that's not exactly true. I didn't fire him. He quit on me. I think Rico was hoping I would replace Max as his surrogate father, and it obviously didn't work out. So he vanished. He said he was going to Haymarket for fresh produce, but he never came back from the errand."

"But that's not what really happened," I said.

Marshall Zander squirmed in the plump leather seat.

I went on, "I talked to the police. Rico was killed in a traffic accident."

He applied the brakes suddenly, a stupid if typical driver's response on Storrow Drive.

"I know that!" he said with a loud sob. "But did you expect me to tell my staff that an employee was killed?"

"It was the truth."

"You don't understand," he said. "Hotel service is like theater. It must be a dream world where everything happens for the comfort of the guests."

That sounded like theater of the wimps to me. I asked him, "Why should a traffic accident in Boston upset your guests?"

"You never know how people will react. But I believed it was judicious to tell the staff that I had released Rico from service. That was to be the hotel's official stand. The staff always knows what's really going on, but they also know enough to accept what I tell them."

Except perhaps Rico.

Marshall Zander placed his hand on my thigh and felt around my leg muscles. His touch was revolting. But I repeated to myself those famous words: Close your eyes and think of England.

By the time we approached the airport he'd removed his hand from my leg.

"Does flying bother you?" he asked.

"No," I said. "I'm a Gemini. Air sign, you know."

"I'm petrified of heights myself."

"Is that why you live in a penthouse?"

"I never go out on the deck. Maybe you can help me overcome my fear." Once more he put his hand over mine. This time I couldn't control the reflex, and I pulled away in revulsion. I'm sure he noticed.

We arrived at the terminal and he pulled over to the curb.

He handed me his personal card. "Call me collect from London," he said. "Tell me when you're returning and I'll pick you up."

"Thanks, but—"

"I insist," he said with that boggy-eyed look of his.

"Sure," I said, eager to placate him but with no intention of calling. I got out of his car, grabbed my bag from the back compartment, and slammed the door closed. The loud bang marked my freedom. The cockpit of his car, however luxurious, had been too close for me. He waved once more, altogether too friendly, and pulled away from the curb. I was relieved to be on my own, with only the slightest twinge of guilt that Marshall Zander's money was making it all possible.

Inside the terminal, after I'd checked in, I called Nicole one more time. The answering service was still taking her calls, so I left a message that I was en route to London and would see her in a couple of days. Then I called Rafik again and left a message on his answering machine.

"I'm having tea in London. Please feed the cat."

Twenty-four hours earlier we'd been exploring bondage and discipline, and now it was tea and cats.

The airliner was cruising high over the Atlantic, and I had just taken my first forkful of beef Wellington cooked to order when I realized I had no idea where to find Mireille Rubinskaya in London. Too bad Sharleen McChannel hadn't provided a more complete itinerary.

16

Dance Ballerina Dance

Have you ever been awakened with the smell of French-press coffee, hot buttered crumpets, sliced fresh fruit, and soft breakfast cheese, all while flying at forty-one thousand feet? And with impeccable service, no less? If a first-class flight to Europe was any indication of life on that side of the ocean, I was ready to consider a big move. However, shortly after touchdown—eight A.M. local time—I faced coach-class reality once again. Though I'd flown like royalty, I quickly discovered that a hired car from Heathrow Airport into London would cost the equivalent of half a week's tips—a good week—which was extravagant even for me. And since I was no longer on Marshall Zander's dime, down I went into London's legendary Tube.

But riding the Underground into town was both enjoyable and instructive, like a free tour of the city's outskirts. For much of the ride, the train remained on the surface and trundled past backyards and alleys and all the signs of real people's lives—pale plump women gabbing over fences, their clotheslines hung with laundry swaying in breezy counterpoint to their morning magpie gossip; mechanics in overalls, their twisted bodies half-consumed by the open bonnets of the ailing trucks or cars; and youngsters racing each other on bicycles, or else scuffling hand-to-hand. It was almost like passing through the back lot of a movie set.

I got off the train at South Kensington and walked the short distance to my hotel. This neighborhood was different from what I'd seen on the train ride into town. Here were rows of Edwardian townhouses, all uniform and tidy and white, bounded by gleaming black wrought-iron railings and distinguished only by their front-door treatments and the occasional bed of chaste paperwhites or showy azaleas. It was the kind of stuff you see a lot on Sunday-night public television.

I found my hotel, complete with its French name. Though all traces of Olde England had been removed by the Greek owners, one thing they hadn't been able to renovate was the view: My room faced the Victoria and Albert Museum directly across the street. Couldn't get much more Brit than that.

It was ten o'clock, not too soon to set about my mission to find Mireille Rubinskaya. And I figured the most direct way to find a prima ballerina was to call the ballet companies. As far as I knew, London had only one major classical company, the Royal Ballet. However it took far more than one telephone call to locate my quarry, for whoever answered would cheerfully give me an alternate number to try. This went on until five attempts later a woman finally said that yes, she could take a message for Miss Rubinskaya, and no, she could not release her address or telephone number to me. I told her it was urgent that I speak with Mireille, and that I was in London as Max Harkey's representative.

"I shall give her your message," said the woman. "And I shall ring you back with her reply."

Along with my telephone number, she asked the name of the hotel, which I told her.

"Don't forget to mention Max Harkey," I said.

"I have made a note of that, Mr. Kraychik. Good-bye."

I waited impatiently for her call, which came a half-hour later. She told me that Mireille Rubinskaya would meet me at three o'clock sharp at the Connaught Hotel. A rendezvous there implied that the young ballerina was already an *assoluta*.

I took a long hot shower and put on fresh clothes, then set out for my meeting with Mireille. It was early yet, but I decided to walk partway and make a brief shopping tour of London. I bought a map in the hotel lobby, then walked a few blocks along Brompton Road to a café, another place with a French name. I ordered a *café pressé* and a fruit-and-cream pastry, then planned my route to the Connaught Hotel.

The first stop was Harrods, where I toured the legendary food halls. The main room was a vast tiled chamber, much like an enormous Roman bath. Its glazed walls glistened like white ice with vivid hand-painted borders. Food items exotic and pedestrian were displayed below in sparkling glass cases, lavishly arranged like goods at Cartier. The produce section purveyed fruits from around the world, all clearly labeled by name and country of origin, including MacIntosh apples from Maine, U.S.A.—proof that we were still a recognized colony.

From Harrods I took the Tube to Piccadilly Circus. To get to the train I had to go down, down, down numerous escalators. A mile below the earth's crust, or so it felt, I waited for the train, which arrived in minutes—an unlikely event in New World Boston. Once the doors slid shut, the train accelerated to a raucous velocity that verged on self-destruction. Yet the sturdy coaches tolerated the abuse very well, had obviously done so for many years, and probably would continue for many more—much like myself, I thought.

The chaos and excitement of Piccadilly Circus—which is actually a gigantic traffic rotary, and not a performance arena per se—caused me to exclaim aloud, "I'm in London."

On my walk up Piccadilly toward the Connaught Hotel I stopped at Fortnum & Mason. If Harrods was luxurious, Fortnum & Mason was regal. I half expected the security guard to ask for my pedigree documents. But the place was well attended by people from other countries, and not everyone looked like royal blood. I decided to buy some violet- and rose-flavored chocolate creams for Rafik, something to renew the romance of our love, at least for myself. The clerk rang up the sale—a huge sum until I realized that it was in mere pounds sterling, and that my cost in dollars would be even more. Ah, what price romance? Just then an East Indian princess wafted by in a billowing silk sari, oblivious to the luxury around her. When I saw her eyes I was stunned, for they were too familiar. They were the eyes of Sharleen McChannel. How was it possible? I wondered. How could she be here in London as well? Had she been on the same flight? And why was she no longer posing as La Duchessa? I was about to approach her, but she had vanished. Perhaps it had been a jet-lag hallucination.

At the Burlington Arcade I bought Nicole a cigarette holder. If she was trying to smoke less, she might as well play the grande dame while she did. And finally, at Maitland's Chemists I found a small green bottle of balsam cologne that rekindled a distant memory of my first meeting with Lieutenant Branco. I bought it, not certain whether I would keep it for myself or present it to him, since he was almost part of the family now.

It was exactly three o'clock when I walked through the flower-bordered entrance to the Connaught Hotel, a red brick building on Carlos Place, just off Grosvenor Square. Though warm and inviting, the hotel also had the sacrosanct air of a museum, a living testament to the zenith of late nineteenth-century refinement. The wood-panelled lobby resembled a gentleman's private study more than a common egress for the guests. And if I was thinking in words like that, the Victorian energy was clearly still present and affecting.

I'd paused to admire an arrangement of tiny white lilies and fresh-cut fuchsia when a slender young man in dark vest and striped pants approached me.

"May I be of assistance?" he said, which I interpreted as "Who are you and what are you doing here?" I told him my name and he said, "Ah, yes, Mr. Kraychick," with perfect Czech vowels and consonants. "Mademoiselle Rubinskaya apologizes. She will be detained, and suggests you should await her in the lounge." He directed me there.

In the lounge the bar waiter escorted me to a reserved table set within a bay window that faced the bar on the opposite side of the room. I settled myself into a heavy tub-back armchair upholstered in dark leather, and ordered a martini. The lounge reflected the same past glory as the hotel lobby: walls panelled in chocolate brown oak; a brass chandelier with faceted glass shades; a pair of mounted deer heads; numerous paintings of hunting dogs; a huge portrait of Charles II, and another of an anonymous lady whose billowing salmon-pink skirt matched exactly the color on some of the pillows on the scallop-backed sofa directly below it. The carpet throughout had a muted red lozenge pattern, and was reassuringly worn.

The bar itself had no rail for standing, so it was an open stage for the bartender—in British, the barman—to ply his art. Against the backdrop of a wall-sized mirror and shelves full of Victorian glass decanters and vases, the barman, dressed in his white tunic coat, gathered the makings for my cocktail. He conferred on the bar tools and the liquors the same reverence a Shakespearean actor allows to spoken syllables. He prepared the drink on a small raised section at the center of the bar. All was accomplished quietly, within the shadows of sound. Even the tinkle of ice swirling against the long glass stirring rod was muted. Meanwhile the bar waiter re-entered the lounge from a swinging door off to one side, carrying on his tray a porcelain bowl filled with—good lord! Potato chips? Then in one long, continuous, graceful phrase worthy of a danseur noble, he swept my cocktail from the bar, placed it upon his tray, glided to my table, and delivered both drink and comestible to me, all with the most liquid movement and the barest hush of sound. I restrained myself from applauding him.

He said, "Some fresh crisps for you."

And I couldn't help remarking, "You move beautifully."

He replied with a modest nod. "Kind of you, sir."

And I'd guessed right about the snack. It was potato chips—or more correctly, crisps—but I'd not expected them to be made especially for me and my cocktail at that moment. The only problem facing me was in the serenity of the Connaught Lounge, how was I supposed to enjoy those warm, crunchy wafers of flash-fried potato? Was it some kind of test? Was this what finally separated the aristocracy from the commoners? The mastery of silent mastication?

I chose a small crisp from the top of the mound, one that might fit completely into my big mouth and be suitably muffled. Yet in that microsecond of temporo-mandibular activity, when the bespoke potato crisp was about to be shattered between my Slavic chops, *that* was precisely when all the whisperings of conversation throughout the lounge arrived simultaneously at a hiatus, just in time for the big *crunch!*

A confounded silence followed. But within those dazed moments, as after any epiphany, when the other guests began to comprehend what had transpired, what they had witnessed firsthand in the sanctum sanctorum of the Connaught lounge—that someone had actually *eaten* a crisp—then, one by one, at various tables, people began to try the forbidden wafers themselves, until finally the lounge itself, that bastion of late Victorian high manners, resounded with a well-tempered fugue of crunching and noshing. The barman caught my eye and gave a quick wink.

Then entered Mireille Rubinskaya, limping on crutches and looking like a wounded swan, ethereal and pale. She was extremely small and fragile, but had enormous sad eyes, dark convincing eyes, eyes suitable for the great tragic roles, just like her great-aunt back in Boston, the venerable Madame Rubinskaya herself. Despite the crutches, Mireille moved like a graceful apparition, a lost being from the spirit world of romantic ballet who had taken on a mortal form for these few hours. Her long black hair only enhanced her pallor. She embodied the Old World artist, too sensitive and too vulnerable to hardship, not like her counterparts in Boston, who were of the earth: evolved, improved, and tough.

I stood up to greet her. She balanced herself on one crutch and proffered a lovely pale hand.

"You've brought news of Max, then?" she said eagerly, dispensing with formalities.

"News?" I replied. "Don't you know?"

"That he's dead? Of course!"

She pulled her hand away abruptly, then lowered herself into her chair and laid the crutches next to her.

"I apologize for the inconvenience," I said, eyeing the crutches. I had completely forgotten about her injury, which Max Harkey had described to us the night of his dinner. "We could have met upstairs in your room."

She smiled politely. "One does not live at the Connaught," she said, correcting my gaffe with the grace of a sledgehammer. How was I supposed to know what one did and did not do at the Connaught? "But I couldn't very well see you in my flat," she continued, "since I have no idea who you are, except that you claim to be Max's representative here from the States."

"That's true to a degree."

"And what exactly is that degree?" she asked with chilly reserve.

"I'm not officially connected to Max," I said, "but I had to convince you to see me."

"Bravo then, Mr. Kraychik. Your ruse worked. But what is so urgent that you must lie in order to see me?"

"I'm trying to find Max's killer."

Mireille's strong dramatic features seemed to dissolve as her jaw fell open. "Are you saying he was murdered, then?"

"Yes," I replied.

At that moment the bar waiter appeared with a tray bearing a complete tea service that included exquisite porcelain pieces containing the tea, milk, and sugar, along with a tiered plate of sterling silver arranged with puff-pastry savories, finger sandwiches, miniature scones, petit fours, and fresh berries. On the bottom tier were numerous small bowls of assorted marmalades, and two larger ones mounded with Devon cream that looked deliciously firm and spreadable. But the kaleidoscope of treats now before us did nothing to ease Mireille's shock at hearing the fact that Max Harkey had not died naturally but had been killed.

"I am certain that you are lying to me. I don't know what you want, Mr. Kraychik, but your cruelty in saying that Max—"

"I'm sorry you learned it this way," I said.

"Why didn't my aunt tell me about it, then?"

Mireille had raised her voice. I remained quiet. She continued rather loudly, "Aunt Rubi told me that Max had suffered a heart attack and had died instantly. But now, here you are with an absurd story about a murder."

"I'm really sorry. I thought you knew. Surely the newspapers—"

"No, Mr. Kraychik. I did not know. I haven't been well and I haven't been reading newspapers either."

Boorishly self-conscious, I took a slug of my martini.

Then, as if to nullify our bad start, Mireille exercised consummate British decorum and proceeded with her tea. "They are so kind to remember the extra cream for me," she said vapidly. "I am supposed to be gaining weight." She pressed a chunk of heavy Devon cream and a spoonful of rose-petal marmalade onto a tiny scone and placed it in her mouth. Then she closed her eyes and let the morsel soften and crumble within. A glow rose in her pale cheeks. She dispatched her heavenly tidbit with a delicate swallow, then opened her eyes.

"Better?" I asked.

"Yes, thank you," she replied.

"Can you tell me about your relationship to Max Harkey?"

"There isn't much to tell you," she said in a vain attempt to shrug off my question. But her large eyes failed her. She avoided my gaze and looked toward her teacup as she poured. She seemed to address the teacup instead of me. "I suspected that something horrible had happened. My dear aunt seemed to be protecting me again. I just never thought . . ." Mireille then put her hand to her throat and gasped softly. Once again her complexion became ashen, and she slumped back into her chair.

"Are you all right?" I asked.

She held up her other hand as if to ward me off, then closed her eyes and became extremely quiet, almost not breathing. I caught the eye of the bar waiter, who was already heading toward our table.

"May I assist you?" he said to her.

She opened her eyes to him and said, "I'm fine, thank you. It always happens after the first bit of food, but it passes quickly."

Thus dismissed, the bar waiter left us alone.

Mireille looked at me with her big sad eyes.

"You see," she said in a whisper, "I'm pregnant."

"Ah," was all I could manage while my mind raced to the most obvious conclusion. I reached quickly for my cocktail, but the glass arrived at my lips empty.

"It's made me quite sick," she said. "Between that and my injury, I couldn't possibly travel. Otherwise I would have come to Boston immediately after Max's death."

"You look so thin to be pregnant," I said stupidly.

"I know. I was concerned about that too, but the doctors tell me that everything is fine now. I should start gaining weight soon. I may even have breasts."

Her directness unnerved me a bit. Then our eyes met, and my instinct told me that my first guess had been right, but still I had to say it, to confirm it with her. My whisper seemed loud enough for the entire lounge to hear.

"Is it Max's child?"

Mireille nodded vigorously, and for a moment her tired eyes glistened with pure joy. We had a common bond with her love for Max Harkey and my pursuit of his killer.

I said, "Did you know Max kept a diary?"

"Of course," she answered, proving the existence of the mysterious missing diary.

"Had you ever read it?"

"I'm sure it was private," she said quickly.

I pressed her. "But had you read it?" To my mind Mireille Rubinskaya had already played her trump card by telling me that she was carrying Max Harkey's child. So why was she pretending to be so moral about reading his personal diary? I said, "It may hold the answer to Max's murder."

"How?"

"He may have written about his relationships with other people."

"I'm certain that he did," she said.

"And with brutal candor," I added.

Mireille hesitated. It's never easy to confess that you've casually rummaged through someone else's most private affairs, even your lover's.

I said, "Do you want his killer to go free?"

"Of course not!" she said quickly.

Just then the bar waiter reappeared with a fresh cocktail for me. He quickly surveyed the table, and then, psychic to the core, asked nothing before vanishing again.

Mireille sighed. "I've told no one," she said. "But yes, I did read his diary. I think he wanted me to, since he always left it where I was sure to find it. I read it every day until he returned to Boston. I told myself it was the only way to be sure of his love for me."

"Had he proposed to you then?"

"Yes," she said. "But he never knew about the child. I suffered vertigo and fell during rehearsal. The ballet company was concerned only about my knee and saw the accident as a tragedy. But to me it was a small price for carrying Max's child."

"So you loved him?"

"All my life. But it had been so complicated. He was always like part of the family, yet I had always loved him more than I should have. All my youth I dreamed of our love but never believed it could happen."

"Why not?"

"Isn't it obvious? I'm so much younger."

"Sometimes that doesn't matter," I said.

Mireille Rubinskaya looked at me as though I was the stupidest boy on a grade-school field trip.

"Don't you see?" she said. "My great-aunt loved him too."

Oh dear, I thought.

Mireille went on. "Aunt Rubi raised me after I'd lost my parents. I was only twelve, but I was already dancing seriously, preparing for a career. The timing couldn't have been more propitious for a young girl to face the first great love in her life. Living with my aunt I saw

Max Harkey often, perhaps too often. And as much as I tried to avoid Max, I felt destined to fall in love with him. And I could never tell my aunt about it for fear of her wrath. I may have been young, but I sensed her feelings for Max, and they were exactly like mine."

"Did he know how you felt back then?"

"I was precocious enough to know not to tell him, but I'm sure my eyes and my body gave me away. Whenever he came to visit, I had to make excuses to run away. I'm sure Aunt Rubi knew as well. There were awful scenes between us, though nothing explicit was ever said. It was obvious to me that we both wanted the same man, and one of us was too old and the other too young. So I sacrificed myself to ballet. The pursuit of art became my whole life. It was the easiest solution."

Whew! I thought.

Mireille continued, "And the last time Max was in London, all those years of denial between us finally culminated in a single night. What had preceded that moment no longer had any meaning, for we knew that we would spend the rest of our lives together, or else die."

Strong stuff, I thought, thankful for my martini.

Mireille said, "It sounds melodramatic, but there wasn't a moment's doubt for either of us."

"Except that you had to read Max Harkey's diary to be sure."

Mireille's face colored slightly.

I said, "How much of this does your great-aunt know?"

"Max promised to tell her everything when he returned to Boston, but I don't know if he got the chance. When Aunt Rubi called me after Max's death, we spoke only about him and about my injury. Nothing else."

"So as far as you know . . ." I said.

Mireille completed my sentence. "My dear Aunt Rubi knows nothing about the baby."

"Unless she's got that diary," I said.

"What do you mean?" said Mireille with alarm.

"It's disappeared. The police never found it among Max's possessions."

"Then how did you know about it?"

"Max's houseboy mentioned it to me, then got killed shortly after."

"No!" she said.

"Yes," I said sadly. "Now can you tell me what was in it?"

Mireille still resisted. I promised her I'd keep whatever she told me confidential, unless it would guarantee finding Max's killer. That seemed to unlock her rigid secrecy.

She began, "Max was a marvelous journalist. He wrote about everything."

"I only want to hear about the people in his life. Did he say anything about Alissa Kortland?"

"My other rival," replied Mireille with a small laugh. "Yes, Max had had relations with her. But you see, they had no past together, not the way Max and I did. Max didn't love her. He barely knew her. His life could go on easily without her, despite any momentary passions they'd shared."

"Is that what he said?" I asked.

"I'm paraphrasing it, of course. The details were much more lurid. Apparently she is a nymphomaniac, and quite good at it."

"Did that disturb you?"

"Why should it? My connection with Max . . . You don't quite understand how a woman can feel, do you?"

"Sometimes," I said ruefully.

Mireille explained it simply. "Alissa was like a decoration for Max. A toy."

"And you?" I asked.

"I was Max's future," she said confidently.

Heady stuff, but I wanted to know what else was in that diary. Then it occurred to me to ask her directly. "Do you have the diary now?"

She stared at me with her big, sad, brown eyes—what had those eyes seen that she wasn't telling me?—and she said, "Max took it back to Boston with him."

"You're certain?"

She spoke somewhat sharply. "If I had the diary and I thought it would help you, I would show it to you. As it is, you probably know more about me now than anyone else, other than Max. Perhaps because you're a total stranger, yet you seem compassionate."

Which one of us was acting out a role now? Was I an objective bystander honestly relating to this beautiful if wounded young creature? Or was she an elusive sprite telling fabulous lies to please me?

"Did Max write anything about Toni di Natale?" I asked.

"The conductor?"

I nodded.

Mireille said, "Max knew that she desired him, but he never encouraged her. Apparently she is a real talent, and Max didn't want to risk her musical assistance for the sake of a quick toss. He respected her work."

"How noble," I said.

"It's true."

"Then what about his feelings for your aunt? Did he write about Madame Rubinskaya?"

Mireille said, "More than anyone else."

"Including you?"

I sensed her pulling back.

"I'd rather not discuss that part of it."

"But just minutes ago you offered to show me the diary if you had it."

"But I don't have it," she said. "And if I did, perhaps I'd change my mind now."

"Does it incriminate your great-aunt?"

"Haven't you asked enough questions?" she said. Then she closed her eyes and complained, "I'm feeling tired." That talent for quick-change emotions seemed to run in the family. Mireille signaled for the bar waiter and asked him to call a cab for her.

While we waited, I asked if there was anything in Max Harkey's diary about Scott Molloy. She reluctantly told me that Max had felt protective toward Scott.

"No sex, then?" I asked bluntly.

"Max had stopped all that back in his early teens."

I suppose that made him a rare model of psychosexual health, except perhaps for impregnating his mentor's grand-niece, a woman young enough to be his daughter.

I begged one more question of Mireille.

"I must go," she protested.

"Think of Max's killer," I said.

She replied, "You're making me wish I'd never admitted looking at that diary. It *is* personal, you know."

"Please," I begged. "You're the only one who can tell me, now that the diary has vanished."

Finally she acquiesced, and I asked about Marshall Zander.

"As far as I know," she said, "Max and he were once best friends.

Apparently back then Marshall had hoped that Max would be more than that to him. That's probably why he gave all that money to Max's ballet company."

"That's all?"

Mireille added, almost regretfully, "It wasn't in the diary, but I know that Max was plagued by it, by the idea that Marshall's hope of love never died."

Her cab arrived. She pulled herself up onto her crutches.

"I'm sorry I can't offer you a lift," she said courteously, yet unable to contain her eagerness to escape. One emotion had been honest, at least.

"I don't know how to thank you," I said.

She smiled wanly. "Find Max's killer. That's enough."

The doorman escorted her out to her cab, and she was gone. Too late I realized that I'd forgotten to ask her if Max had ever mentioned Rafik. It would have been a choice tidbit to offer him on my return, the secret truths from Max Harkey's diary.

I asked the bar waiter for our bill.

With a beneficent smile he said, "I've taken care of it."

"Really? That's extremely kind of you."

"The Connaught is proud of its service."

I offered him a generous tip, but he politely refused it, claiming that gratuities weren't customary there. I thanked him again and headed back to my hotel, quite pleased to have received such hospitality.

Back at my hotel I confirmed my return flight for the next morning, then called Rafik to tell him what time I'd be arriving in Boston. He wasn't home, so I left a forlorn message on his answering machine. Then I called Nicole at the shop to give her the same message, but Ramon told me that she had left early that day. Thus defeated and alone, feeling abandoned by my nearest and dearest, I took myself to supper and then to the theater. I chose a popular and long-running comedy, a murder mystery highly recommended by the hotel staff. Trouble was, it had been on the boards so long that the actors and actresses were robots, nothing at all like the evasive and ephemeral characters in the drama of my private life.

When I checked out of my hotel the next morning I faced an astronomical bill, even though Hanni my travel agent had prepaid the room. A huge charge had been added by the Connaught Hotel—the bar tab for the afternoon I'd spent with Mireille Rubinskaya. When I asked the clerk how that charge had got on my room bill, he explained that the secretary from the Royal Ballet had given the Connaught my name and my hotel, and that as a trade courtesy a few of the most reputable hotels throughout London still accepted the charges incurred by their guests at other fine places like the Connaught—adding their own service charges, of course. I guessed I was supposed to be grateful for the favor. But after the previous day's carefree shopping spree for my friends in Boston, I prayed that my plastic would handle the unexpected hotel bill. Fortunately the gods of credit were watching over me, for my charge limit had been miraculously increased overnight. Apparently the purchases I'd made in the various London shops had tripped a computer flag on my account and marked me as an international big-time spender. Accordingly, up went the limit.

Later at the airport I got through immigration without a hitch. The flight departed on time, and six first-class hours later I was safely taxiing on Boston tarmac. No one met me at the airport, and after the cab ride home no cat greeted me at the door. Two telephone calls, one to Rafik and one to Nicole, yielded nothing, and no messages had been left on my machine. Taped to the refrigerator door—a guarantee that I would see it—was a hastily written note from Rafik explaining that he had taken Sugar Baby to his apartment. Abduct me, abduct my cat.

I poured myself a shot of bourbon and toasted my own homecoming.

"Welcome home," I said to the empty rooms. "We all missed you terribly."

Among the mail was an envelope addressed in handwriting I didn't recognize. I opened it and a key fell out. The note inside read, "They wouldn't make a copy, so this is the original one. Give it back before Mr. Zander finds out I took it. Beijos, Rico."

Getting the key for me had been Rico's last gesture of goodwill, and I couldn't even thank him for it. I put the key in my pants pocket, and lay down on the sofa to plan my next move. If nothing else, that afternoon I would ransom my cat from my lover.

But instead I found myself weeping for my *tesão*, now dead and gone.

17

Just Face the Music and Dance

I'd dozed off, and the sound of the telephone woke me at four o'clock. It was Marshall Zander.

"Welcome home," he said.

"How did you know I was back?"

"I called the airline and checked all their passenger lists."

That sounded like an exercise in grim determination.

"You didn't call me," he said. "I wanted to pick you up."

"I guess I misplaced your card."

"What are you doing now?" he asked.

I felt my defenses rising fast. I'd been hoping to hear from Rafik or Nicole, not this guy.

"I'm resting," I said. "It was a long flight."

"What are you wearing?"

"What do you mean?"

"Can't you guess?" he said with a nervous laugh. "How would you like to go for a nice relaxing ride?"

I hedged. "Maybe another time."

"It's no trouble," he said. "I'm downstairs right now."

Damn car phones.

He added, "The passenger seat looks so lonely without you."

Was "passenger seat" a euphemism for his lap?

"I paid your way to London," he said. "Now won't you let me take you for a ride? Please?" He verged on whining.

What price gratitude? I told him I'd be down shortly. Perhaps I could finagle a lift to Rafik's place to pick up Sugar Baby. And the short jaunt to my lover's apartment might remind Marshall Zander that, conjugally speaking at least, I was not available.

When I got downstairs I found Marshall waiting in his sporty car. He'd removed the hard top for his late afternoon cruise, and he looked almost appealing behind the wheel. Maybe my eyes were dazzled by the red lacquer paint gleaming in the setting sunlight, or perhaps my nose was distracted by the heady scent of the plump leather seats. But, no, something had changed about the man himself. There was some brighter aspect in his face, his eyes maybe. Yes. That was it. Marshall Zander's eyes were now lit with a new look of desire. And sitting in his car like that, all decked out with money and power, he appeared almost handsome, at least from the shoulders up. Fact is, I knew that the remaining ninety percent of his body was a mess.

I got in the car and was fastening my seat belt when I felt his rough dry hand grab onto mine.

"What are you doing?" I said and tried to pull my hand from his.

"Just saying hello."

His eyes were full of lust. I stared back coldly until he released my hand. He put the car in gear and started to drive.

"Where would you like to go?" he asked eagerly.

No secluded groves, that was for sure. I quickly defused any romantic ideas by telling him I was meeting Rafik at his place.

"Sure," he said. But then, as if to bolster his own confidence in the face of rejection, he said cheerily, "How was London?"

"What little I saw was wonderful."

"I know the city well. I'd like to show it to you sometime."

I left his offer open and replied with a jab of reality.

"Mireille Rubinskaya told me that you were in love with Max Harkey."

The traffic light turned red and he rolled to a smooth stop. He turned to me with mournful eyes.

"Is that a crime?" he said, almost accusingly. "Is it wrong to love someone and hope that they might return the feeling? I can't help it that I don't look like Max's beautiful dancers. But my feelings are just as strong as a beautiful person's, perhaps even more so."

The light turned green and we were moving again.

"The trouble with Max," he continued, "was that he never had to love anyone back. He was always desirable. Just seeing him, people became infatuated with him, threw themselves at him."

"Did you?"

"Never."

"Wasn't all the money you gave him just a substitute for the love he wouldn't accept?"

"You make it sound dirty," he said.

"A lot of people say that about the truth."

"I know the truth. I'm not ashamed to admit that I loved Max. But it wasn't for his body."

I directed him to Rafik's apartment, where he double-parked the car. I thanked him and was about to get out when he held onto my arm. The car was idling quietly but his pleading eyes were in overdrive.

"I like you a lot," he said.

"I'm with Rafik."

"That didn't stop you with Rico," he said sharply.

His remark left me speechless. I felt the key to Max Harkey's apartment in my pants pocket—the key that Rico had risked his safety to get for me. Its point was stabbing my hip.

"Don't get me wrong," said Marshall Zander. "Casual sex doesn't bother me. In fact, I've been doing some thinking, and I've come up with an idea that might interest you. I'd like to make you an offer—actually to both you and Rafik."

No three-ways, pal. Sooner Toni di Natale than you.

Marshall said, "I hope you'll take it in the right spirit. It's the only way I can show you how much I like you."

Still unable to speak, I stared at him.

He went on. "Since Max's death and Rico's death I've been extremely lonely. I need companionship, male companionship. And now I've met you, and I like you a lot. You're not the kind of person who uses other people. I can trust you. So if you would be willing to be my friend—just friends—I'm sure I could influence the board of directors to appoint Rafik as the new artistic director of the Boston City Ballet."

Preposterous, I thought, yet he went on.

"I make a very good friend."

And some people make a very good apple pandowdy.

He continued, "I will always be there for you. I'm not the kind of person who lets people down. I'm just like you."

The only sounds I heard for the next few seconds were the ticking of the dashboard clock and murmur of the powerful engine.

Finally I spoke. "Forgive me," I said with a shaking voice, "but you sound desperate for sex." And no one on the face of the earth understood that syndrome better than I.

Marshall Zander averted his gaze and looked downward—ironically, at his crotch.

"I wouldn't mind if it turned out that way with you," he said.

I pulled my arm away from him and muttered, "In all my days at the styling chair I've never been propositioned like this."

"But I do like you."

"If you say anything often enough, you'll believe it."

"But it's true. It's not just sex," he said earnestly. "I think a lot of you. Why don't you talk it over with Rafik? It's not a chance everyone gets every day. Surely you both want his career to advance. This would be a major achievement for him."

But at whose expense?

"I'll tell him, all right," I said. I got out of the car and closed the door. "Thanks for the lift."

Marshall Zander sat in his car and watched me hurry toward the front door of Rafik's apartment building. Fortunately we both have keys to each other's places, so even if Rafik wasn't home, I'd be able to get inside, away from Marshall Zander, and be with my beloved feline. I rang the doorbell, and hallelujah! My man's voice came sailing over the intercom.

"J'écoute."

"Open up," I said urgently. Then well out of earshot of Marshall Zander I added, "There's a big troll chasing me."

Rafik buzzed me in. I turned and waved good-bye to Marshall Zander who then raced the big German engine and drove off in a loud squeal of rubber. Was it something I didn't say?

I bounded up the stairs two at a time. Rafik had left his apartment door ajar. When I entered I found him down on the floor playing with Sugar Baby on the rug near his bed. I got down too, then rolled onto my side and mewed and purred for attention. Sugar Baby stretched

herself out to touch me with her front paws. I stretched myself out
to touch Rafik the same way.

"I forgot to bring your gift," I said.

"Chocolate?"

"How did you know?"

Rafik smiled. "You always give me what you want yourself."

Like now, I thought.

Ten minutes later we were laughing noisily on the rug after a quick
and sticky round of "hello."

"Welcome home," said Rafik. "Nicole has called me many times.
I told her I was missing your calls too. I am sorry."

"Rehearsals again?"

"Soon you will understand why I am working so hard."

"Never," I said.

I told Rafik about my meeting with Mireille Rubinskaya and what
she'd told me about Max Harkey's diary.

"Were there any words about me?" he asked.

"I forgot to ask."

Rafik snarled playfully. "Two things you forget. Soon you will
forget who I am."

"How can I forget you?" I said. "You are my life. Of course, I can
never remember you the way Max Harkey did—with his big, long,
shiny Bösendorfer."

"It is a beautiful piano."

"So what more could he have said in his diary to show how he felt
about you?"

Rafik answered, "He could say I was the best person to direct the
ballet company after him."

Even though Rafik knew that decision lay with the board of directors, he had given me the perfect lead-in to tell him about Marshall
Zander's bizarre proposition. I related his offer with the calculated
coolness of a brain surgeon explaining the lousy odds of recovery to
a patient, all in the hope that Rafik's instinct would rise victorious and
he would declare resoundingly, *"C'est fou!"*

But instead Rafik pondered Marshall Zander's proposal seriously,
as though he might actually consider the offer. Was it possible? I felt
the skin around my nipples prickle. What would happen if Rafik
agreed? Could I sacrifice myself to become Marshall Zander's consort

and provide my lover the artistic opportunity of his life? Or would Rafik's "yes" mark the end of "us" just like that? Easy sex on the rug, a good laugh, and then never to be together again because of his absurd response to an absurd proposal.

Rafik delivered his verdict.

"I will answer him myself. If I am the director of the Boston City Ballet, I will earn it myself, from my respect for art and my love for the dancers."

That's my man.

He invited me to stay the night with him. What would you have done?

The next morning we set off together with Sugar Baby nestled in the cat carrier. I accompanied Rafik to the ballet studio, where I planned to initiate a scheme I'd dreamed up last night—literally dreamed up—while sleeping secure in his arms. I was conducting a group interrogation with all the people who knew Max Harkey, the kind of ensemble scene popular in British manor-house mysteries. Like a stage director I was setting all the players at cross-purposes, so that the truth eventually rose up from the chaos and conflict. The only problem was, in real life I had no manor house in which to act out my dream. And then I realized that, thanks to Rico, I did hold the key to a fabulous pied-à-terre: Max Harkey's own apartment. And every character from my dream could be found at the studios of the Boston City Ballet.

Inside the lobby of the ballet studios Rafik said good-bye to me before he went to teach class.

"After class I will tell Marshall about my decision," he said. "Do not say anything to him."

"Mum's the word, love. He's all yours. Shall I come to the rehearsal tonight?"

"No," he said shortly. "Please be patient, Stani. Soon you will know why."

It was just as well that Rafik didn't want me at rehearsal to see his secret work yet. For my part I hadn't told him about my dream or how I was planning to make it a reality that evening. Rafik went into the teacher's room and I set to work on my mischief. I intended to snag my potential party guests with the irresistible bait of exclusivity, the same ploy that market researchers use to con people into attending their focus groups: You and only you can solve our predicament. Demographic superiority would compel them all to attend my soirée, for every one of them at some point had been a contender for Max Harkey's love.

Alissa Kortland and Scott Molloy were stretching their long limbs on the carpeted floor. I knelt down near them and spoke quietly.

"It's good to see you both together again."

Scott glared at me and said, "What do you want now? Last time I talked to you, all I got was trouble."

"I thought we had a good talk."

"I'm sorry I told you anything. It was too personal."

I'd seen it happen often enough, where the trust that encourages intimacy gets twisted into resentment.

"We're both still the same people, Scott. Actually, I'm having a little party this evening and I'd like you both to come."

The two dancers looked at me blankly.

"Whatever for?" asked Alissa.

"I'm playing the faculty wife to Rafik," I replied.

Scott scowled at me and said, "Whose idea was that?"

"Mine," I answered. "I've just returned from London, where I met Mireille Rubinskaya."

That caused no visible response from either dancer.

I murmured seductively, "She gave me Max Harkey's diary."

Both heads turned quickly to face me.

I went on, "I think you'd both find it interesting."

"Where is this party?" said Alissa.

"At Max Harkey's place."

Their startled faces caused me to shush them before they spoke out.

"It's all right," I said.

"What time?" they asked in unison.

"Six o'clock."

"Will there be food?" asked Scott. "We have a big rehearsal tonight. We'll have to eat sometime."

"There'll be food," I said reluctantly. "See you then. And don't tell anyone."

"Why not?" said Alissa.

"I'm not supposed to have the diary."

As I rose to go, Alissa said, "Is that your cat?"

"Yes," I said, and proudly turned the cat carrier to display Sugar Baby to them.

"She's beautiful."

"Of course she is," I said. "She's a princess."

Scott Molloy smirked and said, "The daughter of a queen."

Alissa slapped him lightly on shoulder.

Rafik passed by and went into the studio, a cue to all the lounging dancers to file in quickly after him. They took their places at the barre, Rafik commanded them into first position, and class began. I watched his virile form while I waited around for another of my potential party guests to appear. According to Rafik, she was at the studios that morning making final arrangements for the big rehearsal that evening. Patience, I thought. Like the best hair work, sleuthing took time and patience. The payoff would follow. And follow it did.

Toni di Natale entered the lobby with her usual bustle of lively energy. She saw me waiting there and came by.

"Isn't he handsome?" she said, refering to Rafik.

"I'd have to agree," I replied.

Then she noticed Sugar Baby and said, "What a pretty cat!" She knelt down and ran her fingers lightly along the door of the carrier. "Who is the prettiest girl in all Back Bay?" she said, inflecting her voice with typical kitty foolishness. Sugar Baby bestowed a blasé flick of her tongue on Toni's fingertips.

I said, "I'd like you to come to a small reception I've planned for this evening."

"Bad timing, I'm afraid. We have a big rehearsal tonight."

"Then you should eat something beforehand, and I'll have food."

"What time?" she said.

"Six o'clock."

"Well, I suppose that leaves enough time before rehearsal. Tonight is the first run-through with full orchestra, and that's always a thrill. What's the occasion?"

"You probably know that I've just returned from London."

"No, I didn't."

"Rafik didn't tell you, then?"

"I haven't talked to him except in rehearsals," she said as she kneaded the soft fur under Sugar Baby's chin. "There's so much to do, and opening night is just days away. What were you doing in London?"

"I saw Mireille Rubinskaya."

"Oh," said Toni absently.

Brum-brum-brum, went Sugar Baby.

"She gave me Max Harkey's diary," I said.

"Did she?" Toni was trying hard to appear unaffected by me, but like Sugar Baby, was responding in spite of herself. "How indiscreet of her," she added.

"Not really," I said. "She wanted to help me find Max's killer."

"And have you?" she asked slyly.

"I'm very close now."

"Where is this reception?"

"At Max's place."

Toni blanched. "How did you—?"

"It's a secret. It's against police orders."

"Then why are you doing it?"

"I had a visitation."

"You're mad," she said with a big laugh. "No wonder Rafik loves you. Well, I'm game for your mysterious party." She stood up and faced me. "See you at six, then."

"Remember, it's a secret," I said again.

"A secret," she repeated, as though humoring an idiot.

Just moments after she left me standing in the lobby, Jason Sears entered from the main corridor, along with Marshall Zander. When Marshall saw me, he turned back and vanished into the corridor. That was lucky, because I certainly didn't want him to know I had his key to Max Harkey's place. It would only prove that I had conspired with Rico to get it.

I intercepted Jason Sears on his way out.

"Are you free this evening?" I said.

"What?" he said, vexed by my question. "Who are you?"

"You met me at Max Harkey's place the night he was killed. I was with Rafik."

Jason Sears studied me impatiently, like a trick question on a chemistry exam.

"The hairdresser," he said finally.

"That's right."

"So what do you want?"

I whispered, "Can you come to Max Harkey's apartment at six o'clock?"

"What is this secrecy? Max Harkey is dead."

"Shhhhh!"

"I've heard you like to play cloak and dagger. But I've no time for it. I've just made special arrangements to use the piano in the performance hall. I'm on my way there now. It's the only chance I'll get to play the instrument before tonight's rehearsal. So to put it bluntly, I cannot attend your Nancy Drew colloquium this evening."

I retorted, "Don't you use her name in vain."

Jason Sears stormed out of the lobby. I imagined his piano playing would be quite a performance too.

Sugar Baby pressed her nose against the wire door of the carrier. I grazed it lightly with the side of my finger. "We don't need him anyway," I said to her, then quickly scanned the lobby to see if anyone had caught me talking to my cat in public like a dotty old lady.

One more person remained on my guest list. I went to the teacher's room and knocked on the door. Moments later it swung open to reveal the small stocky form of Madame Rubinskaya. The room behind her was veiled with smoke.

"Rafik is in class," she said curtly.

"I know. I came to talk to you."

She noticed Sugar Baby in the carrier. "You have cat?"

"Yes."

"My Verushka is afraid of cats. They scratch her nose."

"Madame," I said. "Can you come to Max Harkey's apartment tonight?"

"How you can ask me such a thing?"

"I've located his diary, and I want to share it with the people who knew him. But it's strictly confidential. Don't tell anyone else."

Her eyes were mistrustful. "I think you are making bad joke."

"I'm serious. I haven't even told the police about it."

"Why don't you let Maxi rest in peace. You have no respect for death."

"I'm going to find his killer."

She set her eyes on me while the smoke from her cigarette wafted up between us. She shook her head disdainfully.

"Again I see you are just ridiculous boy."

"Please come tonight," I said. "Six o'clock."

Without another word, but staring intently into my eyes, she pushed the door slowly closed in my face.

I left the studios and set out for home with Sugar Baby in the carrier. On the way I stopped in at Snips to say hello to Nicole. She was genuinely pleased and relieved to see me, but seconds later was scolding me for running off to London on a whim, calling me irresponsible and all that.

"Wait'll you hear what I'm doing tonight, doll."

I told her about my planned event at Max Harkey's place.

"Does Lieutenant Branco know about this?"

"No way, doll."

"How are you going to get in there?"

"I have a key. By the way, has Branco made any progress on the case?"

"He certainly hasn't had time to run off to London."

"Too busy at home, eh?"

"You never mind about that," she said sharply.

"Just don't tell him about tonight. There's no danger, no heroics. I'm just playing a little psychological parlor game to get all the facts out and organized. If Branco had cooperated and let me see the police reports, I probably wouldn't be driven to such drastic measures."

Nicole said, "You always find a reason to do what you want, Stanley, so don't blame the lieutenant for this absurd scheme of yours."

"Promise you won't tell him."

She smiled. "I couldn't keep a straight face."

"I'll see you tomorrow, doll." I kissed her and headed toward the door.

"Don't forget the cat," she said.

Oops.

I took Sugar Baby home and played a lengthy round of mouse with her. Then I finally unpacked my bag from London. Then I showered again and put on fresh clothes. At 4:30 I set out for Max Harkey's place. In one hand I carried a small wrapped parcel from London, and in the other a bag of cheese and crackers for my party guests. Then, as I was passing a trendy charcuterie, I considered getting something more substantial for my guests. After all, I had promised them they'd be fed. And though hospitality wasn't critical to the success of my venture, Scott Molloy and Alissa Kortland *were* dancers, and dancers needed fuel. Besides, if food could show love, perhaps it could also persuade.

So, laden with two large bagfuls of expensive and aromatic savories—I'd purposely chosen a lot of rich fatty items that my body-conscious guests were likely to avoid and leave for me—I stopped in at Station D for another round of mouse, this time with Lieutenant Branco.

"Something smells good," he greeted me.

"Hungry?" I asked.

"And thirsty," he said. "But I'm having dinner in a little while. Don't want to spoil my appetite. I hear you were in London."

"True," I said. "And I brought you something."

I gave him the small wrapped parcel from London.

"For me?" he said.

"No other."

"Max Harkey's diary?" he said with great hope.

"Two more guesses, Lieutenant."

Branco opened my gift and examined the bottle inside. It was the balsam cologne I'd found at Maitland's. He let out a small approving whistle.

"This one is hard to find," he said.

"Not for a member of the jet set," I replied.

"Thanks," he said.

I shrugged, but I also felt my neck redden.

Branco said, "On a more serious matter, I got the lab report on your friend's motor scooter. Turns out the brake cables had been nicked. They were rigged to fail at the worst possible time, under heavy pressure."

"Like coming to a stoplight at the bottom of Beacon Hill."

Branco nodded solemnly.

I asked, "Are you any closer to an answer?"

"There's one piece of evidence that still hasn't materialized."

"Max Harkey's diary," I said.

Branco nodded.

I said, "No wonder you were hoping that's what my present was."

Branco said, "When I heard you were in London, I thought you might get lucky and find it there."

"I came close."

Branco smirked. "It's probably been destroyed by now."

"I'll find it," I said.

"How are you going to do that?"

"With this food."

"Are you keeping something from me?" asked the cop.

Did I dare tell him that my attempted showdown was probably going to look more like a Tupperware party than a carefully staged interrogation? "Just be ready, Lieutenant," I said. "I plan to have Max Harkey's killer for you within twenty-four hours."

Branco chuckled and waved me off. "Go to your party."

18
The Next to the Last Tango

It was just after five-thirty when I let myself into Max Harkey's flat at the Appleton. Fortunately the locks had not been changed yet. The darkness inside the flat and the still air and the lack of any sound were mildly disturbing, the way a museum can be after hours.

I found some platters in the kitchen and set out the food. It was then that I got the final inspiration of how best to spend the short time I'd be with these people. I went searching through the sprawling flat for a particular item, something I was certain Max Harkey had owned because of my familiarity with Rafik's work as a choreographer. I found it in what appeared to be Max Harkey's study. It was an artist's easel with a large sketch pad on it. Rafik often used one just like it for roughing out costume designs and preliminary stage blocking. Since Max Harkey had been his mentor, I assumed that Rafik had adopted the technique from him. I set the easel up in the living room and awaited my guests.

Alissa, Toni, and Scott arrived together shortly after six o'clock. They'd obviously walked *tous les trois* from the studios, and they brought a noisy festive energy in with them. I cautioned them to remain quiet, since we were all technically trespassing. They were blithely unaffected by my warning, and instead the group of three headed straight for the food.

"You invited us," said Toni di Natale, chomping on a slice of roulade. "Now don't go making all kinds of rules. Let's have some fun before rehearsal tonight."

Theater people. Perhaps they knew better how to shrug off the petty concerns of life.

"There's one more guest," I said. "But I have a feeling she won't be here."

"Let's get started," said Scott, who'd piled his plate full of food.

Alissa added, "We only have an hour." She'd put less food on the plate she was holding, but then I saw that she'd divided her meal between two plates. So much for the idea of leftovers.

"Yes," said Toni. "Only an hour. Rehearsal starts at seven. It was so nice of you to have this reception for us."

"But—" I began.

"And so clever to have it here," she went on. "No one can bother us because no one knows where we are. Perhaps we can finally toast Max with the kind of impromptu party he could never enjoy or even imagine. Here's to you, Max!" she said. She raised a bottle of Italian mineral water in the air.

"Read us his diary while we're eating," said Alissa.

"Spill it all for us," said Scott, who was clearly enjoying his food and his limp double entendre.

Meanwhile I was flabbergasted by their energy. Here I'd been planning to get to the root of things, to delve seriously into the events of the night Max Harkey was killed, to find the missing pieces, to identify his killer. And instead I'd created a boisterous party. I stood up to make a formal announcement.

"I owe you all an apology. I don't have the diary."

But my statement caused peals of laughter among them. These folks were making a debacle of my investigation. Perhaps the pressures of rehearsal and the imminent opening-night performance had made them punchy. Their defenses had been tried to the point where they could no longer control their behavior. The question was, How far did that lack of control extend?

"Lighten up," said Toni. "Max was too serious and look where it got him. He didn't even get to see the new season open."

I said, "Max Harkey's serious nature was hardly the cause of his death."

"We all know it was a knife," said Alissa.

"But who was holding the knife?" I said. "Was it one of you?"

The room went instantly quiet.

"Please," said Scott. "If you don't have the diary, then let's just eat and go back to work."

"Sure," I said. "And let Max's killer go free."

Alissa said, "He's dead. It's done. The estate is settled. What good is finding the killer? It's not going to bring Max back."

I moved toward the easel. It was time for the game.

"I happen to know that all three of you sought Max's affections at one time. And now it's obvious that you've all lost the contest to Mireille Rubinskaya. Ergo, I assume that you resented Max for withdrawing from the sexual arena so abruptly, and for settling down so easily. After only one sexual encounter with Mireille, Max Harkey was forever unavailable to any of you."

"This sounds like a soap opera," said Alissa.

"If the shoe fits," muttered Scott. Alissa glared at him.

I continued, "I'm assuming that nobody in this room killed Max Harkey."

Toni said, "Thanks for that, at least."

"I'm also assuming that you—I should include myself—we have all lied about some of the things we've said so far to protect our egos or our reputations."

"Like now?" said Scott.

"Shut up," said Alissa.

"Continue, Professor," said Toni.

I did. "And despite those lies some little bits of truth always manage to slip out. And sometimes those fragments stick to other bits of truth to create a bigger piece of truth. That's when we enter the realm of danger. The payoff comes when enough of the stuff sticks together to convict the killer."

Scott remarked, "So what are you saying? Is this going to be some kind of encounter group?"

"No," I said. "I was thinking of something lighter, like a parlor game. We could call it 'My Last Time with Max.' "

Toni laughed heartily. At least someone appreciated my kind of levity.

I went on, "The only rule of the game is you don't have to tell the truth, as long as you know the truth."

"What good is that?" asked Alissa.

"You'll see," I said.

On the easel I drew a large grid. Across the top I filled in times in half-hour increments, and down the side I listed the names of the three people present.

"On this grid I'm going to map everybody's actions the night of the party for every hour. Each square on the grid will contain part of someone's version of what happened that night."

Scott demanded, "Where's your name?"

"I hardly knew Max."

"But Rafik did," said Toni.

"Yeah," added Scott. "Maybe you killed Max because you were jealous of his professional relationship with Rafik."

"That's ridiculous," I countered.

"Fair is fair," said Alissa.

"But I brought the food," I protested weakly.

Scott snapped his fingers and pointed to the easel.

"Names," he said, just like a man. "Yours and Rafik's."

So I added my name to the grid and then Rafik's under it. As I did so I felt a calmness spreading within me. Had I passed some milestone of emotional growth? Was I about to testify before them all, to share my version of the stormy saga of Stan and Rafik? Recovery be damned. No way!

"What about Madame?" said Alissa.

I added Madame Rubinskaya's name to the grid.

"And Marshall Zander?" said Scott.

Good, I thought. We've finally got the two real suspects.

"Anyone else?" I said in my best impersonation of a facilitator. No one answered. I said, "What about Jason Sears?"

Toni quickly interjected, "He barely knew Max, and besides, he didn't stay for the party."

"Put his name down anyway," said Scott. "Nobody gets away this time."

As I scrunched Jason's name onto the bottom of the chart, I thought, They're hungry to implicate anyone else to divert suspicion from themselves.

I turned to face them, and Scott said, "Now that we're ready to play police station, you go first."

"Sure," I said, figuring I'd gain their confidence if I was agreeable. I started filling in the grid with my own version of the night Max

Harkey was murdered. I annotated my entries with a running commentary to liven up the drama of the otherwise dreary night I'd spent alone.

10:30—Stumble out of Max's place. See Big Red parked on the sidewalk.

11:00—Arrive home and cry myself to sleep.

12:00—Awake. Sob melodramatically.

1:00—Ditto throughout night.

6:30—Phone call from Rafik.

7:00—Arrive back at Max's.

"As you can see," I said, "until I got the telephone call from Rafik, I spent the night rather uneventfully."

"Pitifully, I'd say," muttered Scott.

Unfazed, I went on. "So, since my night was so dull, I'd like to speculate on what some of the other people were doing."

I proceeded to fill in some of the empty boxes on the grid, specifically:

11:30—Max home alone.

12:00—Madame walks dog.

3:00—Scott cruises Esplanade.

"Hey!" said Scott. "What are you doing? Those aren't your boxes."

"But it's my game."

Scott said, "I'll tell you what I did myself."

"Be my guest," I said.

So his story began.

"I left Max's place with Alissa around eleven. I walked her home. Then I . . ." He looked at Alissa. Her eyes held a tiny warning, which Scott chose not to heed. He continued, "I asked her if I could come up."

"Nice alibi," I said.

"Except she told me I was being silly."

Through clenched teeth Alissa muttered, "You bastard."

"And then what?" I asked.

"And then," he said. "And then . . ."

"Well?" said Toni.

"Tell them," said Alissa. "Now that you've ruined both our alibis. You might as well finally say it."

Scott said, "I went back to Max's flat."

Almost predictable, I thought.

"When was that?" I asked.

"I don't know. I walked around for a long time. After Alissa humiliated me, I had to build up the courage to do it, to go to Max. It was a big step for me, like my last chance for his love. I'd been trying and trying with women, but it didn't work. It was Max I really wanted."

"So you went back to his place?"

"Yes."

"And told him how you felt?"

"No."

"No?"

"No!"

"Then what did happen?"

"I rang his apartment but he didn't answer. Then I saw the front door was broken, so I went up to his place. The door was open." Scott's chin began quivering uncontrollably. "Max was at the piano. The blood was all over him. I knew he was . . ."

He stopped and I pressed him to go on.

"What time was it?" I said.

"I don't know."

"Was the sun coming up?"

"I don't know!" he yelled.

Then he broke down into violent sobs. I made a move to comfort him, but he pushed me away. Likewise he resisted Toni's attempt to hold and quiet him. Meanwhile, Alissa sat and watched with a cool satisfied stare. She seemed to be enjoying Scott's pain and defeat, as though she had a vested interest in keeping him that way, and subservient to her.

Toni grimaced at me. "Well done," she said.

I sighed. "My parties always turn out like this."

Then Alissa spoke up sharply. "Well, I went back too, and I can assure you that Max was not dead when I got there."

"What time?" I said quickly, leaping toward the easel.

"It was . . ." Alissa fumbled. "I don't know, damn you! Do you think people look at their watches all the time?"

"Just go on," encouraged Toni, after glaring at me.

The young ballerina said, "I wanted Max to reconsider his decision to cancel *The Phoenix.*"

"Cancel?" I said. "But he'd just cast you in the part that night."

Toni added quickly, "After you left the party, Max told us that he had changed his mind and was going to cancel *The Phoenix* for the entire season."

"Really?" I said. Both women nodded.

"So," continued Alissa, "In the same night I had won and lost the major coup of my dancing career. When Max had cast me in the role against Madame's wishes I felt a great victory. It put me above her in importance, which is as it should be with dancers. But then Max changed his mind and said no. So I went back later and tried to reason with him. That's when he told me he had reconsidered his decision to cast me against Madame's wishes, and that's why he decided to cancel *The Phoenix* altogether. When I told him I couldn't accept that, he laughed and said that I had nothing to say about it. In fact, he told me that he and I were finished as well. That's what we really fought about. He said we'd had our fling with each other and got what we wanted and that it was over. But I wasn't going to let him off that easy. I started hitting him, hard. He grabbed me and tried to overpower me. I felt he was going to transform our fight into a sexual contest. He always did that, and I was fed up with it. So when he began thrusting his hips against mine, I pulled back just far enough to knee him in the groin. Then I kicked him hard—a full-force battement to his jaw— and sent him sprawling back into that big bronze statue. He hit his head and was dazed. When I went to help him, he screamed at me, called me a—never mind. Then he passed out. He was breathing regularly, so I assumed he'd be all right. I left quickly. That's the last time I saw him alive. I didn't believe that I'd killed him then. Later when I learned that he'd been murdered, I assumed I was the killer. I didn't plan to kill him, although he'd made me so angry that I never regretted hurting him."

Like the village idiot, I stood at the easel with the marking pen in my hand. Toni's jaw was in her lap. And Scott was crying quietly.

Alissa's story was absurd. "Did you tell the police all this?" I asked her.

"Of course not. I wasn't going to admit that I was the last person to see Max alive."

"If your story has any truth in it, you weren't," I said. "Someone dragged him to the piano and stabbed him there. The blood was localized around the piano."

Scott had recovered enough from his crying to say, "It wasn't me. Max was already dead when I got there."

"But between Alissa's visit and yours, someone went into Max's apartment, dragged him unconscious to the piano, and cut the arteries in his thighs."

Toni caught my gaze on her and said, "Don't look at me like that. I was with Rafik all night. We took a long walk after leaving Max's place, talking about work and love. When we got to my hotel, Jason wouldn't let me in the room."

"It's all right, Toni," I said. "You don't have to explain."

"But I want to. I want to set the story straight with you once and for all. Jason's jealousy that night alarmed Rafik, even though I tried to assure him it happened all the time. It was one more thing that Rafik and I had in common, our jealous lovers."

"But—"

"I was prepared to take another room in the hotel that night, but they were full up. Rafik offered me his place, saying that he would stay with you that night. But I didn't want him to disturb you. From what I could see, you needed time away from each other to cool down. So I stayed with him in his place. And he insisted I take the bed while he took the floor. So, for your information, Rafik is still all yours." She finished her spiel with a righteous grin.

"I know," I said. "I know." I was utterly beyond jealousy now. "But what I don't know is which one of the two remaining people delivered the coup de grace to Max Harkey."

"Wouldn't it be wise to leave it to the police?" Toni said. Then she checked her watch. "It's almost time for rehearsal."

The three of them got up to leave, and I followed them to the door. Scott and Alissa were glum and left without a word. Toni said to me, "This ought to be some show tonight, thanks to you."

They left me and I closed up Max Harkey's apartment. Before going down one floor to confront Madame Rubinskaya, I considered calling Lieutenant Branco. But then I figured I'd be safe enough facing the old woman alone. If she had managed to kill Max Harkey, it was only because he'd been unconscious at the time, while from all indications I seemed to be awake.

When I pressed the buzzer, Madame's dog Verushka began squealing behind the door and scratching at it. Moments later I heard the old woman murmur to the animal and try to pacify it. Then she spoke sharply through the door.

"Who is there?"

"Stan Kraychik."

"Who?"

"The friend of Rafik."

Through the big door came the various metallic sounds of locks and bars being disengaged on the other side. Then it slipped open a few inches, and Verushka's black muzzle appeared and sniffed the air nervously. Higher up I caught the quick glint of Madame Rubinskaya's eyes before she released the final chain and opened the door for me.

A heavy, sickly-sweet odor emanated from her foyer, and I unfairly assumed it was Verushka.

"Tank God you come," said Madame. "I have so much now to tell you."

A confession already? I entered the foyer. Madame closed the big door and methodically refastened all the locks and chains.

I said, "Why didn't you come up to Max Harkey's place?"

"I could not go back there."

"Why? Because of what you did to him?"

"You don't know what happens here tonight."

"I want to know what happened the night Max Harkey was killed."

Madame Rubinskaya heaved a weary sigh. "You are like the police," she said. "First I get us something to eat." And she shuffled toward her kitchen. "You are hungry?" she said.

The question must have registered with Verushka, for she wagged her tail energetically and trotted after Madame.

"No," I replied, and followed them both.

"You are sure?"

I stood in the doorway to her kitchen.

"Madame Rubinskaya, how can I think of food when I suspect that you might have killed Max Harkey and Rico?"

"What! What you are saying? That I am killer? Me?"

"You can save the histrionics. I see through you."

"And what you see?" she said. "You see old woman. You see bitter woman. You see tired woman. But do you see killer? Why would I kill that boy?"

"Because he knew that after you killed Max you took the diary and the musical score."

My accusations caused Madame Rubinskaya to grab onto the edge of the kitchen counter to steady herself. *"Bozhe!"* she said. "You are like dancer who tries and tries until she does it right. You don't care what else is happening. Only your idea. Only your world. Nothing else."

She pulled herself up straight, then filled two tall glasses with hot tea. She put them on a tray with some pastries and walked past me toward her sitting room.

"Come," she said. "Now you will have good reward. You will be happy now because you will know the truth." She put the tray on the coffee table, then sat in her big cushioned chair. Verushka settled at her feet and I sat facing her from the sofa.

The stage was set for her big scene, and she began.

She said, "You know what it means, icon?"

I nodded and then gestured to the Byzantine image of Christ mounted high in one ceiling corner of the room.

"Yes," said Madame. "That is icon. But also was my grandmother icon in all Russia. She was symbol for romantic ballet. She was like saint. She was *Rubinskaya.*"

Madame put several spoonfuls of sugar into her tea and stirred it.

"Take tea," she said.

I took the other glass, now wary of being captive not to a killer but to a lonely old woman living vicariously through her ancestors, much like our domestic aristocrats from the antebellum South, the people who wrap gifts at Neiman Marcus but manage to apprise you of the glory days when their daddy's folks owned vast plantations of sugar and cotton.

Madame Rubinskaya continued her litany. "For my grandmother was created the role of *The Phoenix* when she was young ballerina, and she dances it for her whole career. In Russia *The Phoenix* was more famous than Pavlova's *Dying Swan.* Did you know that?"

"No," I said.

"Is true. And she was smart in business too. She made—how do you say?—copy and write?"

"Copyright?"

Madame Rubinskaya nodded and smiled. "Copyright. My grandmother made copyright on that ballet so no one could dance without her permission."

A precedent for a dancer in imperial Russia, I thought.

"And she leaves to my mother, and my mother leaves to me that copyright, so now only I can give the permission to dance *The Phoenix*. You understand?"

"Yes," I said. "So your mother was a dancer?"

"No. She had no music in her blood, and such bad feet, no arch. My brother and I have good bodies for dancer, and I became ballerina. But my brother's daughter, that is Mireille's mother, she is just like our mother. No music in her blood. But still she keeps the name Rubinskaya."

I'd heard the notion among dancers that natural talent often skipped a generation. Madame Rubinskaya's lineage seem to confirm the myth.

"You had no children yourself?" I asked.

"I never marry."

"Yet you are called Madame."

"It is title of respect for old woman." She repeated the word as if savoring its irony. "Respect," she said with a snigger. "That is why I took the music from Maxi's piano. It is mine. I have the right to take it. *The Phoenix* is sacred. It was not performed for two generations. So when it comes back on stage, it must be with Russian ballerina. But Maxi was saying that American girl can dance *The Phoenix*. That was not right. He has no respect for that role. It was for Mireille, only Mireille. No other girl."

"Is that why you killed him?"

"He was destroying Mireille's career. He makes love to her, and then he deserts her."

"But he didn't," I said. "Max was going to—"

"I know what happens in London," she said. "I have strong connection to my great-niece. She would never fall, never. But Maxi comes back from London, and I know what happens over there. He breaks her heart. I know how he is with girls, but I never thought he would do that to Mireille."

"But Mireille isn't broken-hearted." I said.

"She says she loves Maxi, but in her heart she knows he ruins her career and her life. She falls on her knee, and she will never dance again."

"But it will heal, Madame."

"When the knee is hurt you never dance the same."

"Madame, you don't understand. Mireille is—"

"No! You don't understand. Now you listen to me! No one ever listens to old people. We are not crazy. We are just tired. We see too much pain. I was young girl once too. I had dreams, just like you, maybe more. I had scholarship in St. Petersburg at Imperial Ballet School. I have everything there—warmth, food, security. I learn new ideals, ideals of art. Ballet was my survival. Ballet was my life. It comes before my friends or my family or even God."

She paused to sip at her tea, and I attempted to hasten her story. I had a killer to convict, after all.

I said, "And you lost everything in the revolution."

"I escape with my brother to Europe. My grandmother gave me the music for *The Phoenix,* piano score and full orchestra. I still have. Then I became character dancer. You know what is?"

"Yes," I said, recalling that she had already told me that during an earlier visit here. "It's very exciting stuff."

Madame gave a modest shrug. "Is mostly tricks."

"That's not true. There's a lot of passion in character dancing. The best of it makes your blood boil."

"But is not romantic, not like *The Phoenix.*"

"Did you ever dance that role?" I asked.

She pondered the question as if she had to recover a lost answer. Then she said sadly, "I was not good enough."

"But Mireille was?"

"Mireille was perfect. Her debut will be first time the name Rubinskaya is onstage in America. *The Phoenix* will make her famous around the world."

No wonder she was so angry over Max Harkey's decision. He'd cast Alissa Kortland in the role almost whimsically, while for Madame Rubinskaya, her grandniece's debut was to revitalize a long-dormant line of great artists.

"When did you meet Max Harkey?" I said.

"I was teaching already in France. Forty-five I was, and I was not dancing anymore." Then she added somewhat proudly, "Character roles are very strenuous."

"I know," I said agreeably.

"Maxi was young dancer from America. He was trying to make his career in Europe. His looks and temperament did not suit American taste at that time. He was too . . ." Something caught in her throat, and she coughed harshly until it cleared. "Too much cigarettes," she said. "My lungs will be smoked ham."

"You were saying about Max?"

Madame Rubinskaya raised her eyebrows. "Maxi was too sexual. His face was all beautiful angles, eyes so bright, and his body—even when he died he was like a god. And it was rare, just like now in ballet, that he likes girls. Really likes. Not pretending like in Russia, where some men must hide their true feelings." She added quickly, "I hope I don't offend you."

"Hardly," I said. "I freely acknowledge the existence of good-looking heterosexual men."

"That was Maxi!" she said. "When he is partnering a girl, he holds her, and supports her, and caresses her like he is making her ready for him. Like he is going to make love."

Madame placed her glass of tea on the table and sighed quietly.

"How long did he study with you?" I said.

"He was already good dancer. He wanted to be choreographer. I encourage him, but his talent is too big for me. He makes many friends with wealthy men, and sometimes their wives too." She smiled playfully. "So many times he is almost caught. But he is serious too. He forms a small company, and it makes a big success."

"When did he meet Marshall Zander?"

Madame's brow furrowed. "Sometime then," she said. "That is when we come to America to make the Boston City Ballet."

"That was about twenty years ago."

"Yes," said Madame. "Maybe more." But her storytelling fires had been extinguished by my mention of Marshall Zander. "I like very much to live in Boston, especially in winter. It reminds me when I was student in St. Petersburg, all those clothes, and the snow, and the cold, and the frost on the window glass."

"Not the summer?"

"Ach! Too hot."

"So you've been with the company here ever since its beginning."

"Maxi and me, we start it! We do everything. He did choreography, and he has good head for business. But I train the dancers. I give Maxi his material. Like artist has paint or sculptor has clay, Maxi has dancers. And I make them for him."

"And now the Boston City Ballet has an international reputation for changing the shape of classical dance."

"Maxi and I never have such ideas. We never try to make progressive ballet. But the whole world was always looking at Maxi for what they should do next. That is what change him. Now he has reputation, one that comes by surprise from outside. If Maxi stayed on his own ideals, he would be all right."

Maybe even still alive, I thought.

"But instead he follows what the world is saying about him. He believes everybody else, and forgets about his art. And that is when he becomes a monster."

"A monster? What do you mean?" I said. I wanted to hear more of these suppressed feelings. "Please tell me more, Madame. How was Max Harkey a monster?"

She said, "Suddenly Maxi sees I am old woman. He wants to throw me away. He has no more humor. He runs away from me. So I leave him alone. I don't bother him. I do my job. I give good class. But now Maxi thinks he is God."

"Madame Rubinskaya, what happened that night?"

"You were there. You saw. It was wonderful party, big success, until Maxi makes announcement about *The Phoenix,* even though Mireille cannot dance. That was proof he turns against me. I never think he would do that, give role to young American girl. He deceives me, and in my heart I want to show him how angry I am. But I go home."

"And then you went out again, to the ballet studio."

"Yes . . ." she said tentatively.

"What?"

"Something else happen that night I don't tell anyone."

"But you want to tell me."

"Yes," said Madame Rubinskaya. "I will tell you to prove that I kill no one. Maybe I feel the passion to kill, and maybe I make many mistakes, but I did not kill Maxi."

"What happened, then?"

She offered me a plate of sweets. "You want cookie?" she said. Was she trying to distract me? Or did she simply need a brief intermission for herself?

"No," I replied. "Please go on."

"So," she said. "After I come home, then later I hear noises from Maxi's apartment upstairs. Part of his big room is over us here."

I pressed her. "What kind of noises?"

"I hear loud angry voices. Then becomes quiet. Then more shouting again."

"Men's or women's voices?"

"Eh?"

"Were they men or women who were shouting?"

Madame's eyes narrowed as she tried to recreate the sounds of that evening in her head.

"I hear Maxi, and then I hear a girl. Then I hear crash on floor. Big sound, like maybe the statue is falling. Even Rushka was nervous then. She was running and barking. Then all is quiet up there. Quiet, quiet. So . . ."

"So you went up to see."

"Yes," she said.

"And Max was on the floor lying against the big sculpture."

"How you know about that?" said the old woman. Yet her question confirmed at least one part of Alissa Kortland's version of the events that night.

"Alissa told me that she fought with Max."

"So *she* kill him!"

"No, Madame. They fought because Max had changed his mind later that night. He realized his error in casting Alissa as *The Phoenix*, so instead he was canceling the piece altogether."

This news seemed to strike the old woman like a blow.

"Maxi change his mind?" she said.

"Yes. You see, Max had kept his promise to you after all. *The Phoenix* would not be performed without Mireille. And when Alissa left him, Max was still alive. He was only unconscious. Someone else dragged him to the piano and killed him there."

I wondered again, Could this old woman have done it? It would have been a kind of infanticide. Yet all that unexpressed passion between them might have driven her to kill him. But was she that kind of person? Did she possess that ability to kill someone knowingly? Or had it been done in a moment of ultimate and literal *carelessness,* when a person cares about nothing but the action at hand. Even if the act was not premeditated, Madame had been under grave emotional stress that had reached its peak that night. Passion might have spurred her on.

Finally she said, "I know. I know Maxi was still alive. How I know? I check his breathing." She sounded as though she was ready at last to tell the truth. "So I am making call to the police, and then I see on his piano the score for *The Phoenix*. And I think what Maxi wants to do, and I think what that role is for me and for Mireille, and then I think I will not help him. I will leave him there. He gets what he deserves. I did not know that he change his mind. How can I know that? So I take the music and come back here. Then I smoke cigarettes and think what to do next."

"And that's when you decided to go to the ballet studios."

"Yes. I want to be away from him."

"And that's when his killer arrived."

"Ach, what a mistake I did!" Her eyes were filling with tears, and for the first time I believed they might be real. She continued, "Maybe I did not kill Maxi with the knife, but now I see that I leave him there for his killer. So I kill him too. I should help him that night, and instead I was cursing his soul."

She got up from her chair and I asked where she was going.

"I will light candle for him now."

She went to a credenza and opened one of the top drawers from which she produced a small votive candle. She brought it back and set it down on the coffee table between us, then lit it.

"Perhaps it is too late," she said, "but I pray that Maxi will understand why I did not help him. I thought he was betraying me. I will pray for his soul."

"There's a part of him that's still alive," I said. "You wouldn't let me tell you earlier, but I have other news from Mireille in London. She is pregnant. And Max intended to marry her."

Madame Rubinskaya then let out a long horrible cry, and broke down into violent sobbing. And here I thought I'd told her some good news. Her crying continued, and I began to feel awkward about sitting there. Like I said before, I don't seem to have what it takes to bear up under other people's real pain and sorrow.

Finally Madame stopped crying. Then she picked up her head and blew out the candle. She gave a small shiver.

I said, "Since you didn't know about Max and Mireille, I guess you don't have Max's diary either. I thought you did."

"Marshall say that too, that I have diary."

"When?"

"I told you, he was here tonight."

"No, you didn't, Madame."

"He comes to tell me about his love for Maxi, like he is making confession to his mother. Then he tells me that he loves Maxi so much, but Maxi always likes girls, so he gets mad at him. Marshall tells me this! He is like brokenhearted girl. And then he says he will go to the police and tell them everything."

"He's going to confess?"

Madame shrugged weakly. "I have no more strength to think. I am too tired."

"Madame, I think you might be in shock. I'm going to call for help."

"No," she said. "I will be all right."

"But I'm concerned you might . . ."

She looked at me quizzically. "You are thinking I will hurt myself? I am not a coward. Perhaps I made big mistake—many mistakes. But I will face them. I never run away."

That was a relief. One thing this case didn't need was a dramatic suicide attached to it, some meticulously executed act of self-retribution, Madame Ekaterina Rubinskaya's last show.

"I'm going to leave you now. Just lock the door and don't let anyone in. Promise?"

She nodded quietly, then followed me to the door. When I'd left her, I heard all the mechanical sounds of security as Madame resealed the door to her apartment. While I was waiting for the elevator I checked my watch. It was just after eight o'clock. Rafik would be rehearsing. Branco was probably dining with Nicole. I decided to go to Station D anyway. I'd report everything I'd just found out to one of Branco's assistants. Then I'd go home and have a quiet night with Sugar Baby.

Just as the elevator arrived I heard a voice behind me.

"I missed your soirée at Max's place."

19

Totentanz

"Did you forget to invite me?"

More than the suppressed anger that tinged his voice, it was the sickly smell of rotting fruit that identified Marshall Zander standing behind me.

"I guess I did," I replied. "Sorry."

"No you're not," he said. "That's twice you've forgotten me. Maybe you'd like to forget me altogether."

How could the same sentiment—almost to the word—create such opposite reactions in me? With Rafik it had intensified my desire to conjoin. With Marshall Zander it caused revulsion.

He said, "Is that how you thank me for flying you to London? You're almost as ungrateful as Max was."

"I didn't see the need," I began weakly.

Marshall pushed me into the elevator.

"Let's go for a ride," he said.

The elevator descended noiselessly, but my panic escalated. Here, finally, was Max Harkey's killer. My blood pulsed so hard that my eyes throbbed with the pressure. My mouth went dry and I began to see white patches of light dance before me. Breathe, I told myself. Focus on the breath. Take the air in and then let it out. Disregard the reek of his body. One thought at a time.

"Your lover spoke to me today," he said. "He refused my offer. I must say he wasn't very chivalrous about it, except regarding you. I think he's ready to die for you. It must be nice to be loved by someone that much."

"Where is Rafik?" I said. "What have you done?"

I made a move toward him, but suddenly he brandished a stiletto. I saw his hand squeezing the hilt of the dagger nervously. The slender blade flashed brightly. It was the perfect instrument for slicing into the femoral arteries.

"Where's your courage now?" he said.

The elevator stopped and the door slid open. He used the knife to point the way out.

"After you," he said with mock courtesy.

We left the Appleton and walked toward his car. There would be no wind in our hair for this ride. The hard top was securely attached now.

"Get in," he said.

I did. But I was already imagining myself leaping from the car and fleeing from him. I could surely outrun him. I would sprint all the way to Station D, taking the alleys and footpaths so that he couldn't pursue me in the car. I would scream bloody murder all the way. He would never catch me, and I'd be safe.

But before he closed the car door, Marshall pulled a heavy chain from around the back of the seat and secured it with a big padlock across my belly. Some chastity belt, I thought.

He got in behind the wheel and pulled away.

He said, "Even if Rafik didn't accept my original offer, I'm sure you both want to see his work performed on opening night, don't you?"

I didn't answer him.

"I know you do," he said. "And it would be a shame to have the performance canceled, especially after all the time and effort Rafik has spent on it. Did he ever tell you what it's about? I know it was supposed to be a big secret, but I doubt that lovers like you can keep secrets from each other."

I stayed mute.

"It's really touching," he said. "Rafik's new ballet was inspired by you. It's all about the most perfect male couple in Boston. It's even got a fancy title—*Uomo giocoso.* 'Playful Man.' Isn't that sweet? Well, tonight we'll see how far your playful love for each other goes in real life."

He said nothing more for the remainder of our short ride, but he did keep the sleek dagger visible at all times. I wondered what it was going to feel like to be slashed with the razorlike edge of that knife.

Marshall pulled the car into the underground garage of the Copley Palace and parked it in his reserved space. He got out, then came and opened my door and unchained me from the seat. His private elevator was right near his parking space, yet he felt the need to brandish that slender glistening blade at me for those few steps. Once inside the wood-paneled chamber he must have felt safer, because as we began our long ascent he softened his voice and his manner.

"All I'm asking from you is some companionship tonight. Do you think you can manage that for your lover's sake?"

I realized at that moment, with myself in mortal danger, that somewhere else in the city of Boston Rafik was making art with Toni di Natale and a whole company of dancers. And somewhere else Nicole was having dinner with Lieutenant Branco. Who knew where I was? The unsettling answer was, Nobody.

Once we were inside his suite Marshall Zander double-locked the doors. The lights were extremely low and he dimmed them even more. What might have been a romantic gesture only increased my dread, especially with him wielding that knife.

"Would you like a drink?" he said.

I didn't answer.

He said, "I want to celebrate tonight." He pulled me roughly toward the wet bar and went behind it to make himself a drink, always keeping that naked blade close by. The wall of plate glass behind him opened out onto the balcony, which was still under reconstruction. Beyond the railing the broad cityscape of Boston's lights sparkled invitingly under a clear night sky. I wondered how many other people in that glittering terrain were facing the same kind of danger I was.

Marshall half-filled a tumbler with scotch and drained it in a few noisy gulps. He refilled it, then took another glass, filled it with ice, and poured some gin into it.

"See?" he said, pushing the glass of gin toward me. "I even remember what you like to drink. Does Rafik do that for you?"

I finally spoke. "Rafik mixes me a proper martini."

"Is that what you want me to do for you?"

"I don't want anything from you."

"But tonight is an important night. I want you to be happy and comfortable with me. Tonight is when everything turns out the way it's supposed to."

He left the two bottles of liquor on top of the bar and came around to my side. He offered me a bar stool.

"Don't be afraid," he said.

I sat down warily and he pulled another stool close to me.

"I don't want to hurt you. I just want company." He sat down and pressed one of his heavy legs against mine. Fortunately both his hands were occupied—one hovering over the stiletto and the other holding his drink.

"I knew Max for over twenty years," he said. "And for all that time I never thought of hurting him, not for real. See, I believed if I waited long enough Max would come home to me. I waited for him and I deserved him."

He clinked his glass heavily against mine.

"I want to drink to you and Rafik, to the kind of love that works out right. Aren't you going to drink to that?"

Faced with the possibility of never seeing my lover again, I thought of Rafik and took a big mouthful of gin. It seemed to help the situation.

Marshall asked, "Do you want to hear how Max and I met?"

I nodded, even though it was probably the last thing in the world I wanted to hear at that moment. But I was facing a big nervous beast, a dangerous creature that had been caged and frustrated so long that the slightest snap of a twig might launch it into a killing rampage. Maybe if I appeared to cooperate I could lull him into calmness. I didn't know what else to do. No one knew where I was. All I had to play with at that moment was time. Perhaps I could stall the inevitable long enough for a deus ex machina to pick my name out of the cosmic bingo basket and rescue me.

Marshall began his tale. "I was vacationing in Biarritz one summer. My mother wanted to get me off her back. Do your parents have money?"

I suppressed a laugh.

Marshall continued. "Well, mine were shits, but they were filthy rich. I mean *filthy*. You can't imagine how much money we had. I still don't know what I'm worth. I've got a full-time staff of accountants and lawyers just to keep track of it all, and they don't even know. But you know what? That money compensates for an awful lot."

He gulped at his scotch, then went on.

"My folks hated me. They hated everybody. The only thing they loved was their money. And the joke was, they acted as if the money was some kind of award for their superior taste and intellect, when the fact was it all started with my grandfather's deli in the Bronx. The Zander empire was born in Zandlinski's Deli. That's a good one, huh? Then by some fluke of luck my grandfather kept expanding the business until he landed up with a chain of supermarkets clear across the country."

Marshall Zander raised his glass. "Here's to Grandpa!" he said, then noisily drained the contents. He poured himself another drink and went on. "By the time the old geezer died, he had already been buying hotels. And here we are in the final result." He spread his arms to encompass the panoramic view of Boston by night. "All mine." He leaned toward me, one hand still grasping that stiletto. "Just give me the word and it's yours too."

I said, "You were telling me how you met Max."

"Max," he said. "Max! Where's Max?" he shouted. Then he said quietly, "When I quit medical school Mother was so ashamed she sent me to Biarritz. That's where I met Max. I liked him right from the start, and he liked me too. I don't think it was just my money, but I didn't hide it either. That's the kind of place it is. You throw your money around. So Max and I got friendly and did things together for a while, go out and stuff like that. God, he looked unbelievable on the beach. And finally one day I had to tell him how I really felt about him."

Marshall sucked down some more scotch, as though he needed Dutch courage to confront Max Harkey again.

"What happened?" I asked.

"Oh, it was awful. Max gave me that look. You know that look? You go out with someone for a while, and then you go to touch them and they give you that look."

Marshall cocked his head and eyed me like an animal that has just sensed a change in its environment.

"You did that to me too," he said.

"Can we stay with Max?" I said nervously.

"Sure," he said. "Max now, you later." He laughed as though he'd made a joke, then he passed his fat tongue over his lips. "All that time Max was flirting with me, and then suddenly it was 'Oh, no! Not that!' So I was okay about it. I just went after some of the other guys there. It was easy. You give them money and they love you forever."

Marshall gazed into his glass of scotch. Though it wasn't yet empty, he poured more in. He didn't return his free hand to the dagger, but it was still lying on top of the bar, close to him.

"Shit!" he said suddenly.

"What?"

"You know what he did to me once? One time at dinner Max started preaching to me about my sex life and how dangerous it was. I had a renter with me that night and I was kind of insulted, not to mention what the renter must have thought. But then, Max started flirting with the guy. Imagine that? I had a paid companion, and Max was going after him—Max, who was supposed to be straight. So I got mad and threw my drink at Max and left the table." Marshall shook his head and chuckled as though amused by his own anecdote. Then he continued, "I went back there two hours later to have a peaceful meal by myself, and damn it if Max wasn't still there with that same hustler. They were laughing and having a grand time together. So I went up to Max and demanded an explanation. Max grinned from ear to ear and told me that the young man was a dancer, and they were discussing modern choreography. And you know, that's when I really knew I was in love with him. So the next day I gave Max a blank check and told him to start his own ballet company."

"Did you two ever have sex?"

"Never. Max liked women, plain and simple. We stayed friends, but it was hard for me because I always hoped Max would change his mind. I think that was what linked me to him, the promise of his body. And all I had to do to keep him close was write a check. That was one thing I was good at. And that was exactly what he got from me, the promise of my money. We needed each other for different things, and that was what kept us connected."

Now, in spite of Marshall Zander's precarious mental state and my dubious future, I was curious to know what had changed between them, so I asked him what happened.

He said, "You like this story, eh? You like hearing about Max and me?"

Had my unchecked curiosity about other people's business finally careened onto its final course?

Marshall grinned with satisfaction and continued.

"After more than twenty years of waiting for Max, of putting up with all his women—married ones, single ones, old and young—after all that time, Max met that dancer in London and he was never the same. He told me that something had clicked, and I laughed at him. But in fact I saw that something was changed in him. He acted as if he didn't need me anymore. When he came back from London he told me he was going to marry her. He'd already changed his will to leave most of his estate to her. Mind you, that was everything he acquired because of my help. Maybe all those women he had over the years were painful for me, but at least they were temporary. But marriage and family weren't temporary. He said he didn't need me anymore."

"I'm sure he still needed you in his own way."

"No. He was through with me. He wasn't even throwing crumbs anymore. That's why I needed his diary. I had to know how he really felt. Did he really love that girl?"

"Yes," I said, realizing too late that I was purposely provoking him.

"How do you know?"

"She told me."

"What does she know? She'd say anything. I need that diary. That's where the answer is, in Max's own writing."

"But you already have it," I said.

"No, I don't."

I said, "You took it after you killed him."

Marshall's face froze. He picked up the stiletto and stared at it. Then he got up off his bar stool and stood facing me. Then with all his strength he screamed, "I never killed him!"

He started toward the center of the room, but he was unsteady from the liquor. He faltered for a second, then caught his balance.

"Max!" he yelled out. "Max, I'm sorry. Come back. I promise to be good. Please. Come back!"

In his moment of madness I saw a small hope for my own salvation. While he stood in a daze waiting for Max Harkey to answer him, I surreptitiously lifted the receiver off the nearby telephone. I hoped the concierge downstairs would notice that the phone was off the hook. If he was worth his salt he would listen in for a while, spy on us, like most people in the service industry. And perhaps he would also hear trouble and come up, and I would be rescued.

Marshall caught my slight movement in his peripheral vision. I tried to conceal it by standing up myself.

"What are you doing?" he demanded.

"Just stretching my legs." I moved cautiously away from the bar toward the sofa in the center of the room and said, "Can we sit here for a while?"

"You want to get more comfortable, eh?"

"Right," I said.

He came and sat next to me on the leather sofa, the exact place where I'd enjoyed my brief romp with Rico. Marshall was toying with the knife now, making its shiny blade glint in the dimness. I realized that what scared me most was his clumsiness with that weapon. Max Harkey had been an easy target because he was unconscious. But I imagined Marshall tripping and hurtling his bulky body at mine in his clumsy gorilla way, flailing to keep his balance and lashing randomly with that finely honed blade. Distance was the key to my survival. That, and my quick reflexes.

I said, "Can you tell me what happened that night?"

He spoke to the knife blade as he recounted his version of the events the evening Max Harkey was killed.

"I did go back to his place. There was something important I had to tell Max, and it couldn't wait. The production of *The Phoenix* could create serious legal problems, since the company didn't yet have the performance rights for the work. We were having trouble finding who owned the copyright, if anybody."

I said, "But Max had already decided to take *The Phoenix* off the program."

"He never told me that," said Marshall Zander.

"He said it to everyone at the party. You knew about the cancellation, so why did you really go back that night?"

"It doesn't matter," he said quickly. "It doesn't matter why. The point is I did go back. I had to see Max just one more time alone. I had to talk him out of marrying that bitch. When I got there the door was open, so I went in. Rico was nowhere around, and Max was lying at the base of the Brancuşi. He was wearing that silk robe I'd brought him from Hong Kong. It was open and everything was showing. And . . ." Marshall faltered. "I guess I got turned on. Max's legs were still as smooth and muscular as when he was dancing. It's remarkable—his body never seemed to age. I went to him. He was still breathing, and there was no blood. I shook him and spoke to him. All he said to me was, "Get out, you cunt!" Then when he saw it was me, he laughed. Then he went out again. That's when I dragged him to the piano and hauled him up onto the bench."

"Why?"

"Because he loved that piano more than anything else he owned. That's where I wanted to have him. His bathrobe slipped open again. God, what a sight! And it was finally all mine."

"Don't go on," I said. "Please."

"But I did," replied Marshall. "I did go on. After twenty years of waiting I finally got what I wanted from Max Harkey's sacred body."

"And then, like a spider, you killed him."

"I told you I did not kill Max! I loved him too much. Killing him would be too common. What I did was sacrifice him. That's how our love finally culminated—in a beautiful sacrifice."

"And you knew exactly where to cut him."

"Yes, in those beautiful thighs. The blood pulsed out at first, almost like he was coming again. I used his robe to block the spurting and make it run down his legs. After a few minutes it slowed down, and finally it stopped."

Just like that, I thought. No pain, no panic. Just the draining away of life from a body.

Marshall said, "But now I want him back. I can't go on without him. Who else can cause me such exquisite pain and frustration? Only my parents, and they're both dead. Even the parasitic hustlers I hire can't be as heartless and cruel as Max was with me. They do it only for the money, and they're lousy actors. But Max and I were the real thing. Just like you and Rafik. We were destined for each other. It began long before I gave him his ballet company. Whatever I did for Max came out of my love for him. Our relationship was not based on money. It was based on passion and sacrifice."

Gosh, I thought. That's exactly what I thought my relationship with Rafik was founded on. And at that instant I promised myself that if I survived this nightmare, I would take each moment with Rafik the way it came, without questions, without analysis, without conditions. I wanted no more of passion and sacrifice if this was where they led. And if I survived tonight I would also lock away the kitchen knives.

Suddenly the door buzzer sounded. It was my deus ex machina, the concierge. I was saved!

Marshall however was now keen and alert as a wild animal. "What's that?" he said. "They know never to bother me."

He got up to go to the door and on the way he turned off all the room lights. Then he warned me, "Don't do anything stupid. I have nothing to lose."

It was the concierge at the door. I heard him asking Marshall Zander in his fawning manner if there was any trouble, since his telephone had been left off the hook.

My jailer assured the concierge that everything was fine.

"I'm having some personal therapy," he said. "It's been difficult for me since I lost my friend." He was holding the stiletto behind his back. "So please leave us alone."

"Very good, sir," said the concierge.

Obsequious bastard, I thought. He was listening to us over the phone. Didn't he hear anything we said? I was about to yell out, "He's got a goddamn knife behind his back!"

But the concierge had departed without further question.

Marshall Zander relocked the doors and came back in. The only light still on now was under the bar. He stopped there and poured himself another drink. Then he calmly replaced the telephone receiver in its cradle, and then, in one violent twisting sweep of his big body grabbed the telephone and ripped the connecting cord from the wall. A small table was upset, and the lamp on top of it crashed to the floor. Marshall Zander then noticed my cocktail on top of the bar where I'd left it.

"Aren't you drinking?" he said. "Don't you want to celebrate my special night?"

"What so special about it?"

Marshall Zander grinned at me, but it was same demented grin that King Kong used on Fay Wray.

"Tonight is the night I get what I want. I'm so tired of rejection," he said. "Everyone says no. Rico refused me, too."

"Is that why you rigged the brakes on his scooter?"

"He was meddling, just like you. He already knew too much about me, and he was bound to figure out what had happened. So if I'm going to pay for two murders, I have nothing to lose by getting what I want from you, whatever it takes."

In a flash I saw myself unconscious like Max Harkey, with Marshall Zander rooting around my crotch. Unconsciousness was the only state in which I'd be able to tolerate his mouth anywhere on my body.

"But you don't even like me," I protested.

"That doesn't matter anymore," said Marshall Zander. "I just want to know that I can get what I want. And all I want right now is to hold you. Just to hold you. Just for a little while."

The city lights outside cast a dim light on us. Marshall twirled the stiletto in his hand, and the blade flashed like a surgeon's scalpel.

I said, "And after you hold me a little bit, then what? Will you want to kiss me a little bit too? And then stick your tongue in my mouth a little bit? And rip my clothes off and cut me up and fuck a little bit?"

"No," he said. "That's not what I want."

"Then what do you want?"

"I want Max. I want my Max back."

"Too late, pal. You killed him."

Suddenly he lunged for me and pressed his big soft face against mine. He tried to thrust his tongue into my mouth. It was like a warm slug burrowing into me. The smell of his body nauseated me. I pushed him away. He was already breathing hard.

He said, "That was for the trip to London. Now I want payment for your lover's ballet."

Again he thrust his heavy body onto mine, and this time pressed me deep into the cushions of the leather sofa. He pinned both my hands behind me, and I felt the blade of the stiletto brush against my wrist. Not the hands, I thought. Not the hands.

"Why don't you cooperate?" he said. "Just pretend you like me. Is that so much to ask?"

"In your case," I said, "yes!"

Bondage was no fun when the act was for real. I was being forced into dirty fighting—but then our match was hardly within a gentleman's code of honor. Those yoga stretches would finally come in handy. All that flexibility and range of motion in my strong legs let me coil the muscles up and then release the energy and ram my knee directly into Marshall's groin. He screamed and doubled up. His body sank heavily onto me. I wrestled around underneath him, trying to free myself. At the split second I'd squirmed free of him, I felt something brush against my left butt cheek. I pushed myself off and away from the sofa, but my usual spring wasn't there. Something was wrong.

"I'll get you," he said.

"You'll have to catch me first."

That's when I felt a warm wet sensation on my fanny. I put my hand there and it came back sticky. I smelled my fingers. The metallic odor proved I was bleeding. Just as I'd slipped away from him, Marshall Zander had knifed me in the butt. I felt the pain rising fast, almost as though my awareness of the wound was causing it to hurt.

Marshall Zander was crouched on the sofa, groaning softly. I got down on the floor and crept away from him. The city lights outside glowed softly through the long walls of plate glass windows. That's when I figured out where I might be safer from him. In the darkness I crawled on all fours toward the big grand piano, which sat directly in the way of the sliding doors that opened onto the outside balcony.

I got under the piano and pulled against one of the doors, but it wouldn't budge. In the darkness my fingers fluttered frantically around the door frame to locate the locking device. It was probably some high-tech electronic gizmo controlled from an office buried somewhere in the belly of the hotel. But no, I found it—one of those simple screw mechanisms. That's exactly when the room lights came up bright and blazing.

"I see you," said Marshall Zander.

From under the piano I saw his big feet lumbering toward me. I untwisted the locking screw on the door as quickly as I could, all the while feeling the seat of my pants getting wetter and warmer with my blood. I knew I was losing it fast. Just as I finally disengaged the lock, Marshall grabbed my feet.

Reflexively I kicked at him and he backed off, no match for my high-action feet. I heaved at the sliding door until it slid open enough for me to squeeze through. The outside air blew onto my face. I would be saved!

But just then I sensed the grand piano above me being moved. Marshall heaved at the massive instrument until he had rolled it aside and completely exposed me. Desperately I pushed myself through the half-open door, but not fast enough. Marshall was on top of me again. He was swinging wildly, and the dagger hissed through the air in front of my face. I grabbed his wrist to keep the knife away from me, but I lost my grip for just one instant and felt the blade slice into my shoulder. I grabbed onto his wrist again. There was no pain, not yet. The blade was so sharp it had performed its job mercifully, without tearing the flesh. I heard myself think with absurd calmness, "He is killing me."

But I wasn't about to go down without calling once more on my Slavic legacy, my super-strong legs. From my crouch I focused everything that was still alive in me down into my thighs and knees. I coiled my whole body up even tighter, compressed every cell that had the potential for movement, and then released it all in one atomic push against the floor. I sprang up like a killer whale breaching high out of the water. Marshall Zander was thrown back onto the piano, which gave me enough time to stumble out onto the balcony.

The rush of cool night air felt good on my body. Except for the sparkle of city lights far below, it was dark out there, but in that darkness was my safety. I prayed that the renovations on the balcony hadn't progressed far enough to have the lights connected yet. I hobbled my way cautiously toward a large potted tree silhouetted amidst the rubble of marble slabs and brass railings scattered about the balcony surface. I had at least a slim hope of surviving out here, for I had recalled Marshall Zander's fear of heights. Chances were he wouldn't follow me outside, especially in the darkness. Trouble was, how would I summon help? Semaphore signals? I could stay out on the balcony and bleed to death, or I could go back inside and get my throat slashed. Some choice. Unfortunately I wasn't going to have the choice, for Marshall was now standing in the doorway that opened onto the balcony.

"I know you're out there," he said. "I can smell your blood."

Like any good predator, he knew he had wounded me, and he recognized his clear advantage despite his phobia.

"All I have to do is follow your trail."

The pull of blood was strong, yet his voice sounded a bit uncertain. Was his fear beginning to paralyze him? Or was I hoping for a miracle?

"I'm sorry," he said. "I didn't want it to turn out this way. I just wanted to feel your body. I'm not a killer. Everything just went wrong. It wasn't supposed to be like this."

He made his way slowly toward where I was hiding behind the large concrete urn. He kept his body crouched down close to the floor of the balcony as though that would protect him from falling to the ground forty-five stories below. He crept like a crab, with one hand always holding onto something to steady his shaky footing.

I saw another potted tree farther away from him and next to the railing right at the balcony's edge. It would take a measure of courage that I prayed he didn't have for him to follow me that close to the edge of the building. I set off toward that tree, but my fanny failed me. That big push I'd given to my legs to get Marshall Zander off my back had sent more blood into those muscles, and now that same blood had dripped and splattered onto the polished marble slabs scattered about the balcony. My attempted scurry to safety became a kind of limp-and-drag movement, a signal of easy prey.

Marshall saw me making for the edge of the balcony. "Get back from there," he said. "It's dangerous."

"For who?" I said, forgetting in the urgency of the moment the only rule of grammar I ever knew.

He changed his direction and headed toward me. I dragged myself toward the big urn near the edge, but I wasn't going to make it. I saw him stand up and come at me, still brandishing the knife. I pulled myself up and staggered toward the balcony railing. I felt the blood almost streaming off me now. He lunged at me, and I swooned and fell to the side. And then I heard the sounds—three of them, one right after the other, all within a half second. The first was a sliding, slippery sound, like the *whoosh* of a leather sole without traction on a wet marble slab. And the second sound was the high musical clang of English forged steel falling against polished marble. And the third was the heavy fluttering of some huge desperate object not meant to be airborne.

With my one usable arm, I hauled myself up and looked over the railing. Marshall Zander was falling through space, and I was Fay Wray watching her ardent pursuer plummet from the Empire State Building. The blundering ape shrank to a pathetic monkey, a fitting end for the man who was afraid of heights, yet dared to live in the highest, most spacious penthouse in Boston.

Had it been an accident? Or was it an intentional leap?

Had it really happened?

It took me a long time to drag myself back inside. I was still conscious enough to be worried about losing so much blood. That would be the last irony, to die now. I called 911, and they told me that the accident had already been reported and the police were on their way.

"I need an ambulance," I said, but they'd already hung up.

I set out for the elevator, but stumbled and fell just before I got there. It seemed as if hours passed. Why wasn't anyone coming to save me? Then I realized I should have called the desk for help. What would that arrogant concierge have to say to me now?

Finally I got into the elevator and back down to the main lobby. I was dripping blood everywhere as I staggered my way through crowds of screaming hotel guests on my way outside. I had to get out to the sidewalk to see what had happened.

The police were already out there with their usual chaos of light and sound. One plainclothes cop stood out from all the others in uniform. It was Lieutenant Branco, crouched over Marshall Zander's smashed-up body on the sidewalk. He turned to see me standing there like a battle-bloodied soldier.

"I should have guessed," he said. "You told me you'd get him."

"I didn't kill him, Lieutenant."

"Then who did?"

It took all my remaining strength to deliver the line with a straight face.

"Beauty, Lieutenant. It was Beauty killed the beast."

And then I blacked out.

20
Coda

Three days later I was back at work, the hero of Snips Salon. Fanny and shoulder stitched closed, and my arm in a sling, I was regaling our clients with my feats of bravery, including the unit of blood I'd received from none other than Lieutenant Branco himself. He'd ridden with me in the ambulance to the emergency room, and when it was evident that I needed blood, he offered his. Who would have thought that the beefy cop and I would have exactly the same blood type, right down to the rare Rh_o variant (D^u)? In all my fantasies about Lieutenant Branco, I'd never imagined that kinship with him.

In the days that followed, I was notified by an attorney that Rico had drawn up a will and had named me the recipient of all the kitchen equipment and appliances that he'd inherited from Max Harkey. I don't think he even got a chance to use the stuff before he died. But it sure caused a big change in my life. I agreed to look for a place with Rafik, if only to house Max Harkey's Bösendorfer Imperial and Rico's household legacy.

At Snips I was chatting with one of Ramon's clients when Nicole handed me a large international air express envelope.

"This just came for you, darling," she said. "I thought I'd help by opening it."

"Sure, doll," I said. "No more secrets between us."

"Says who?" she replied.

From the envelope fell an American Express cashier's check for five hundred dollars and two full-fare round-trip first-class tickets to Italy.

Inside the envelope was a letter from La Duchessa, aka Sharleen McChannel. It read: "Thank you for trusting me and performing magic with my hair. You are a rare gentleman. The check, though small, is for your fine work, and the tickets are for your vacation. You must come and visit me in Firenze. My villa is your home."

Nicole raised one eyebrow. "A villa, no less," she said.

I said, "Maybe those affirmations really work."

After closing time Nikki and I went back to my office. We'd both brought a change of clothes for our big night out, the opening night of the spring ballet season. We donned our glamour togs—Nicole lined my sling with an Hermès scarf—then we sat down for a cocktail while we awaited our driver.

Nicole said, "Are you sure you don't want to go to the theater early?"

"No, doll. Rafik told me honestly that he didn't want me backstage tonight. He insisted that I see his new work from out front the first time. And I'll do whatever he wants."

"I wonder how long that's going to last."

"As long as you and Vito do," I said.

"That is completely different."

"It's exactly the same," I retorted.

A robust knock on the alley door signaled the arrival of our driver, Lieutenant Branco himself. There's nothing like a police escort for opening night at the ballet—provided you don't have to ride in a squad car.

Branco entered the shop with a great rush of energy, looking fine in a double-breasted suit of midnight-blue wool with a faint gray chalkstripe. He and Nicole exchanged polite greetings.

I said, "It's okay, you two. Go ahead. I won't faint."

Nicole countered, "Whatever do you mean, Stanley?"

"You can kiss in front of me. It's all right."

"But why would we do that?" she said.

Branco looked at me then said to Nicole, "Is he still on those painkillers?"

Nicole answered him, "He insists that we are Romeo and Juliet."

Branco grinned and showed his big white teeth.

"Wishful thinking," he said.

"On whose part?" I asked.

Nicole replied, "You're not ready for the truth."

Abruptly changing tack, Branco said to me, "You want to guess what arrived on my desk today by special courier from British Air?"

"Max Harkey's diary," I said.

Branco grunted. "How did you know?"

"Where could it have been except lost, Lieutenant?"

"Well, you're right," said Branco. "Turns out Max Harkey left it on the airplane the day he returned to Boston. When British Air couldn't reach him, they finally sent it to us."

"Can I see it?" I said.

"Until this case is officially closed, Stan, the answer is no."

Nicole said, "I still don't understand why Max Harkey never identified his killer in any of those phone calls."

"He never made a phone call, Nikki. He went from unconscious to dead without knowing who killed him."

Branco nodded in accord.

Nicole said, "Who phoned, then?"

"Who else, doll? Marshall Zander knew the police could trace any calls made to them, so he made the first 911 call from Max Harkey's penthouse pretending to be Max, right after he killed him. Then he called again as himself from his car phone right after he left Max's place, claiming that's where he received Max's urgent call for help."

Branco said, "I should have seen through Zander's alibi for his whereabouts. Cruising around town at the exact time that Max Harkey was killed looked suspect, but we had no hard evidence on Zander. From where we stood, Max Harkey had made that call to us himself."

"So even phone traps aren't foolproof," I said.

Branco grunted.

"And the front door of the Appleton?" I said.

Branco replied, "Zander's attempt to imply a vandal, most likely."

The three of us went out the alley door and got into the big dark sedan Branco had parked back there. On the way to the theater I got to stretch out on the back seat, which took some of the pressure off my sore rump.

The Boston Performance Center glittered with the excitement and glamour of a ballet opening night. We had house seats in the orchestra, and mercifully I was on the aisle, so I could stretch my leg out and shift the weight off my wounded cheek. I was reading the program when I realized the importance of this night for Rafik. It was his first commissioned work for the Boston City Ballet, a full-length piece he'd created especially for them. Though Rafik had restaged many of his other works on the company, this night marked a world première, and before an extremely critical audience too.

In his program notes Rafik described the piece *Uomo giocoso* as a paean to the adventure of love that he and I shared. He said he wanted to express the challenges and rewards of spending his life with me, and I squirmed in my seat, anticipating a mawkish display of my life on stage.

Sitting next to me, Nicole said, "Pain, dear?"

"Heartburn," I replied.

Uomo giocoso was set to George Gershwin's Concerto in F. The work was dedicated to me. There was my name, Stan Kraychik, right there in the program. The premier performance was in memory of Max Harkey. *The Phoenix* would not be performed this season, if ever. Maybe its era had passed. Times change, after all, and there's no better way to initiate change than with new art. Ergo, *Uomo giocoso*.

There were three soloists. Scott Molloy portrayed me on stage, and I finally comprehended why he'd always been studying my moves and gestures so carefully in real life. Rafik portrayed himself, in a role that required more drama than ballet technique, and I fell in love with him again, just like the first time. Alissa Kortland played the third role, the metaphoric role, the role of jealousy and mystery in our love. Rafik was even confessing his own participation in our conflicts and resolutions. The most moving part for me was during the plaintive trumpet solo in the second movement. It was a beautiful *pas de trois* for all three of them—or us—Rafik, Stan, and the outside forces that affected us.

With *Uomo giocoso* Rafik had taken all his difficult experiences with me and had refracted them into a work of art that focused on the essence of why we were together. Through dance he was trying to show that the difficulties between us were external to the positive forces that kept us together.

The corps de ballet had challenging ensemble work during all three movements, especially when some of the corps members danced in canonic imitation of the three soloists. Their dancing seemed to symbolize the potential and far-reaching effects all our actions have on others, the ripples that can result from the simplest action on one person's part.

Jason Sears played the piano with bravura, Toni di Natale conducted the orchestra with panache, and love conquered all. Rafik's creativity had finally obliterated my cynicism.

The ovation lasted for fifteen minutes. *Uomo giocoso* was, as Rafik later said, *un succès fou*—wildly, insanely, ridiculously successful. True, it helped that the opening night audience was well attended by gays. But even Branco had stood and applauded with the others.

After the performance Nicole and Branco and I headed backstage to congratulate Rafik. He was surrounded by people, but Branco cleared the way for me and protected my arm in its sling as I made my way to Rafik. I saw Madame Rubinskaya standing next to him. She looked dazed with pleasure.

When I got to Rafik, he lifted his long arms to quiet the big mob. Then he put one arm on my shoulder and announced to everyone, "Here is my inspiration."

And right there in front of everyone, dancers and audience, musicians and stage crew, cops and civilians, gays and straights, Rafik and I embraced and kissed each other brazenly on the mouth, a lingering, loving kiss. Applause followed by all. Yes, even Lieutenant Branco.

Nicole asked Rafik, "After this wonderful premièr, what's next?"

Rafik answered, "Stani and I will go *en vacances.*"

"How did you know?" I said.

But before he could answer me, Madame Rubinskaya scowled at his remark. "What you are saying? You cannot take vacation. You are teaching class tomorrow morning."

I said, "But it wouldn't be until summer."

"Oh," replied Madame. Then she softened her face with a smile, as if to overrule her first hasty decree. "So maybe by then you will both deserve vacation."

But how had Rafik learned about the trip? I was planning to surprise him later that night with the tickets. Had La Duchessa already sent him a psychic message?

"How did you know?" I asked him again.

Rafik winked at me and whispered in my ear.

"I always know how to fix a wounded hero."